Heirs & Spares

BETWIXT THE SHEETS EDITION

THE REALM, BOOK I

JENNIE L. SPOHR

This book is a work of fiction. Names, characters, businesses, organizations, places, events, and incidents are either a product of the author's imagination or are used fictitiously. Any resemblance to actual persons, living or dead, events, or locales is entirely coincidental.

Published by River Grove Books

Austin, TX

www.rivergrovebooks.com

Copyright © 2013 2025 Jennie L. Spohr

Distributed by River Grove Books

Design and composition by Jennie L. Spohr

Cover design by Greenleaf Book Group

Publisher's Cataloging-in-Publication data is available.

Print ISBN: 978-1-63299-965-8

eBook ISBN: 978-1-63299-966-5

Second Edition

Contents

The Realm Series
by Jennie L. Spohr

Heirs & Spares
Heirs & Spares, Betwixt the Sheets
God & King
God & King, Betwixt the Sheets *
Crown & Thorns
Crown & Thorns, Betwixt the Sheets *
Sword & Shield, novella

*coming in 2025

For those of us who like our (k)nights with a dose of spice.

Map

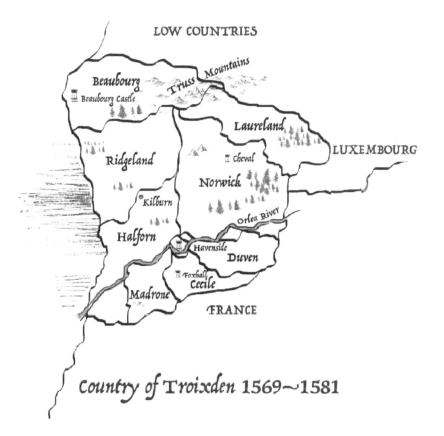

LOW COUNTRIES

Beaubourg
Beaubourg Castle

Truss Mountains

Laureland

LUXEMBOURG

Ridgeland

cheval

Norwick

Kilburn

Orlea River

Halforn

Havenside

Duven

Foxhall
Cecile

Madrone

FRANCE

Country of Troixden 1569~1581

Milady

"He can't be serious." A blonde curl escaped Lady Margaux's headdress and quivered with the ire of its mistress.

Robert, Duke of Norwick, seated behind his desk piled high with papers, arched a black brow, considering his sister. "While the king isn't thrilled, he has steeled himself to his duty. And while he does so, I am in charge here at the palace. This should please you."

He signed a contract with a flourish, blew off the blotting dust, and handed the parchment to his secretary, whom he dismissed with a flick. Making his way to the front of his desk, he perched on the edge looking like a self-satisfied raven. "Besides, we need an heir — one of Troixden blood, not of some foreign land that will pitch us into war with the Germans or the French."

"Save your lecture for council! You recalled me to court for this? Even your tiresome wife hinted that I—"

Robert stilled her with a look. She waited for his entourage to exit, smiling sweetly at the bows they gave her. With the close of the door she was at him again.

"How dare my own brother go along in recommending His

Majesty look outside court for such a match? Have you no heed for your family?"

Robert was up and twisting her arm before she could move. She yelped. "Keep your voice down!" he hissed. "You come here screaming like a banshee about succession when King James's grave is barely cold, William one month on the throne, and I next in line?"

He thrust her away and she tripped onto a waiting settee, her wine-red skirt a cloud swelling about her. "Don't pretend you have no interest in the throne. Friend or no, you want your boys in our fair cousin's place."

Robert turned to the girl he had once protected, the girl he had played knight and princess with, rescuing her from fiery dragons and their fiery father alike. Now she sat there, a shrill annoyance, twitching her nose like a rodent. Perhaps not a rodent — her nose was far too lovely for that, even he could admit.

"And how does your becoming queen get me or mine any closer to the throne? My sons would be well behind any brats you'd bear—"

"Perhaps I wouldn't have any brats." She crossed her arms and frowned out the windows at the early summer gloom.

"The king will have children — it's the entire point of the marriage. And knowing William, well, he'll be fathering children like Abraham."

"There are ways women know to keep children from coming."

Robert walked over to frown down upon her. "'Tis repugnant, what you speak of."

"And what if the king should pass before I conceive?"

Robert jerked her off the settee and steered her, shoulders first, into the stone wall. "You come to my rooms in the middle of the day while the king's away and speak of his death!" She had the grace to flinch. "Do you not think all eyes are upon me? Do you think because he and I are old friends I'm immune to his vengeance?"

He held her until her perfect face crumpled like a crushed flower then walked back to his desk. "Guards!"

Margaux stood where he left her, shriveled against the wall like a dead spider. His guards came in an instant.

"Please show my sister the door." Without looking up from his papers, he added, "and my lady, I trust I won't be hearing from you anytime soon."

She straightened to her full height, regal as ever, gave Robert a trifling curtsy, and preceded the guards out, leaving him alone with his discomfited thoughts.

In the far-flung duchy of Beaubourg, where the Truss Mountains tumble soft and green to the sea, Annelore squatted in her garden, plunging her grimy, bloodied hands into the cool earth, extracting the last of the sage. She frowned at one wilted, brown-stemmed sprig.

Plants died, of course, but most merely drooped or refused to thrive, silently bearing their grievances only to sprout anew the next year. The blacksmith's leg she and her maid Mary realigned that morning would not be so resilient.

Sitting back on her haunches, she brushed a tendril of hair off her cheek, leaving a streak of earth in its place.

"Annelore!" Her father leaned out the kitchen window, calling into the sunny June day. "Annnaaaaa!"

"Mhm?" She looked up. Even from that distance she saw the mirth in his face.

"Anna! Bryan is here—you must come to see. Comport yourself; make haste."

Hoisting herself up, she pushed through the kitchen door.

"Papa," she said, "certainly Bryan has seen me in much worse." And she him, to be sure.

"Have you forgot what this week is, my dear?" Her father ruffled her hair. "Or do you forget your friend unless he's in front of your smudged nose?"

Anna clapped her hands. She thought her mood couldn't be lifted, but this—how could she have forgotten? "And here I have nothing to congratulate him with."

"I daresay your smile will be sufficient," the duke said, smiling in his own turn.

She tore through the castle, tossing her filthy apron on the Great Hall table as she flew past. Washing her hands as best she could, she pinched extra color into her cheeks, and hurried to the stable yard.

She stopped short. There was Bryan, mounted on his steed in full chain-mail regalia—quite literally glowing.

"Bryan!" she called with a wave. "Or do I say Sir Bryan now?"

He dismounted, fell into a bow, and doffed his helmet, revealing all that golden hair.

Laughing, she ran to him. "Our very own knight, newly minted!"

"My lady," he said, then lifted her and swung around, laughing himself. "Yes, 'tis true."

"Well done," she said when he put her down. "And what of court? What of the new king? Even more wicked than his brother? What wore the ladies? What did they serve you?"

"Questions, questions—you're worse than my mother." He held out his arm. "But let's walk and I'll tell you all there is to tell, starting with silk—the ladies wear burgundy silk."

She looped her arm through his. "Blast, and here I am in blue taffeta."

"Even in a woolen tunic you would shine like a princess amongst all of those painted peacocks."

Clucking her tongue she looked down at her hands and frowned at stubbed nails filled with sediment. "Court has no use for Beaubourg and I have no use for it."

They set off to their favorite spot, the willow leaning by the stream at the far end of the east meadow.

"Oh, I think we'd make a fine pair there. Don't you?" Bryan said. "The Knight of Beaubourg and his lady love?"

"Court just seems a whole other world," she said. "As if you've traveled home from the Far East. And I suppose the ladies were no less exotic."

They came to the willow. Bryan, reaching for her, lost his footing and the two tumbled giggling to the soft moss below.

Sun dappled their faces and a soft breeze lifted the tree branches like a swishing skirt over their heads. Anna lay on her back, weaving her fingers through new summer grass, while Bryan, propped on an elbow as best he could, picked up a lock of her chestnut hair and wrapped it around his finger.

"May I be lashed severely if I thought even one held a candle to you, my love." He gave her forehead a kiss. It was dry. Quick.

"I see they haven't spared your education in the art of courtly love." She smirked at him.

He laughed, gave a drawn-out sigh and threw himself, chiming, onto his back. "You vex me, Anna. One day I think you love me, the next you don't. One day we're to marry and care for your father in his dotage, the next you shall never marry and I'll be cast out to haunt the lands sad and alone."

"Well, then, shall we find out today's answer?" She picked a clover daisy and began to pluck its petals. "I love you, I love you not, I love you, I love you not—"

Bryan grabbed the flower, tossed it aside, and seized both her hands. "Annelore, hear me." She cocked an eyebrow at his sudden zeal.

"Now don't tease," he said. "Being knighted—it's made me take a firmer look at the future. Even the king is casting about for a wife. I too want my future to be secure, to be settled. You know I've planned for us . . ." He looked into her dark eyes and swallowed. "You'll be twenty-one by month's end, well past time to marry—"

"And my father will finally relent to any suitors I may have, yes, we've discussed this." She kissed him gently on the hand, but he scowled and pulled away.

"Bryan, you know you're the nearest and dearest person in the world to me, forsaking Father and Mary. Be of good cheer. Why would he refuse you?" She picked up his fallen right hand, intertwining their fingers.

"But you'll tell him, won't you? That it's what we both want?" He searched her face. "We can start our own little family soon—the girls will look like you and the boys like me, and—"

"And any second now you'll be naming our grandchildren." She patted his hand and smiled at his frown. "Come now, tell me more of court."

Relenting his talk of love, he relaxed against the tree and told her of the grandeur of Palace Havenside, its courtiers and feasts, animation increasing. Then he spoke of the new king.

A fuzzy image of the king—then a young prince—floated to mind. He was giving her flowers . . . . But she shook the thought away, knowing the cruelty of his family all too well.

"He's surely a brute. Just like the rest of them, God rest their souls—if He must."

"He's no brute, Anna. He—"

"He what?" She could feel her cheeks turn hot. It was enough that Bryan had to serve this king—to risk his life, but to extol the monstrous man? "I for one have had enough of his family. Beaubourg's wool market sold more than ever this year, but our farmers saw no profit—though I'm sure the crown did. Not to mention the—"

"Anna, I tell you, this William . . ." He paused. "There's something in his countenance—something in his manner of being, in the set of his jaw . . . I can't describe it." He looked up, as if the right words might be found in the wind. "I would follow the man wherever ordered, even straight down the road to hell."

"Well then, perhaps you could marry him and all our problems would be solved."

"Don't." He shook his head then sighed. "Speaking of hell and marriage, this waiting for us to wed grinds my soul."

"I say again, *Sir Bryan*," she gave him a wink, "you must wait 'til Father is at his leisure—"

He interrupted her with a kiss full on the lips. This one was also quick, but wet. Forceful. She broke away and stood, dusting off her skirts.

"I must bid you *adieu* for a time," she said, "but come sup with us —we are to fête you properly."

"Mother won't have it." He gave her a half smile. "She's impatient to hear more of court and the goings-on."

She backed slowly away from him up the hill. "For heaven's sake bring her along, and your brothers and Charity too. That's an official order from the House of Carver and the Duke of Beaubourg."

With that, she turned heel and ran back home. When she reached the castle's outer gate, she looked back at their tree and saw him still sitting beneath, plucking a clover daisy, sun splattering his chainmail with shocks of light.

What ever was she going to do with him.

* * *

Anna returned home to find her father doling out coins to a royal messenger at the foot of the Great Hall table. The little man doffed his feathered cap and left the duke with a letter sealed in thick, red wax.

"Well, what news?"

"'Tis from the king," he said.

She rolled her eyes. Not him again. She stared at her father.

He stared back. "You'd like me to read it?"

Anna pursed her lips. "If it's not too much trouble."

He turned it round and round, ever so slowly broke the great seal with a knobby finger, and began to read. To himself.

"Out loud, Papa, out loud."

The duke's mouth curled at the edges, eyes twinkling. "But of course, my lady—if you demand it."

"Papa!" She stamped a foot, but couldn't help a grin.

He grinned, cleared his throat, and began. *"From His Royal Highness, King William the Second of the Mighty Kingdom of Troixden, to His Grace the Honorable Duke Stephen of Beaubourg* et cetera, et cetera . . ." He scanned the letter, lips twitching. "Ah! Here's the meat: *On a matter of both personal and national import, Our Royal Person shall arrive to Castle Beaubourg on the fifth of June, the year of Our Lord fifteen-hundred and sixty-nine. All persons of the House of Carver are obligated to attend—"*

"June fifth? That's the morrow!"

"The courier said there were some delays on the road . . ."

While the duke continued reading Anna hollered for Mary, who was already peering over the balcony.

"I've started on the beds," Mary called down, "and I suppose we'll be having to strangle the swans for feasting."

"Surely not!" Anna looked over at her father. "We don't want things too pleasant, lest His Majesty want Beaubourg for himself. For why else would he lower himself to come here? We've been disdained by court for years."

The duke, still reading, frowned.

"Papa?"

"We must ready the castle—no time to waste. You as well, my dear—and until the royal party leaves, there'll be no more digging about like a mole."

She was about to make retort, but glanced at her hands and thought better of it.

CHAPTER 2

His Highness

The royal carriage was stuck—again—leaving the freshly crowned King William II and Daniel, Duke of Cecile, standing in the mud under a hastily erected canopy. It did not put the king in a courting frame of mind.

As William's closest friend and advisor, Daniel was as new to Council Table as the king to his throne. It was against all tradition to name a novice to such high standing, an unpopular decision in any case thanks to Daniel's being a bastard, in lineage if not in manner. But the king was happy to have his friend by his side again.

Except at the moment. At the moment, William could have wrung his wiry neck. Although, to be fair, much of his anger derived from endless talk about the inevitable royal marriage.

"Can she not be pretty and witty as well as willing?" William said.

"I don't see why not, Majesty." Daniel said. "*You're* quite regal, you're—"

William rolled his eyes. "You sound like a courtier wanting another title."

"I think you've done enough for me already." Daniel looked at his feet. "But truly, sire, you've nothing to worry on."

Daniel kept talking, but William had heard it all before. With the effects of his family's disastrous bloody reigns still lingering, and the heretical Germans hoping to take a bite out of his realm, the crown needed security. The country needed stability. William needed heirs and spares and he needed them soon.

"Negotiating with England for the hand of Elizabeth appeals more and more at the moment." William watched his men working valiantly, and thus far fruitlessly, to dislodge the carriage wheels from the thick mud.

Daniel smiled in his quiet way. "You've been out of the realm these fifteen years in lands hostile to the Holy Father. To marry a heretic—"

"I know, I know." William eyed his straining men, itching to put his own shoulder to the task. "Besides, she's too aged for our purposes—though not much more so than my creaky self." He created haphazard rivers and tributaries in the sludge with his foot. "But at least I'd be dry. And her mind would make me merry. And I daresay, if our past acquaintance is any indication, she wouldn't find the idea abhorrent."

Daniel watched the progress of William's miniature riverbed for a minute, frowned and looked up at him. "You're but thirty, sire. And since when has Your Majesty ever balked in the face of such exploits as—"

"'Tis William when just the two of us." He clapped his friend on the back. "Didn't think I had to tell you that twice. And as for exploits, I've never had to tromp through fields, forests, and foulness in such absurd costume." He held up his arms, modeling his damp royal finery. "As king come a-courting, I cut a damned sorry sight."

Daniel scratched his temple in consideration.

"Yes, friend," William said, "I'll give you all the gold in the realm if you can spin this yarn into something agreeable."

Daniel swallowed a smile. "We can head south, turn back to—"

"Turn back?" William said. "As you say, our people already have a foul opinion of their sovereign. Shall they now find a little mud forces him to retreat?"

"They shan't, Majes—William."

"Then let's review our route. Again." William rubbed his large hands together as if to magic away the damp. "Why on earth we started by going north . . ."

"Seven duchies. Seven ladies. Seven chances to charm your people — "

"I'm sure the people of Hosmer were quite charmed as we sloshed through town in a hail of filth and rain, not even stopping for a royal wave."

"Hosmer is not even the halfway point," Daniel said, "and we'd already been delayed over four hours. We may have to skip Beaubourg entirely — "

William looked up at the canopy just as a large drop of rain hit him square on the nose. He swore.

"We'll not skip it. Though the duke will have to wait." He massaged his jaw, feeling the scrape of its close-cropped stubble. "As will the rest."

At the rate they were moving, the Duke of Beaubourg would have to wait quite a while.

* * *

That evening, when Anna retired to her chamber, Mary was standing ready with a hot bath and Anna's most luxurious gown hung to air.

"Ugh," she said, stretching her arms, "what a day, and what a morrow."

To Anna, Mary was frozen in time, smelling of spice-bread, roses, and a curious blend of tinctures. As a child Anna had spent many a night nestled against Mary's ample bosom as the nurse sang away the witches and goblins.

"What a day indeed, m'dear. Now off with your filthy clothes and into the tub."

Mary helped Anna out of her day dress and into the copper bath in front of the fire, then set to scrubbing Anna's hair with a frenzy normally reserved for an outbreak of lice.

"Do you want me to go bald?" Anna turned to her nurse who, holding the ends of Anna's dripping tresses in her calloused hands, continued unabated to thwack the dark locks into submission.

"Mary, do you think he means to take our lands?"

Mary stopped, looked square at Anna, opened her mouth, seemed to reconsider, then snapped it shut. "I'll be saying nothing about the whole matter—I'm just a servant here, after all."

"Don't be ridiculous, Mary." Anna shook her head. Everyone was so peculiar today. Even the mottled cat Mae sulked under the bed, refusing to come out. Perhaps it was the approaching dark clouds from the sea harkening yet another storm that put them all to such brooding.

Anna resettled herself in the deep tub. "Once he sees our natural splendors, how could he not want them for the crown?" she said. "And then what would happen to us all?" If she had to start wearing scrapped wool again to keep food on the tables of her people, she would do it.

"Well, m'love, as I said, I'll not say a thing about it." Mary helped Anna out of the bath and into a towel, then her shift. "'Cepting I think he's here for some other reason altogether."

Anna saw tears starting in Mary's eyes. "Mary, for heaven's sake, whatever is the matter?"

She thought of her father. Was he going to be called away? How could she manage running Beaubourg by herself?

"Tell me or I shan't sleep a wink!"

Mary patted her head as if she were a welp. "'Tis nothing, dearie. The early summer winds are making me head fuzzy." She went about turning down the bed, Anna following right behind.

"Tell me or I'll leave my candle burning all night and read the whole of St. Paul's epistles. Aloud. In the Greek."

"You wouldn't do that to your old Mary, now would y'?" She wouldn't meet Anna's eyes.

"If it's about Papa . . ."

"Don't be playing on me weak heart. I told you 'tis not my place. But I daresay you've nothing to badger me about."

Anna sighed. She would not be getting more information from her unusually tight-lipped maid. Perhaps things would be clearer in the morning. She climbed into bed and opened her Bible.

While Protestantism was gaining purchase in other lands, the

Pope still held sway in Troixden. And the gentry were expected to know their Scripture, if only to appear learned. If they had a Bible at all. Anna enjoyed the stories—they fed her sense of adventure and drama. She loved the wisdom and poetry, the epic tales. Every night she read until her candle burned out or her eyes fluttered to a close.

"Not too late, dearie. You'll be needing your sleep."

Anna arched a brow. "For what, pray tell?"

Mary shook her head and Anna smiled through a yawn. "I'm tired—and in Leviticus. I'll soon be asleep."

Mary gave her one last lingering look and wiped a creased eye.

* * *

It was getting on eleven the following evening, and the entire House of Carver, from the lowest stable hand to the duke himself, stood at attention in Castle Beaubourg's courtyard. The rain was misting, a fine drizzle that showed no sign of abating.

Anna had been up and down and up and down what seemed like twenty times that day. No one dared touch the feast—now gone cold —and no one dared take a bit of leisure, lest His High and Mighty arrive without warning. They had been kept apprised of the king's halting progress by a succession of messengers, all claiming His Majesty would arrive soon, the last one having left them a half-hour ago.

He'd been due early that afternoon.

Blast these royals! Anna shivered in her damp gown. *Selfish, slow, full of their own airs. The butcher's wife due with her babe any moment and Mary and me stuck here . . . .*

She heard the thick clomp of hooves fast approaching. No doubt another fleet of messengers. She'd go to bed after this final insult, king or no.

Just as she turned to beg permission from her father, horses tore into the yard, mud flying, whining and wet, their riders bedraggled in their court dress. A tall, cloaked man at the center dismounted in haste, barely waiting for his black beast to halt, the others scrambling after him.

"Your Grace," the man said, striding to her father, not bothering to pull back his hood. His boots were covered with mud. How disrespectful of her father's rank and wait! They were all alike, no matter what Bryan said.

"Please accept our most humble apologies for our tardiness," the man said. "It seems the weather up north frowns upon our journey. And as you can tell from our state, we have been stuck a long while."

"Your Majesty," her father said, bowing, then taking the king's proffered hand and kissing his ring. "'Tis a trifle to wait upon such an honor. Please, let us retire to dryness and warmth."

Anna gasped, unsure whether to be appalled or astounded at this behavior. The two men entered the castle followed by another four of the king's party. Anna heard the king's deep voice booming out.

"Our carriage shall be along at some point. Hopefully by the time of our needed departure."

"Certainly, sire, my men shall attend to every need," her father replied. "They'll soon be about seeing to your steed. A creature of rare beauty, I might add."

Their voices faded and Mary caught hold of Anna's arm, pulling her to the foyer.

"Ye look a fright." She busied about Anna's hair, which had frizzled in the damp.

"What does it matter? I shall retire and make my official appearance in the morning." She didn't care how the king would look upon such a breach. It served him right, keeping them waiting like this. Weather! What a paltry excuse.

"You'll do no such thing, dearie," Mary said, moving to re-fluff Anna's sleeves. "'Tis the king who's here, not some horse trader."

"And the king needs to learn his manners."

"By flouting your own? Nay, Anna, you were raised better, if I say so meself." Mary gave a final shake to Anna's skirts. "Maybe with the light so dim he'll not see dirt on the hem."

Anna stood glowering as more laughter echoed in the hall.

"Out with you." Mary gave her a little shove on the backside.

Anna stumbled the few steps to the archway leading to the

sunken hall where the men had all sat down to eat, the king at the far end—in her father's usual place—her father to the king's right.

The hall was darker than normal, as if the gloom from outside had drifted in with the king's party and hung over the table. She could barely make out the men's faces closest to her, shadowed as they all were by the pall that even a surplus of candles could not pierce.

She stopped on the top stair, unsure whether to enter there or go around through the hallway to her father. The laughter crested and she noticed the king joining in. He glanced in her direction, stroking his cheek. His smile faded. Even at such a distance she could feel his eyes bore through her. Her heart sped like a sparrow under Mae's paw.

Benches and chairs scraped the stone floor as the men rose to honor her entrance. All but the king. He remained seated, watching. She furrowed her brow at him and saw the flicker of a smirk break. So she was entertaining, was she?

"Your Highness," her father said, hurrying to her side, "may I present my daughter, the Lady Annelore Matilda of Beaubourg."

Anna curtsied low, glad to avoid the king's sharp eyes.

"Lady Annelore," the king said, "we are pleased. And hope you accept our regrets for the lateness of the hour. Please, join us at table."

At *her* table. "Thank you, Majesty," she said. She rose and moved to the lone open seat at the far end between two of the royal party, a thin blonde man and an older one, heavy and balding. She sat without ceremony, took a long swig of wine and set her goblet down with too much force, hushing the conversation enough to attract Bryan's attention. He gave her a sheepish look from across the table.

She picked up a fork and stabbed at a piece of cold venison. Meat secure, mouth open, and morsel halfway to its mark, she looked up to find the king still staring at her. She put her bite down slowly, her eyes following it to her plate.

Dammit! Stop looking at me with those blasted eyes!

"By all means, dear lady, eat," he said. The men were silent, everyone now watching her.

"Begging your pardon, Majesty," she said, eyes glued to her plate. "As we long awaited your party, I had not a moment to eat since noontime." She knew it was rude, but she couldn't help it. At least it should stop his stares.

"Of course," the king said. She felt his eyes leave her and then, her breath return. "Your Grace, tell me more of your stables."

This was the cue for the rest of the men to resume eating and talking. How skittish they all seemed, all save the two flanking her. The one to her left, the big one, reached out and patted her forearm.

"Pay no heed, my lady," he said. She glanced up to find hazel eyes dancing in the dim candlelight. "I especially enjoy the plum sauce with the venison. Finer plum sauce is not even found in Havenside, I daresay." His smile was so sincere she couldn't help smiling back.

"The Duke of Halforn at your service, my lady." He made a little twirling salute with his hand. "And the gentleman to your right is His Grace, the Duke of Cecile."

Cecile turned to her and nodded with a perfunctory smile. "My lady, it is indeed a pleasure. And His Grace is correct— the plum sauce surpasses that of even Rome."

"Your Grace has been to Rome?"

His pale cheeks flushed. She had not been able to mask her eagerness.

"Yes, my lady, but I did not mean to boast, only to compliment the sauce."

"But of course. I merely wish to—it's just that—please, Your Grace, speak to me of your travels."

Daniel acquiesced with almost enough details to satisfy her, the jolly Halforn interjecting his wit until the talk of travels finally subsided.

"So 'tis true. Your Ladyship has a learned mind," Halforn said after a mouthful of sweetbread. "If only my daughters would take a lesson from you, my dear."

"How have you heard such, Your Grace?" How could anyone outside of Beaubourg have heard anything about her, let alone the state of her mind? Ah, but of course: Bryan had just returned from court.

Halforn laughed. "Why, it's our business to know of all the ladies of the land —"

"What His Grace means to say —" Cecile started, but the voice of the king rose above them.

"We are afraid there's no remedy, Your Grace, as we are already so delayed. We really must away tomorrow morning. Please do not take it as any reflection upon your hospitality."

"Of course not, sire," her father said. "I only wished you to have the time you needed, as the matter is of such import."

"Worry not," the king said. "Things shall present themselves much more clearly after a night's rest. If her ladyship would be so inclined as to break fast with us, we do not believe our early departure will hamper the matter."

"If that be the case, Highness," Anna said, "I shall to bed now, if you please." The king raised his thick brows at her.

Her father sat stunned. "Please excuse my daughter, Highness, she is used to less formality, as in usual circumstances only she and I are at table."

"Think nothing of it, Your Grace," the king said. "A lady who speaks her mind is one to be admired, is she not?" Several at the table called out "Here, here!" and raised their glasses in a toast. To her or the king she could not tell.

She pushed herself away from the table. "Then I shall —"

"You have our leave," the king said, fixing her in mid-rise with that unnerving stare of his. How dare he make her feel so small in her own home? But of course, that's what kings did best.

"Majesty," she said, dipping into the faintest of curtsies and meeting his gaze with the force of her own, "the distinct honor of your presence has been mine. Please continue to enjoy our hospitality as seems fitting to you."

With that she turned from all those men with their disconcerted faces and left them to grovel before their tyrant of a king.

* * *

The morning came bright and clear as the sound of men and hooves from the stable yard below wakened Anna. Mary had laid out a pretty, yet perfectly average, day dress for her—apparently she had not been called to break fast with the king. She lay still, listening to snippets of conversation that floated to her ears.

"A hearty thanks for your hospitality, Your Grace."

A reply from her father she couldn't make out. "Yes, we shall see you soon." The king's voice.

See you soon? Oh Papa, no—he couldn't be leaving!

She threw off her sheets and ran to the window. The plump duke was shaking hands with her father, grasping his arm and laughing. The Duke of Halforn. He was merry enough last evening. Now she loathed him.

The king, about to climb into his carriage, glanced up. He caught Anna looking at him and gave her a quick nod before she could duck. Just as the night before, his gaze glued her to the floor.

"Fair journey, Majesty, milords," her father called as the last of the men mounted. "Farewell, Your Grace, and to your fair daughter, highest compliments of your king."

With that His Royal Highness settled into the carriage, the Duke of Cecile in his wake.

Anna turned from the window. "I must find out what's going on, and if you won't tell me, Mary—as I'm sure you know the whole of it—I'll just have to force it from Father."

"If that be your mind, dearie, I shan't be changing it." She tried to help Anna dress, but Anna wouldn't stay still. "It all started with this business of Bryan's being knighted—Mary, tie me!—perhaps 'tis all to do with that."

Not caring to glance in a mirror, Anna hurried to the door, but then ran back and gave Mary a tight hug.

"Oh, Mary, I couldn't stand being separated from Papa. What am I to do?"

"You'll find out soon enough. Now off with you."

Anna tore down the staircase and into the Great Hall, where she found her father meeting with his horse master, Jeffrey.

She stopped short at the bottom of the stairs. "Father?"

The two men were hunched over some sort of ledger, the table still showing remnants of a sumptuous breakfast. The duke's one vice was horses. He searched the country for the fastest, prettiest, smartest, heartiest ones he could find, and his stables were the envy of many beyond Beaubourg.

"Father, I must speak with you."

"Tush, you know we don't stand on ceremony." He smiled broadly, opening his arms in welcome.

"I fear my temper in front of Master Jeffrey, begging his pardon."

The duke turned to his faithful horseman. "Would you excuse us please? I shall find you in the stables later." He took in Anna's dour expression. "It may be a while."

She tried with no success to calm herself while Jeffrey took his time gathering and arranging papers. The duke tapped the seat to his right at the head of the table.

"Anna dear, please sit. I have much to tell you." He smiled at her, but the smile didn't reach his eyes. Was he nervous?

He reached for her hands, engulfing them. "My darling daughter, I can't believe it, but the day has come that I may have to bid you goodbye."

She grabbed his forearms, as if she could hold him there forever. "Papa, you can't leave us—"

He unclenched her hands gently. "My dear, you misunderstand. It's you who are to go—to go and be a wife."

I thought Bryan was going to wait. She frowned.

"So he's asked you already?" she said. "And you've agreed?"

Her father cocked his head. "But however did you know, my dear? And are you pleased?"

"Certainly Bryan and I have long—"

"Bryan?" he said. "I've never intended your hand for him." He gave her a quaking smile. "You, my darling daughter, have been given the greatest honor a woman could dare dream. The king has selected you to be among his choices for queen."

Anna's heart dropped to the floor.

"After his tour ends this month, he'll call three of the seven ladies he has seen to court for final review. And I have given my consent should you be among the three. Though I daresay my blessing matters little in the equation."

Anna sat there, still mute, trying to take in words that couldn't possibly mean—

"Annelore, you might be queen."

"No." Her voice was no more than a whisper.

"I can tell you're surprised, as was I when I read the full letter. I'd heard His Majesty was looking for a bride outside of court, but never dared imagine he'd come to Beaubourg." He stopped and took a long look at her. "Annelore?"

Her insides were stone. Worse, the room seemed to careen to the left, tapestries swaying as if on a ship. This was all a horrible mistake, a terrible misunderstanding.

"But . . . I'm to marry Bryan."

"What do you mean?" His face clouded over. "What have you two done?"

"I asked him to wait until my birthday—"

"Are you telling me you've betrothed yourself to Bryan? Without my knowledge or consent?"

Anna could count on one hand the number of times her father had ever spoken to her in that tone of voice.

"Well . . . no. I didn't—I don't know."

He pounded his fist on the table. "Has he defiled you? I'll have his testicles!"

"Papa! How could you think such a thing of him? Of *me*?"

"Are you or are you not bound to each other, girl?" He slammed the table again, the clatter of dishes making her flinch. Her face crumpled in defeat.

"Only by assumption."

He sighed and crossed himself, sinking back into his chair. "Thank the Lord."

"But you know well how close we are—have been for years!" She knew her voice was shrill. "How could you not intend to give him my hand?"

"If that were my intention I'd have betrothed you much, much sooner than this."

"So what—you planned to marry me off to some faceless duke?" She pushed herself to her feet and turned from the table.

"Don't be absurd, Anna." He watched her pace the floor, only half cleaned from the morning's revelry. Sighing, he leaned down to pick up a fallen goblet from the wine-soaked straw and stood.

"Nothing is certain, Anna. His Majesty may very well choose another—he didn't see much of you and—"

"But he's a horrible, selfish old man who'll rob our people blind!"

"Enough!" He stared hard at her, shaking his head. "I raised you better than this—or thought I did."

She quieted, well censured. "You raised me to be useful and happy, Papa. Happy here. With our people, with you."

He came to her and lifted her chin. "Your happiness is the constant demand of my heart. Surely you know that."

"That's why I don't understand." Tears started at the corners of her eyes, but she held them back with a tight swallow.

He gave her a wistful smile. "You were so young when your mother passed. You're so much like her." His eyes glistened too. "I loved her to distraction, Anna. There's nothing in the world I wouldn't have done for her. I risked my very neck to secure her hand. And when she died? Half my soul was buried with her."

"But Bryan—"

"Look me in the eye and tell me you love the boy as much as that."

Seconds passed. Finally she spoke. "'Tis not mere girlish esteem I have for him. As for the king—"

"I know you're fond of Bryan. As for the king, you've spent almost no time with him, which I have. You haven't heard what I have. You didn't even stay until the feast was over. " He sighed. "I promise you, Anna, the king is a man of wisdom and good heart."

He enveloped her in his arms. She sank in, face hangdog against his chest. "If he picks you, you shall marry him."

"But—"

"But," he said, "if he chooses another, then, and only then, will I give Bryan your hand. If that is your true desire."

She looked up at him, her eyes full.

"In the meantime," he said softly, "do not judge the king too quickly. Husband or no, he is our sovereign and must be afforded our fealty."

"I shall try." She stepped back and smoothed her dress.

"And no more bandying about with Bryan until the matter is decided. I know he's your friend, but it doesn't make you or our house look well if you're so familiar with him right now."

Good. All the more reason for the king to choose another.

"Are we agreed, dear?"

"Yes, Papa." *Agreed to make myself the least desirable woman His Majesty has ever come across.*

* * *

Anna returned to her room, face so ashen that Mary hurried to her side.

"How could you not have told me?"

Mary held Anna to her chest and gave her a squeeze. "It weren't my place, dearie. And I didn't know for sure."

Her father might as well have told her she was being shipped off to the Americas. Surely when he finally understood how she felt, he would remove her from the king's consideration. Not that the king would choose her, but what if he did? What argument did she have? She preferred her castle to his? And if she left, who would look after Beaubourg with her father, especially once he . . . . She sniffled, still fighting back tears.

"I didn't think you'd take it so hard," Mary said, "especially as there be six other ladies to consider." She gave Anna's shoulder a squeeze. "Tush, tush. Just try an' see it from your father's eyes."

"My father's eyes are blind." Anna went from Mary's arms to the window.

"You know very well he only wants the very best for you."

"And why are home and Bryan not best? He was good enough to be my playmate and friend and to be always welcome here."

"Bryan's jolly, but ye'll be wanting a husband who'll make something of himself."

"Being knighted isn't making something of oneself?"

Mary sighed and fluffed the bed. "Ye realize you're the envy of all the maids of Troixden—and many outside?"

"Let them have His High and Mighty Majesty then." Anna went to her washbasin and splashed her face with the cool water. Her cheeks were still hot.

"They'll be likely to, more's the pity. We could use a friend in such a high place as queen."

Breathing through her nose like one of her father's unbroken fillies, she scoured her hands. "Don't play on my loyalty to our people." Mary did have a point, but Anna didn't want to hear it. She went to her wardrobe, let out a jagged sigh, and lifted a simple gold-thread hairnet from a hook.

Mary took it and piled Anna's thick locks in. "'Tis not like His Majesty has picked you—after the performance you gave last evening he's no doubt looking eager for the next lady. Why else would he leave without a how-ye-please?"

As soon as Mary finished, Anna returned to pacing, gesticulating as if arguing before a tribunal. "He leaves us standing in the rain, expects us to stay up all hours to fawn on him, then makes an early departure. The man put the whole castle—the whole town—in an uproar over him, then he stays a mere nine hours, most of those asleep."

Mary busied herself about the room, tidying Anna's books, arranging a clean stack of handkerchiefs next to her combs.

"Some of the time there be things even a king can't control."

"Tush." Anna turned to look out the window. Spying her and Bryan's willow, she felt a pang.

"The king's a fine strapping man," Mary said. "Well bred. Stout of heart, so they say."

"I say he's a greedy, selfish brute." She bent to scratch Mae's ear.

Mary shook her head. "Your father may be blind, but so be you, dearie."

* * *

The last night's storm had cleared, but the roads were still slow going. William decided to forego the carriage once out of Beaubourg's sight and continue on horseback now they were headed into hostile territory.

Laureland, Beaubourg's eastern neighbor, jutted out like a horn into the Germanic states of the Holy Roman Empire. The small territory had been unstable for years, made worse in recent times as the conversions to Luther gained swift and dangerous headway.

"Selecting the Earl of Laureland's daughter may look like appeasement," William said, "but I'm not convinced it will quiet the Laurelanders."

"Indeed, Majesty." Halforn took a swig from his flask, full of the Duke of Beaubourg's special stock of amber honey wine.

"We certainly cannot brook outright insurrection," Daniel said.

"As yet, their murmurs hardly amount to that," William said. "I fear a heavy hand will only push them further away. My brother spilt enough of our people's blood. I don't wish to repeat his legacy."

"All the more reason we consider the earl's daughter," Daniel said. He swatted at a horsefly intent on his stark brows.

William took off his cap to thwack at a cloud of gnats. "But I can't marry a rumored heretic."

"The Duke of Norwick doesn't think she's fallen prey to the Protestants," Daniel said. "Of course, I've heard the lady speaks German in the home."

"That doesn't mean she's a heretic," Halforn said.

William laughed, startling his horse. "Did you see the look on our fair archbishop's face when the Queen of England was suggested?"

"I believe," Halforn said, "his face turned the purple of his robes."

"A pus-filled pox he called her," Daniel said.

"Don't forget, she eats Catholic children for breakfast." William swallowed a smile. "Ah, His Eminence will surely fume at a queen from Laureland, devoted Papist or no."

"'Tis rumored this Lady Helena is most cherished," Daniel said. "Sweet-natured, quiet—"

"The opposite of the Lady Annelore, then?" William chuckled.

"Tush, Majesty," Halforn said. "I found the lady charming."

"Indeed I did as well," Daniel said. "She has less polish than the courtiers we're accustomed to, but she appears to have a strong mind—"

"Her lack of courtly manners 'tis not my hesitation," William said.

"Then why did you not send for her this morning?" Halforn said.

William frowned. He'd felt awkward at the thought of waking the lady. Bashful, almost. Something about the way she'd looked at him, like she saw through to his deepest insecurities. He had also never been upbraided in such a cheeky fashion—at least in public.

"Majesty?"

"Truth be told," William said, "I didn't want to spoil her breakfast —or mine. She has the demeanor of a wet cat."

Halforn let out a guffaw and the three men rode on across the forest boundary of Beaubourg and into the belly of the beast.

CHAPTER 3

To Have & Have Not

"Bryan, what am I going to do?"

Anna folded his long, thin fingers in her palm, stroking them over and over as they sat under their willow. Her father was out buying a new horse and would be gone for hours.

She was bone tired, having just returned from helping the butcher's wife give birth. She, Mary, and Bryan's sister Charity were the only women trained at midwifery in town. Not to mention she was in charge of the food dole for the needy, organizing the market licenses, and . . . .

"Bah! He simply must choose another!"

"Why he *would* choose another escapes me." Bryan brought her hand to his lips. "But we'll make sure he does. For you're mine, and I won't let you go."

She frowned, thinking. "If only we could flee to France or something. Or go on pilgrimage—he couldn't interrupt a holy tour."

"Be practical—you know I can't speak French." Then, almost to himself: "Now, the Americas—no one would bother with us if we went that far."

She looked at him as if brie oozed out his ears. "And you say I'm impractical? What would become of Beaubourg?"

"What would become of it if we fled to France or went on

pilgrimage?" His face was flushed. "Besides, I've sworn my fealty — my duty, my life — to His Majesty. I can't leave without his consent."

"I saw nothing in him worth your devotion," she said. "Or has your devotion to me faded?"

He jumped to his feet. "What would my word be to you if I broke my word to him?"

"Then have your king!" She jumped up herself. "I could go of my own accord, you know. I won't be His Majesty's chattel, even if you must."

"You would leave and break your father's heart?" He put both hands on her shoulders, steadying her with his gaze. "And mine? You know I won't let you go, Annelore." He bent down to kiss her cheek, but she turned away with a snort. He could be so thick at times.

"At least in France or Rome I'd be free. And I could return as soon as the king marries."

"We must fix our hopes and prayers on the king selecting another." Bryan pronounced, though looked more desperate than hopeful.

"Indeed. Court considers Beaubourg a trifle. The king gains nothing in me." This had become her internal refrain, the logic to which she'd clung.

Bryan wrapped his arms about her waist. "There you're wrong. For in you, he would gain the world, just as I would lose it."

She looked into his sad, robin's egg eyes. Blast! If there were only some sure way to make her a more unappealing prospect to the king.

"I know that look," Bryan said. "What are you scheming now? Tell me, I can help — let me be a part of it."

She shook her head and sighed. "'Tis as you say, we shall keep and pray until the king marries another."

* * *

After a month of flattering fathers and fluttering eyelashes, William and his men reached Duven, the last duchy on their tour. Gregory,

Duke of Duven, five years William's junior, was one of his favorite councilmen.

"Ah, Your Grace," William said, leaning back in a luxurious leather chair in Gregory's hall, a mug of mead balanced on his thigh, "'tis refreshing to be back in fair company."

"Majesty found his realm unkind?" Gregory asked, sinewed legs stretched toward the hearth.

"Nay, our people are the best in all the lands." William lifted his drink in toast. "My desire to rule them well has only intensified."

"'Tis hard to believe, Duven," Halforn said, resting his mug atop his belly, "but I believe His Highness tires of all these ladies."

"May that never be." William let out a laugh and rubbed his brown stubble. "'Tis not the ladies I despise but everyone tripping over themselves to satisfy. I'd be better pleased if people would just be themselves."

"Sire," Gregory said, placing a hand to his heart, "I promise I shan't simper on my fair sister's behalf, for she does her own self justice. Shall I fetch her?"

William sighed, straightened up, and nodded. He'd met a few ladies who would soothe the country's tension, but what about his? None were what he desired. Perhaps love was not possible, but he had hopes of a wife he could share his mind with. And could she not be pretty? Poor Helena of Laureland looked like a mule. No wonder she was quiet and sweet—it was her only recourse.

If only Catherine were alive. Perhaps under his younger sister's gentle hand there would not be quite such hurry for him to marry. If anyone could placate his people with beauty and grace—and give him time to find a wife to his liking—it was his Cate.

"Your Majesty, may I present Lady Emmaline."

Emmaline curtsied low before him, giving him a chance to admire ample breasts that rose and fell with her quick breath. Her golden hair gleamed even in the dark hall. *Does herself justice indeed.*

The king stood, took her hand to help her up, and kissed it. "My lady, 'tis indeed an honor. Will you not join us for a stroll in the gardens?"

"Nothing would bring me more pleasure, sire," she said, a smile breaking on her wide red lips. William smiled back. *Nor I, my future queen.*

* * *

"Beg pardon?" William had been focused on Emmaline's breasts, not her words: how those breasts would feel up against him, in his hands, their weight and softness and . . . . Dammit it had been too long since he'd bedded anyone.

"I asked if Your Highness preferred hunting to tennis. As I hear you pursue both splendidly."

"It's hard to decide, my lady." He kissed her fingers again, getting a whiff of jasmine. "I suppose the hunt." And his mind was off again. *What a petite waist she has.* But he knew he must not decide based on mere lust. That's how his brother James ended up with a headless queen. He looked from tiny waist to tidy rows of roses in the garden.

"I enjoy the out of doors," he said, "even if not in a hunt."

"As do I, Majesty."

"And when you cannot be outside, my lady, what do you enjoy? To read?" She gave a laugh like a dove and blushed. Adorable.

"I have long since put away such manly pursuits," she said. "Spending my youth at the French court, I realized that not everything is to be learned in books."

"Ah, quite the diplomat, then?" He smiled. Beautiful *and* cultured. Though it was hard to imagine not ever reading.

"Well, I do speak French, so I suppose I could help in some diplomatic capacity." She smiled again, showing off her little dimples. "We ladies proved our worth through music and needlework and other such pursuits." He frowned and she hastened to add, "Of course I would surely love to read anything Your Majesty might suggest. I used to enjoy adventure stories."

"Ah—lovesick knights and sweet young ladies becoming queen?" This time her blush traveled all the way to her cleavage.

He patted her arm and twined it through his. "I should not tease, my dear, as we've only just met."

Lord, she was perfect: raised away from the taint of James's court, eager to please but not fawning, attractive. What did it matter she didn't read? She would if he wanted her to. Turning his eyes back to the landscape, he saw a towering row of hedges.

"What's there?"

"That is our maze, Majesty." She dipped her chin toward the giant shrubbery. "It was built for contemplation, but my brother and I used to play hide-and-seek there as children." She looked up at him with a perky smile and tugged at his arm. "Since Majesty so enjoys the hunt, he must give me a head start."

Without waiting on a response, she hoisted up her pink silk skirts, ran giggling toward a break in the hedges, and then turned to him, all ruddy and glowing. Yes, she would do just fine.

"You must count to ten—nay, twenty!" Giggling again, she scampered out of sight.

It was not seemly for a king to chase after a lady in a hedge-grove. For what would people think he'd done once he found her?

William grinned. *Let the games begin.*

She was not hard to find, what with the giggling and the floral scent in her wake. Though perhaps she wasn't trying too hard. She was tucked behind a wayward branch, a shock of blush enveloped by evergreen and conveniently lodged next to a stone bench. She tittered as he pretended not to see her.

"Why wherever could the lady be?" He sauntered to the bench, still ignoring her, and sat, his leg nestling against her skirts. "I smell her like flowers in the sunshine, as if she is right in my lap." As he said it, he felt familiar heat in his groin. But he must not be too aggressive. She was a lady. A lady he wanted as his wife. Sighing, he looked to his left and pretended to startle. As expected, she giggled.

"Why there you are!" He grinned at her and took her hand. It was smooth, petite, unblemished. Looking her straight in the eyes, he kissed her knuckles, letting his lips linger as his desire rose. She let out a small gasp of pleasure and with the slightest tug, she tumbled onto his waiting thighs.

Eyes grazing her face, he knew there was a certain point at which he would not be able to hold himself back from taking her right on that marble bench. He let those images flash through his mind: his tongue wrapping a pink nipple, his hand under her skirts clutching her ass, her hand on his . . . .

He attacked her mouth, all gentle play gone. He was lost to the need of his body, all thought, all sense evaporating into the yielding of her lips, her limbs.

Surprisingly she returned his passion. No longer the demurring lady, her tongue was not shy in dueling with his, her hands roaming his biceps, his roaming her torso. This certainly was not her first time kissing a man, but he let that twinge of jealousy drive him forward. He nuzzled her chin to the side and slid his lips down her aquiline neck, suckling a clavicle. His hand wrapped her ribs, thumb tracing under her breast over her tight bodice.

"Your Majesty," she breathed, head thrown back. She grabbed the back of his head, pressing him against her. He flicked his tongue over the dip in her throat, felt her swallow a moan. In that moment he knew he could have his way with her. Wanted to have his way with her. Needed to have his way with her.

But would he want this of his queen? A confusion of duty and desire warred within him. As she shifted, arcing up to him, she slipped from his grasp and fell on her undoubtably perfect bottom. He swore under his breath.

Her face turned the color of her dress as he bent to help her stand. She curtsied, stumbling over her words. "I'm so sorry Majesty, I was taken aback, I mean, overwhelmed, I mean I'm not regularly — "

"Please do not apologize," he said, bowing. "'Tis I who must apologize to you. I took advantage of a situation and lost control of my senses."

"I am at your service, sire, I — "

He held up a hand. "That is my point. I should not have put you in a position where you felt obliged to satisfy my bodily whims."

"I wouldn't say I felt *obliged*." She blushed even deeper, if that were possible. "I . . . I rather enjoyed it."

He smiled at her. "As did I, milady. 'Twas still uncouth." He took her hand, turning toward the maze's exit. "Besides, I have a feeling you and I might have all the time in the world to enjoy ourselves, as it were."

"There would be no greater honor, my liege," she said.

Unbidden, the scowling face of the lady from Beaubourg popped in his mind. What was her name? Eleanor? *Someone should have told her it was an honor.* But why did he care? He had his choice by his side. He squeezed her hand again and walked back out into the blazing sun.

* * *

Three days later William was back in his own opulent chambers, spirits aright and refreshed. Just one more task, and off to the hunt.

"Robert, dear cuz,'" he said as the Duke of Norwick entered, "it does my heart good to see you again." He gestured to the walls. "And the palace still in one piece—pigs fly and hell is frozen."

Robert grinned and drew up a chair at William's desk, next to Daniel.

"Despite my best efforts, Wills." He scratched the patch of dark beard under his lower lip. "And all the ladies unmolested to boot—save one."

"You are a rogue," Daniel said. "What would your wife say?"

"Since she be far from court, she needn't say a word." Robert threw his feet on the desk. William smacked his boots, and off the feet went.

"We must pare down this list to three," the king said. Still not quite grasping why they needed to go through all this formality of bringing three women to court when he knew the lady he wanted. But Daniel said it was worth it to appear fair. Why fairness had much to do with his marriage and need for heirs, he wasn't quite sure, but he truly could not think of a time when Daniel was wrong. "I already have Halforn's thoughts."

"I say pick the fairest one and to hell with the rest." Robert thrust his hips up. "At least she'll keep thy royal bed warm."

Daniel turned to Robert with a frown. "There are other considerations."

"Says the man who refuses to marry," William said with a wink, secretly agreeing with his cousin.

"Majesty, my devotion and service is to you and Troixden, a wife and family would only—"

"Tush, Daniel, we only tease," William said. "I know you have my best at heart. Even more so than myself."

"Right," Robert rubbed his hands. "Down to business." He scanned Halforn's notes. "This Helena—Earl of Laureland's daughter? —she sounds a fright."

Daniel shook his head. "Something the queen mother once told me was that royals must always consider the needs of the realm over themselves. I would daresay especially in the case of something so permanent as marriage."

"Of course," William said. "But even if sweet Helena were more . . . comely, could she help bring about the calm we hope for?" He looked out his window to the high green hills. "I suppose we should keep her on the list, at least."

"Halforn, of course, recommends the remaining of his twins," Robert said.

"Sweet as well, but easy to eliminate. She's too close to court to be seen as a queen of the people." William's mouth curved into a half smile. "And God save me, she's daft as the day is long."

"And round as her father," Robert said.

"May we please show respect?" Daniel said. "Especially when she's the daughter of a valued councilman?"

"Must you always be a damp rag?" Robert said.

"Daniel's right," William said, relaxing into his chair behind the desk, his feet on the windowsill. "I'm prepared to take up my cross for God and country."

"I think we can easily remove the ladies of Alsance, Ellington, and Corkle," Daniel said.

"Agreed." William tapped his fingers on the arm of his chair. He knew who he wanted—why could it not be done with? "Duven's sister, Emmaline, she's at the top in my mind. Even you'd be pleased, Robert."

"How pleased?"

William rolled his eyes and turned to Daniel.

"To be sure, she was indeed fair, good-natured—very queenlike, William. And since Duven only arrived at court when you did, she's not a known—or disliked—quantity."

"And she gives good chase." William smirked, remembering her hungry lips. "Frankly, I don't think we need look any further."

"Out of propriety we must at least pick three," Daniel said.

"What about Margaux?" Robert said.

William snorted. "Hardly far from court. You really think your sister would serve the people well?"

"She'd sure as hell serve you." He flashed a wolfish grin.

"You miss the point, Robert," Daniel said.

"I don't think I do. We're in need of heirs, yes?"

"Your sister has many charms," William said. "Perhaps we should at least place her amongst the final three to appease any of her supporters from James's court."

"I could not agree less," Daniel said. Robert glared at him. "Seeking out a woman away from James's court is to calm the people's rage. Margaux would merely inflame them."

William searched Robert's face. "When we left, you wished your sister good riddance and us fair hunting. You seem to have changed your tune."

"She has, shall we say, quieted in your absence."

William let it go with a raised brow and a "Huh."

Daniel turned back to the list. "And what of Lady Annelore of Beaubourg?"

"Beaubourg?" William had been daydreaming of Emmaline again, and not in a way he wished to repeat to Gregory.

"I heard of her insolence toward you," Robert said. "James would've had her stripped and flogged her right there at table."

"Am I my brother?" William said.

Robert looked out the window and scowled.

William thought back. He really had no reason to keep her on the list. She'd been almost recalcitrant, definitely biting, yet there was unexpected fire there. And he remembered how her father's eyes danced as he spoke of her—not as a pawn to gain him more power, but as a treasure to his heart. However happy he might be that his daughter was being considered for royal marriage, he would grieve to part with her.

"She's hardly demure, 'tis true," he said, "but we need a third and I appreciate her pluck."

"But Beaubourg gains you nothing," Robert said.

"Beaubourg would make a fine alliance, actually," Daniel said. "It's known throughout the realm for its hearty people, and being next to Laureland is an added help. Even more than a queen from Laureland or Duven, one from Beaubourg could bring about unity."

Robert threw up his hands. "I thought we'd decided: Helena, Emmaline, and Margaux—"

"I must insist," Daniel said, rising from his chair. "This Annelore has much better prospects—"

William looked out the window again, the light summer breeze playing on his face, then turned back to his friends. Whomever the other two were made no matter. He knew who his queen would be.

"Emmaline of Duven, Helena of Laureland, and Annelore of Beaubourg. Send the letters, Daniel."

Robert let out an extended sigh.

"Cheer up, cuz." William walked around the desk and clasped Robert's shoulder. "Come, let's hunt."

CHAPTER 4

Whom to Serve

The House of Carver had received word three days before. Annelore had been summoned to court for further examination.

She was, of course, beside herself.

She and Mary trudged home from a visit to a milkmaid whose foot had been churned by a cow. They had drained and cooled the swelling and given her a draught to ease the pain. Anna wished she could take a draught herself.

"I don't see why I can't simply withdraw myself from consideration. Surely the king would rather have a willing wife?" She turned to a red-faced and winded Mary. "For heaven's sake, give me the kit —and the bundles." Anna hoisted the burden from her maid. "You should have said something."

Mary leaned against the castle's defensive wall, catching her breath. "I reckon the king'll notice the other ladies being more eager," she said between chest heaves. "You just worry on doing your father and Beaubourg proud."

"I shall be the picture of decorum." Anna wiped her forehead and blew her nose with a loud honk. "I've been practicing demure and contrite smiles 'til my cheeks hurt."

"I can see right through ye to yer bodice lacings, dearie."

"*Moi?*"

"Yes, you! Don't you be shaming your father at court. Besides, I'll be there and stuck to you like butter on bread."

More like manacles on ankles.

"Mary, you know I would never humiliate you or father. Or Beaubourg."

Mary snapped Anna with her apron. "You little schemer. Don't make me watch you night and day like a hawk."

"Worry not Mary, I shall make sure the king is pleased." *Pleased to take another.*

* * *

Robert nudged William, seated on his throne. "What a horrid and measly life we lead, ay?"

"Contain thyself," William said, though he could not help a curve of a smile.

Bernard, the future queen's master chamberman, entered, stamping his staff on the throne room floor with practiced precision.

"Majesty, the ladies are assembled and await your bidding," he said with his breathless timbre.

"Better words have never been uttered in Troixden." Robert looked across the throne to Daniel. "Come now, even you ought to be enjoying this."

"Never thought I'd say this, but Robert's right," William said to Daniel. "Liven up, my friend. Surely this isn't the worst duty to perform?"

"You'd think you two were sixteen again." Daniel shook his head.

"So I'm old, now?" William swatted at Daniel, who ducked away with a grunt.

Bernard cleared his throat. "Majesty, shall we begin?"

William nodded and reaffixed his royal demeanor. He was to select the future queen's ladies-in-waiting so they might serve the three finalists upon their arrivals. Finally, something enjoyable and light, not more intrigues of foreign courts and discomfited lords in his own.

"May I present the Lady Margaux of Norwick," Bernard said.

In swept Margaux, resplendent in deep plum silk, a hair's breadth away from royal purple. Her neck long and white as a swan's, her eyes the color of sapphires, her skin like milk, cheeks high and naturally rouged with bright yellow hair falling in soft waves down her back.

"I daresay you're looking regal, sister." Robert said.

She curtsied slow and low before William, fixing him with her eyes. "Majesty, for your consideration." She tilted her head, giving him a seductive smile.

"Lady Margaux, we would be pleased to have you in our lady's service." At the moment William could not recall why he hadn't kept her on the list for queen.

"As Your Highness desires." She dipped and retreated to the west side of the room.

"May I present the Lady Jane of Cecile," Bernard said. In she came, small and sweet to behold, with dull brown hair and a very pregnant belly. She started to drop into a curtsy, but seeing her hardship, William all but leapt from his throne and down the dais to give her his hand.

"My dear lady, don't exert yourself on our account."

"I thank Your Highness," she said, blushing as she took the royal hand.

"Just think, you may bring our queen luck," William said. Robert chuckled and Jane blushed a deeper red. William squeezed her hand like a fond father. "We are pleased to accept you into our lady's service."

"I thank Your Majesty." She gave a small curtsy, unable to meet his eyes. He kissed her hand and led her to stand by Margaux.

"Sire," Daniel said, "as much as it's an honor to have one from my own lands in service, perhaps you are too hasty? The lady may be at her confinement the time of the wedding."

Lady Jane stared at her hands. She seemed everything a lady-in-waiting ought to be. Quiet, clean, with a kind and soft demeanor. She reminded William of his mother's ladies.

"We shall have Lady Jane as an alternate for the queen to

decide," he said after a moment. "Bernard, please make note and show her every kindness in her fragile state." He turned to the candidate. "My Lady Jane, do not take this to be any question of thy character and fitness to serve. 'Tis merely concern as to the health of your person and your child. May you both be blessed."

The lady bowed her head again, and William returned to his throne.

"May I present the Lady Yvette of Havenside," Bernard said. At this, Robert snapped to attention.

Lady Yvette stepped in front of the three men with the poise of a performer. With large, almond-shaped eyes the color of midnight and hair just as black, her beauty was as exotic as Margaux's was flawless. Her bronze and burnished skin gleamed in her indigo gown. Her hair was swept into a tight chignon at her neck. The sapphire necklace Robert had gifted her hung like a medal, resting just above her cleavage.

"Your Majesty," she said, a hint of an unidentifiable accent coming through as she curtsied before the throne.

"My Lady Yvette, you are indeed welcome to our lady's household." William thought, not for the first time, how lucky a man Robert was. "Counsel her well."

As Yvette took her place with the others, three Council Table members swept in.

"The Dukes of Halforn and Duven, and His Eminence, Archbishop Bartmore," the court caller said.

The two dukes looked about, nervous, the archbishop, chin up, smug.

William waved them in. "Bernard, as much as we are loathe to say this, please see the ladies are refreshed. We shall break from our morning's enjoyment to hear these men."

"Certainly, Majesty." Bernard gave a little dance of a bow.

"Your Graces," William said as Bernard scuttled the ladies back into the larger court, "what brings you here looking like the priests who lost the relic?"

Gregory would not meet William's eyes but glowered at the checkered-marble floor. The archbishop cleared his throat.

"Majesty, it seems one of your selections for queen is unfit to serve."

"What?" William's brows shot up. "Speak plainly, my lords."

"Majesty," Gregory said, twisting the velvet cap in his hand, "I must say I'm ashamed. I certainly should have known. I . . . we . . ."

"Out with it!" The king pounded a fist on his throne.

The archbishop bobbed his head at Gregory like a pigeon. "It seems the Lady Emmaline of Duven is no better than a common whore."

"Eminence!" Halforn said. "That is gravely overstating the matter!"

William reeled. It couldn't be. Not the only woman he actually desired, not that sweet, luminescent pearl.

"Explain, Duven," William said.

The archbishop spoke instead. "She has carried on with a young man for quite some time—"

"We asked the Duke of Duven." William glared at the archbishop. Duven fell to his knees.

"Sire, my wife and I were ignorant, Emmaline being at home and we away—as her guardians, we should never have left her alone. But we thought she was old enough—"

"What is the veracity of the accusations?" William leaned back, head hitting his throne. But he knew. No novice kissed like Emmaline did.

"Would I dare bring false claims?" Bartmore said.

"We mean to hear from Duven," William said through gritted teeth.

Gregory rose from his knees. "I would be the last to believe it, Majesty. But she has confessed it to me through many tears. She is so penitent—she has barely eaten! The affair was only for a month, and it happened a year ago. The boy has since left service—can she not still be considered? She so enjoyed your company."

William turned his eyes to the ceiling. Damn it all to hell. He knew he could not have her—no matter how sorry all parties were, himself most of all. Her dalliance, regardless of how small and far off, was now known. And while he might be persuaded to overlook such a misstep, the same could not be said for the church, nor the realm — they'd not allow him to marry a tainted woman. And would he want to? What did it say of his own virility?

Good God. That left him with the choice between a mule in appearance or a mule in demeanor.

* * *

Anna stood beside wide-open windows in Castle Beaubourg's Great Hall, the cluck and squawk of chickens the cooks had let to graze echoing up to her. A breeze caught the paper the Duke of Cecile read. A smiling Halforn stood by his side, hands clasped across his belly.

She'd been expecting them to collect her tomorrow. But they were early. And had no carriage. Just that bloody document with its bloody wax seal the size of a horseshoe.

"They shall be married on the fourteenth of July, the year of our Lord fifteen-hundred and sixty-nine. Thus has The Right King William the Second declared and decided, God save him, and so it shall be."

An ornery hen voiced shrill displeasure. Daniel rolled up the decree and handed it to her beaming father.

Halforn opened his arms to them all. "May her ladyship and His Majesty be happy and blessed in their marriage. And may Your Grace rejoice in this honor to his house!"

Her father clasped arms with both men, then all three turned to her and bowed, her own face stone.

Later that evening, the sun setting the clouds in the ochre sky ablaze at their edges, Anna's eyes were still glazed as she sat at her desk looking out the window.

She heard the sound of hooves, distant at first, now close. Then she saw him: Armor glowing in the last of the sun's rays, as was his steed. She smiled, her first all day, as she watched him tear through the main gate into the keep and rein in his stallion below her window.

"Annelore!" Bryan shouted, "I've come to take you with me! I shall speak to your father in all haste."

She heard Mary burst through the door, but Anna was already on top of her desk, leaning out the window.

"Annelore Matilda Carver, contain yourself!" Mary hustled to pull her back into the room.

Anna swatted at her but still ducked inside. "'Tis Bryan, come to take me away from my lot."

It wasn't perfect, but it could work, as long as her father wasn't implicated. Bryan could hide her somewhere in the woods at a hunter's cottage or some such until the king married another.

"Mary, quick, help me gather my things—not much, just a change of clothes, my books on herbs, mother's combs, my Bible—"

"Don't be ridiculous." Mary jammed her fists into her waist.

"You dare deny me?"

"You'll go nowhere with that boy."

The two glared at each other, frozen. They felt rather than heard the great main door swing open. The duke's low voice reached them, followed by Bryan's loud one. Both women ran to the window, jostling to see.

Bryan waved his arms, having dismounted, and met her father at the door. Anna distinctly heard Bryan say "never" and "she's mine" and "lest I die," but could make out nothing else.

Her father left him and reentered the castle. Bryan strode to the foot of Anna's tower.

"My lady," he called, "I'm to Havenside now to beg your release from this contract. Do nothing 'til I return. I shall save you, my dearest, despite the ill wishes of your father."

"Bryan, no!" Anna shouted down. "You'll get yourself killed!"

"I know how to handle the king."

"You can't—I'll just come now. Please, Bryan, calm down—"

"I shan't be a fugitive, nor shall you." He was directly below her now.

"This is ill-fated—"

"I shall not rest until you're mine, not just in my heart but in the eyes of the law." He turned to grab his helmet. "Honor me with your favor, Anna."

She threw down a handkerchief, a purple *A* embroidered by her mother's hand. Bryan scrambled to retrieve it. It was all thrilling to be sure, if still foolhardy.

Perhaps the extended ride would calm him, make him see sense. She just needed a hiding place, not all this formality.

"Bryan, don't—oh, just be careful, for heaven's sake. Don't offend him or you'll come back a head on a pike!"

He held the handkerchief to his lips, then stuffed it into his chest armor.

"Have faith, dear heart, for I am a son of Beaubourg, by God—I fear no man, king, or devil!" He mounted his horse and let it loose with a swift kick, yelling back, "To the palace for victory!"

Anna sighed, sliding down to her bed. Would the king really kill him? Or would Bryan even make it to the palace? *Oh Lord, let him sleep it off in the forest.*

She resumed her hurried packing and looked at Mary."You obviously have something to say, so be about it."

"Humph."

"Don't you understand? I can't marry this ogre king! And I can't leave Beaubourg. Bryan seems to be the only one who comprehends this."

Mary started undoing Anna's packing.

"Tush, dearie, we all be quite aware of your mind on the matter. But there be nothing to do about it now. The king willn't concede to a mere knight, no matter how noble his heart and purpose."

Anna frowned, snatching back the shift Mary had just unfolded. Mary caught her hands.

"I met His Majesty once, you know," she said, eyebrows jumping.

Anna frowned at her. She didn't need more mollification.

"'Twas when Princess Catherine died. He came to her door demanding to see her, screaming her name. Nearly broke me heart."

"Was that the fateful trip with Mother?"

"He was the sweetest thing," Mary said, "loving his sister so. He wrote the princess the dearest little letters. I can't imagine he's become a cruel man like his brother and father." She smiled. "And he's a right handsome one, I may add."

"That trip killed Mother! 'Tis their fault she's dead and my wee brother with her." Fresh tears sprang to her eyes. She stormed to her wardrobe, throwing items to the floor. "How can you expect me to go to him?"

There was a soft knock at the door. Mary opened it a crack to find the duke.

"M'lord, I don't know if now be a good time. She's blaming the king for her mum and the world besides."

"Worry not, Mary, I'm not here to scold or cajole, merely to not let the sun go down upon our anger."

"I'll just be down the hall if ye be needing me." Mary opened the door fully and slipped out.

"My darling, darling girl." The duke moved to Anna. "Please don't wound me so with your scorn."

She spun around, brown eyes ablaze. "And yet 'tis you who have scorned me, thrown me to the dogs of court to be torn to pieces. But no matter, for my heart has already been snuffed out."

He let out a heavy sigh. "You are all your mother in beauty but all my daughter in bluster." She allowed him to take her hand. "I've raised you to be a woman of great influence. This marriage to the king gives you that chance—well beyond the scope of Bryan's world, or ours."

"So you would pitch me at a perfect stranger and see if that union is better than a tender, loyal friend?" She snatched her hand away and strode back to her desk, picking up her mother's amethyst paperweight, trying to focus, trying to keep the tears from starting again. How could he not see that it wasn't just Bryan she could not bare be separated from?

"Anna, you are just as I am. Implacably stubborn."

"This is to cheer me?" She plunked the weight back down and turned to her father. How forlorn and weary he looked.

"My heart will leave my very body when you leave this place," he said.

At this, the tears she'd thought were all spent started afresh. He reached out, and she walked into his arms. "Beaubourg is no proper place for a woman of your mind, Anna. Love in a marriage you may not find, but you will find a whole world of ideas and knowledge. To not allow you the chance to explore that world . . ."

"Can not a knight show me the world and its splendor?" She slipped from his embrace and returned to the window, the fresh breeze cooling her wet cheeks.

"Bryan is determined and earnest, but he's young in mind. He's no match for you. I think you know this."

She crinkled her face. Bryan was handsome and fun and adoring, but his wit was never quick. He had no interest in other lands or theology or history. She'd never caught him with a book even. And he would want her to settle into a home life with a little brood of cherubic children and give up her healing and midwifery. But surely that was preferable to marrying this king.

"Papa," she said, "I'm truly sorry for causing you heartache, but I've always believed my life would be here. With you, with Bryan. You can't blame my shock and disappointment."

"Shock I grant thee, but disappointment?" He shook his head. "Our little hamlet may reap much benefit from this—though you mustn't think I send you to the king for the sake of Beaubourg." He walked over to her desk and picked up the paperweight. "I willingly accede to the king because I'm told by those I trust that he's a man of honor and integrity."

She looked down at her shaking hands.

"You are dearer to me than my own life," he said, stroking the cool, jagged stone. "I admit I couldn't bear to part with you for anyone less than a king—this king."

As he replaced the weight on the desk, she put her hand atop his. He sighed.

"Did you not wonder why you weren't married sooner like your peers? This is the kind of opportunity I waited so long for. I love you so very much." Tears had gathered in his eyes. He left her side and sat down, heavily, on the bed. Anna sat next to him.

"Don't cry, else I should have to cry with you, and I fear all my tears are exhausted."

"You have the rare opportunity to be at the center of our country's resurgence," he said. "Word has it that King William will bring us back to the days of fortune and goodwill started by Queen Mother Matilda's short regency on behalf of James."

"But why does everyone suppose this king will be any different from James? If he's such a good and gallant man, where has he been these fifteen years, letting his people waste away under his brother's cruelty? Why was he not here, defending us?"

He smiled at her. "Perhaps you'll ask him."

She made an unladylike grunt. "Why would a king want a country girl like me, who disdains everything to do with him and his court?"

"You sell yourself short, my dear. And who knows? He may help bring about the very change we hope for."

Mary slipped back into the room. "Begging pardon, but 'tis time we got my lady ready for bed."

"Of course, Mary—I'll leave you two." He kissed Anna's smooth forehead. "Remember, Anna, it's because I love you. Everything I do is because I love you so."

William's good mood had carried him all morning. He sat enthroned in the Great Hall, idly watching the ebb and flow of the crowd, occasionally talking with Robert. With a nearly full council to help him govern, a bride secured, and his two closest friends by his side, he finally felt he could tackle this dread job of king.

The only kings he'd seen were bloodthirsty scoundrels, manipulating their courts and their people, bending all to their unquenchable thirst for power. Not just his brother and father, but kings in the lands he'd spent most of his years exploring. To be a king, it seemed, was to be an ass. A wealthy, pampered, war-mongering ass.

And yet, the country needed a strong hand, whatever that looked like. Could a king be strong yet not rapacious? Forceful, yet not cruel?

The court caller roused him from his reverie. "Sir Bryan of Beaubourg to see Your Majesty."

"What a pleasant surprise." William sat up and rubbed his hands together. "We have been wanting to hear tell of your Lady of Beaubourg, sir knight. Come, bend our ear."

"Your Highness," Sir Bryan said, face grim.

William raised his brows in encouragement. "Come, come, speak up."

"Majesty, I must inform you that the Lady Annelore hath prior claim to her hand."

Silence followed this pronouncement. William's heart pounded. "Whatever do you mean, sir?"

"She is already to be wed, Highness." Bryan raised his voice further, his words now loud in the hall.

"Sir knight, you are on dangerous ground," Daniel said. "We have it on all good authority from the duke himself that the lady is free."

William's stomach churned at the thought of losing yet another bride.

"Majesty, with all due respect, the duke was ignorant of our engagement," the knight said.

"*Our* engagement?" William rose from his throne. "Are you to tell us the lady is engaged to *you*? Without her father's consent or, we daresay, our own?" The knight looked to his side to find palace guards edging closer.

"Yes, Highness, we gave ourselves up to each other. In secret."

"You what?" William strode down from the dais, Robert, who'd been loafing in his own chair, followed right behind.

"Do you mean to say the lady is no virgin?" Robert said.

"No!" The knight looked at him, horrified, then turned to William. "No, Majesty, I would never insult her so!"

"Then what do you mean, Sir Bryan?" William said.

Bryan looked back and forth from Robert to Daniel, then at William, now but inches away.

"I . . . she . . . we proclaimed our love and intent to marry by summer's end."

Daniel turned from the knight to William. "This is obviously something he's dreamed up, Highness, and nothing for you to trifle with. Our fair knight is merely mistaken in the formalities involved in a betrothal. The lady is free."

"I love her," Bryan said, "no matter who approves of anything. She was—is—to be my wife."

With Emmaline of Duven, the evidence had been clear. Was Lady Annelore no different, or was the knight's pride merely wounded? And if so, what kind of woman inspired such an idiotic act of bravery? William cocked his head to the side and narrowed his eyes.

"Young knight, you profess your love for our lady and yet you offer no proof she is bound to you. Her father is in ignorance, as was our envoy. Does this not strike you as odd?"

"I was to approach her father after her birthday to ask his blessing. I'm sure that if Your Majesty explained, the good duke would see reason—"

"You would have us dissolve our own betrothal with the lady? After what pains we have taken to select her?" William's deep laugh boomed in the hall, startling eavesdroppers and knight alike.

"But she will not have you, sire!" Bryan drew himself up. "Her heart is mine and mine her own. She will never wed thee. She would die first, and I with her!"

William was at a momentary loss. James would have dragged the knight to the dungeon and lashed him within an inch of his life. William wasn't about to do that, but he couldn't start off his reign allowing young bucks to question his authority.

"Guards!" he called. They shot to attention.

"I will fight for her!" Bryan shouted. The guards seized him by the arms. He kicked wildly, uselessly.

"We shall not show this knave the same ill manners he has shown us," William said. "Let him slay marauders in the woods and write laments to the stars for all we care. Escort him from the city and send him on his way."

He then fixed his eyes on Sir Bryan.

"It may be so that the lady loves you, and you her. And know that it pains us to separate such a stout soul from his lady love. Yet we have the realm to consider. The Lady Annelore shall remain our own.

We pray one day she may grow to love her new home as you claim she loves you." He returned to his throne. "In the meantime, we send you away from our presence until such a time as you are recalled in service. Do not tempt us to further censure."

He waved his arm in dismissal. The guards dragged the knight away to excited looks of the gathered courtiers.

"Daniel," William said, pinning the Duke of Cecile in place with his eyes, "we wish an audience in our chamber. Now."

* * *

William turned on his friend. "How could you have convinced me of a lady already entangled? And with a knight of my own choosing to boot? I'm made a fool yet again."

Did the lady really not wish to be queen? What woman in her right mind wouldn't want a crown upon her head, furs and silks and jewels and fluttering servants, everyone jumping to her bidding before she knew her own need? And he thought dealing with the Germans was convoluted.

"Sire, I sat across from this knight at the Beaubourgian feast and never once did I—nor anyone—notice any special liking or treatment by the lady toward the lad."

"You must not have been looking very hard," William said, pacing. "No wonder she was in such a foul mood."

"I believe 'twas the lateness of the hour—"

"I'm supposed to be the people's king, and my first public royal act will be to thrust apart young love?"

"It won't appear so, truly—"

"Dammit, Daniel, this has become a farce!" William swiped at his desk, sending papers scattering to the floor. Daniel approached with caution.

"Everything will turn out as it should."

"Which is?" He walked to the window, opened it, and took deep breaths of the summer air.

"Lady Annelore will be queen, 'tis simple as that," Daniel said to his back. "What we've seen today is a young man swept up in the courtly call of knighthood and determined to save his first damsel in distress. Nothing more."

"That's the whole point." William turned from the window. "The damsel's in distress."

Daniel gave a half smile. "Perhaps it's only the knight who—"

"And what of my hopes for a happy marriage? I'll be damned if I repeat my parents' union." William threw himself into his ebony desk chair and chewed on his fingers.

A stamp of a staff outside the doors announced Robert's arrival. "So, gentlemen, are we off to hunt a knave and relieve him of his head?"

William scowled. Daniel shook his head at Robert.

"Why are you two brooding like a couple hens?" Robert said. "So the girl fancies another, what of it? Either show her what a real man looks like or find yourself another bride. God knows plenty are willing."

"Like your sister?" Daniel said.

"That's enough." William rose. "The decision's been made. Let ends come where they may. I am, after all, the king, and my word must be held in honor. The Lady Annelore will arrive in less than two weeks' time. And a fortnight from thence we shall be wed, weeping and gnashing of teeth notwithstanding."

He stomped out of his chamber, through the throne room, and back to the fray of court. Not paying heed to his direction, he ran smack into Lady Margaux, who fell curtsying to the floor, fluttering her fan above her bosom.

"Pardon, Your Majesty," she said, "you look peaked. May I—is there any way I might bring you comfort?"

For a moment, William was all the more annoyed to have stumbled into his lady cousin. But on considering the fresh bruise to his pride, he decided having a pretty woman on his arm was just what he needed.

"As a matter of fact, dear cuz,'" he said, loud enough for those near to hear but not so loud as to make it appear he wanted an audience, "a bit of exercise with your lovely person would be most welcome." He reached down for her hand, allowing her to rise, then kissed it. "Shall we retire to the gardens, my dear?"

Margaux took his arm, and he led her through the Great Hall, turning to address the room.

"Come, gentlemen of the chamber, grab ye a fair maid and take a turn with us. And for God's sake someone bring the wine."

* * *

Two nights prior to her departure, Anna was at her desk again. Her last and only hope lay in Bryan's somehow whisking her away. Seeing as she'd heard nothing from him since he left for court, this thin chance faded with each passing hour.

Through the window she saw Mary trudging back from the village. She'd been called away to a birth, and that was some time ago.

"Anna!" she called up. "Get down here—I be needing your assistance!"

Since the official betrothal, the duke had not allowed Anna her usual work, worried she might catch some sickness from a villager. But a birth was another thing entirely. She had assisted at births since she was ten, and was always awed by the struggle and pain a mother endured until, exhausted and exuberant, she brought forth beauty and divinity, all wrapped in swaddling cloths.

"The baby be turned," Mary said as they hastened down the hill into town, "I've managed to wedge him down, but he's still not coming."

They stopped at a three-room shack. The fire was ablaze even in the heat of early July, the air pungent with the smell of blood, spirits, and sweat.

The mother, small except in the belly, and a touch younger than Anna, was reclining in a borrowed birthing chair, her legs bent up like a frog's, crimson sheets spread on the floor beneath her. The girl panted heavily, then sat up with a loud, long howl. She fell back gasping and weeping and speaking in a language Anna had never heard before. It sounded Germanic.

Anna rushed to her side, sat on the edge of the bed by the birthing chair, and grasped her hand and forearm.

"Anna," Mary said as two other castle servants made to swap out the dirtied sheets, "'tis been eighteen hours. She's pushing but she shouldn't be. Nothing I say can make her quit."

"I don't recognize her tongue—"

"Blast, I hoped ye would."

"Where's the father? Perhaps we can have him send for more hands?"

Mary looked at Anna and shook her head. "There be no father, dearie."

Of course Anna knew there were women who made their livings by taking men to their beds, but seeing one in the flesh, so near her own age . . . . *This is what has become of me. I've been prostituted out to the king to get him a son.* She felt sick.

"Wipe that look off your face," Mary said in a tone Anna hadn't heard since she was a child. "We care for everyone, just like the Lord Jesus would, with no mind to money or stature."

Anna looked at her old friend, stricken. "It's not that. 'Tis just . . . I feel connected to her."

"Well then, I hope she's feeling it too. Get down to her face—I have to try and turn the babe again." Anna held the girl's arm and smoothed her forehead with a damp towel. The girl looked terrified.

"Just look at me and be brave," Anna said. "You'll be a mother soon." The girl's face contorted, her eyes looking helplessly into Anna's. She screamed.

"He's turning—his head's down!" Mary said. "He's turned!" She leaned back on her haunches, bloodied to her elbows. "One more tweak and he'll be ready for sure." She reached inside the woman once more. "Now she can push, Anna—let 'er push!"

It took another half-hour. As the baby's head crowned, the mother let out a cry so loud it set the livestock outside the window grunting and whinnying. The baby boy, all slippery and dripping, sailed into the clean sheets that draped Mary's waiting arms. He was the biggest newborn Anna had ever seen—and the mother barely over five feet.

Mary handed the boy to the wet nurse, then turned to the mother. Mary's face turned ashen. "More sheets and hot water—be quick!"

Anna, still entangled in the girl's arms, started to extricate herself but Mary stopped her. "No, dearie, you stay there. Be with her now."

The girl clung desperately to Anna, babbling in her foreign tongue.

"Hush now, hush," Anna said. "You have a beautiful boy. Everything's going to be fine." The mother's eyes rolled back in her head, her grasp went limp in a faint.

"Mary, should I rouse her?"

"Let her rest if she may. You come help with these sheets." Anna went to Mary's side. "Now just push down to stop the flow like usual."

Anna crouched down to help. She didn't know whether it was the turning of the baby, his kicking, or simply the force that sent him into the world, but the mother was torn to her anus. Anna could see the fresh blood and excrement oozing onto the white sheets with each heartbeat. There was some tearing for all women in birth— Anna was accustomed to it—but this? She'd gone through three fresh compresses.

The mother roused, whimpering. She seemed to be gazing through Anna, beholding something no one else could. She gripped the sides of the birthing chair, knuckles white, gasped, then went still.

Mary leaned back against the wall, sighed, and wiped her brow with a blood-smeared forearm. "She be with the angels now."

"But what about the baby? No father and now no mother?" Anna heard a soft weeping from the kitchen. The wet nurse. Mary stood, heavy, and went to the babe while Anna, still in shock herself, tried her best to arrange the dead girl into a dignified position.

Mary was back, not meeting Anna's eyes. "Well, we needn't worry ourselves about the boy," she said. "Sweet Jesus."

Mary wept. She stood there and sobbed, waves rippling through her plump folds. Anna went to her and they held each other as she too joined in the lament. She cried for the baby boy without a chance at life, she cried for a world that would leave a pretty young thing alone in a queer land to breathe her last. She cried for her own mother, dear Julia, gone so many years ago. And with she and Mary leaving in two days' time, leaving the life they had always known and loved, leaving her father all alone, it was all just too much.

One of the castle maids, who was quietly cleaning up around them, pressed her hand to Mary's back, saying, "Go on back to the castle. We'll take care here."

Anna took one lingering last look at the girl and made the sign of the cross above her, mumbling in Latin, for there was no priest to do so.

The light was fading as the two women made their solemn way back to Castle Beaubourg. Neither of them spoke. Anna looked at her dress, arms and face caked with a dead woman's blood and made up her mind: she was going to stop feeling so damned sorry for herself.

CHAPTER 5

The Ladies Wait

The night before Anna was to leave for court she stole away for a final parting with Bryan. He met her at their willow, dressed in his hunting clothes, a small leather pack by the tree trunk, his cloud-white horse nibbling the clover at their feet.

"I should've seen sense when you first proposed it, but 'tis not too late," he said. "Go back to the castle for your cloak and a small bag—"

"The envoy will be here first thing in the morning," Anna said. "We can't risk—"

"Blast the guards!" he grabbed her arms. "We know these lands better than anyone—we'd be well on our way and hid before they even noticed your absence."

She reached up and cupped his cheeks. "The time for fleeing is past, dear heart. You know as well as I that I must away." His face crumpled as he turned his mouth to kiss her palm.

"Why do you make this so much harder for me?" she said.

He reared back. "Harder for you? I'm to sit and watch while another weds and beds my intended."

"And I am to sit and watch while you live out the life I had hoped for," she said, hands on her hips. "I am but a woman. You may seek out better fortune as you please."

"And yet," he said, softer, "I can't remember a day without you a part of it, so what's my fortune if you're gone?" He reached for her and she let herself melt into the shelter of his arms. He rested his face atop her head, swaying. "Can't you see you must away with me?"

She looked into his tender, despondent face. "I can't do that to Father." She pushed a lock of his hair behind his ear. "And you mustn't leave your mother and family. They'd soon be destitute without the money your knighthood provides."

"Dammit, Anna!" He let go of her, throwing his arms in the air. "You're heading to a life of misery and despair—"

"I know where I'm headed, thank you!" Her voice startled his horse, who snorted back at her. "Silly me, I thought my dearest friend would offer me comfort and tenderness in our last moments together."

Bryan leaned his arm and forehead against the willow.

"Oh, Bryan, can we not part in good grace?" She placed her hand on his back. He turned and took her in his arms once more, eyes wet.

"Anna," he said, searching her face, "tell me you love me and I will stay. I will stay and I will find a way for us to be together—"

She shook her head. "The king—"

"Forget about him—just tell me."

"Bryan, I—"

He kissed her, hard, unyielding. Breaking away, he rubbed his face in her hair, repeating her name over and over like a lamentation. But all she felt was cold. Distant. Already lost.

"I love you," she whispered, hoping he would believe it.

* * *

The next morning Anna woke from a fitful sleep to find Mary standing at the end of the bed, arms folded across her chest, biting her lips in barely restrained excitement.

The day had come. What awaited her after her two-day journey to Palace Havenside, she could not fathom. Nor did she want to.

She heaved off her sheets and hoisted her legs over the side of the bed, giving Mary a dark look. "I suppose now's as good a time as any."

She surrendered without verbal complaint to the brushing and tying and smoothing, Mary stifling tears all the way through. There was a tap at the door.

"Annelore, dear? Breakfast is sure to turn to dinner if you don't join us soon."

"I'm almost ready, Papa," she called out. "Come in if you like."

She wore a new goldenrod silk gown with a low neck, a tight waist, and voluminous skirts. He walked to her, arms outstretched and eyes brimming.

"My gorgeous girl, you make an old man weep with pride." He hugged her tight, then reached into the deep pocket of his robe, removed a gilded box, and handed it to her. "My dear, it seems you are not completely dressed."

Anna took the box and opened its heavy gold lid. On a soft green pillow lay a three-strand pearl necklace, a diamond hanging from its center. It was stunning—and it looked familiar.

"'Twas your mother's, child," he said, placing it around her neck. "I've been saving it for such a day as this." He worked the clasp. "I gave it to her on our wedding day. It represents St. Paul's wisdom that a cord of three strands is not easily broken."

"Oh, Papa." Anna's hands leapt to the diamond. "You do me such honor."

Mary burst out a pent-up sob. "Your mum'd be so happy!" She swept them into a hug, laughing and crying in turn. "Ugh, I'll have mussed up my hard work by smooshing you, dearie."

Her father wiped his eyes then took Anna's arm, wrapping it around his.

"Will you do me the honor of presenting you one last time, my darling daughter? For your carriage is ready."

She swallowed, smiled. "Then so am I, Papa."

* * *

And that is how Robert, Duke of Norwick, first beheld his future queen: her head thrown back in jolly laughter at something her father said, glowing like the sun, the stately duke by her side, beaming right back.

Daniel was right again, blast him. She was bloody perfect. His sister didn't stand a hailstorm's chance in hell. He studied her more closely: locks of chestnut hair escaping in soft waves, bright brown eyes, lustrous skin, and a petite but alluring figure. She was more than William could have hoped for—and just maybe she could further his own hopes as well.

* * *

Her father stopped at the final landing, which opened to the whole of the Great Hall. The only man Anna recognized was the Duke of Halforn. She could hear guards clanking and chattering outside. One noble in particular, younger than the rest, dark and brooding, would not take his eyes from her. He had high cheekbones, wavy black hair that fell across his brow, and solid shoulders. The other men showed him such deference, if she didn't know better, she'd think he was the king.

"Gentlemen, my lords," her father called out, "'tis my distinct honor and privilege to present to you the Lady Annelore Matilda of Beaubourg."

He led her through the men, who parted like the sea for Moses, then followed as she sat at her father's right hand, the table already laid with a variety of smoked meats, soft cheese, exotic fruits, French wines, and still-warm breads.

The curious one applauded her as all the rest joined in, shouting hoorays and *long-live-Lady-Annelores*. She didn't realize she'd been holding her breath, but now she exhaled through a half smile, overcome by the pageantry of it all. Everyone ate with gusto except for Anna, who nibbled at a roll and sipped her wine. She felt as if she were watching it all from the balconies above.

The dark, handsome man was introduced to her as Robert, Duke of Norwick—the Dread Duke as Bryan called him. He was the center of attention, telling tales of exploits in Spain and Umbria with the king in their youth. And when her father and Mary led her out through the keep, stopping in front of the royal carriage—dripping in golds and reds, drawn by four white horses with white plumes atop their heads—all eyes were still upon him.

With a flick of an arm murmurs and jostling ceased. Even the horses appeared to be at his call. He bowed theatrically before Anna.

"My lady," he said, "on behalf of His Royal Highness, our dear and faithful King William II, long may he reign, I, Lord Robert, Duke of Norwick, Master of his Majesty's Chamber and Lord Privy Seal, do welcome thee onward to thy new abode and the king's side."

At this he gave her a smile that transformed his face and thrust his hand toward her to help her into the carriage. She reached out to take his arm, but stopped, turned back to her father and hugged him hard.

"My dear girl," he whispered, "hold your head high and brave. For you are a daughter of Beaubourg."

She had to get in that carriage now or she would cry in front of all these men. She nodded, let her father go, and turned to Robert the Dread Duke, smiling as brightly as she could manage.

"I thank Your Grace and am gladdened to attend with you to my liege." She took his arm. He leaned to her with a grin.

"My lady, 'tis indeed my pleasure. I'm at your service. You need only flit your lovely eyes in my direction and I shall grovel about in a most uncivilized manner."

Robert was married, and said to be the king's close and trusted friend. In the world she was entering it seemed that noblemen, married or no, shamelessly spoke thus to the ladies of court. Robert's admiration for her was enjoyable to be sure, but would she return this duke's innuendoes and flirtations? She thought not. Her position was already perilous enough.

She climbed into the carriage, settled herself on a velvet pillow, and stared out the window, regarding the mountains, Mary sinking in across from her. She saw Robert mount his horse in one graceful swoop, wink at her, and with a swift kick to his dappled gray's side, call out, "Onward to the Palace! God save King William and God save the Lady Annelore!"

The train lurched ahead, four knights in front, Robert and another duke flanking her, followed by the rest of the nobles and knights. Once free of the castle keep, they picked up speed and Anna gave herself over to her loss. It was one thing to steel herself in mind, another to be put to the task.

Mary clucked and rubbed Anna's knee. "I know it be tough dearie, but it wouldn't do to be showing a sad face to court."

Anna took a deep, steadying breath and blew her nose. "You're right. And it wouldn't do for this Duke of Norwick to see me thus either, for he'd only babble to the king."

"Right ye are" Mary said. "That one looks trouble to me or I'll be a pig's ear."

Anna managed a laugh at this. Composing herself further, she looked out, eyes landing on the willow where only a month ago she had spent such a pleasant afternoon with Bryan, when she had nothing but happy dreams ahead. Dear Bryan, would she ever see him again? She envisioned him there on his white steed, ready to rescue her from this fate. A fate she knew there was no hope of fighting. She tried to imagine what it would be like to be queen, trussed up in finery but disdained and shut away by her horrid husband.

She was jerked to attention by a commotion surrounding her slowing carriage. She looked around, frantic. What she saw did not calm her. It was Bryan, of all people, charging toward them with his sword aloft.

"Annelore my love, I have come for you!"

Robert veered off and headed toward him.

"Bryan!" Anna shouted, pressing her hands to the window. Did he want to get them both in prison?

Robert circled back to the carriage. "With his sword drawn he doth threaten us all, lady. He will be dealt with swiftly."

"No! Stop!" Heedless, stupid, boy! She saw Norwick roll his eyes.

"Sir Bryan!" Robert shouted. "Sheath your sword and approach at slow pace. If not, take death upon you now."

Bryan had the sense to slow his horse. "I would die for my lady if it brought even the slightest cheer to her heart." Anna palmed her forehead at this pronouncement. But then, perhaps preferring not to be gutted by the Dread Duke, he stowed his sword and rode on toward her still-moving train.

"That's quite close enough," Robert said when Bryan reached the outer rim of her protection. "You may make your petition from where you are. If you make any move I find aggressive or otherwise irksome, your head shall be off before you take another breath."

Bryan gulped and trotted along with the train, craning his neck to get a glimpse of Anna through the guards. "Annelore, these men keep me from you, but they cannot leash my heart."

"Bryan," Anna tried to pry open the window. What on earth had gotten into him?

"This isn't goodbye, for I shall fight for you to the very end!"

"Which may be quite soon," Robert said. "Now off with you before I horrify your lady with the sight of your entrails. Onward double speed!"

The envoy took off at full canter, leaving Bryan in the dust. Undaunted, the young knight spurred his own horse to follow.

"Anna, I love you!"

Anna finally got the window down. She'd written him a note that morning but had forgotten to send it in all the haste. Now she wrapped it in her handkerchief and threw it out the window. All it said was "*I am so sorry.*"

The eagerness on Bryan's face when he dismounted and fetched it made her wince. She had disappointed all his hopes, but it couldn't be helped. Surely he knew that.

Mary slammed the window shut.

"Annelore Matilda Carver," she said, hands pounded to the sides of her hips, "how dare you throw things from the royal carriage? Anyone'd think you were raised in the stables. What will these noblemen think of ye? Sending secret messages to some knight? Hollering out the window for all to hear? For shame, Anna, for shame!"

Anna slouched in her cushions. She knew he was being ridiculous, but she'd broken his heart. She didn't realize she'd made herself look ridiculous too. She glanced out the window and saw Robert scowling down at her. He'd seen her throw the handkerchief.

She thought about the dead prostitute and baby and her resolve to not feel sorry for herself. She thought about how she'd feel if Robert saw her shed a tear. And then she laughed out loud, as if Mary had said something hilarious.

Mary raised her eyebrows to the sky. "Ye've gone mad."

"Not mad," Anna said between peals of false laughter. "I'm simply not giving the Duke of Norwick the satisfaction of thinking I care a wit for what has happened."

"If you be trying to make him think you're loony, then that'll work."

Anna stopped laughing, looked out the window again and saw Bryan far afield, riding parallel to the train, kicking up a dusty wake.

She sighed. "I fear I've made a mess of us all."

* * *

The carriage rolled through Palace Havenside's soaring main gate, straight through the keep and into the lawn square, stopping at the public entrance to the Great Hall.

The doors were shut tight. Better to keep the new queen a mystery. Even the king would not lay eyes upon her again until he lifted her veil at the altar. Anna was unknown to anyone outside of Beaubourg, and apparently it was prudent for her to remain so. She could not fathom why, but the king's orders were law and she had better get used to it.

She peered out at the enormous red stone palace, built to disarm and overwhelm the observer. She had always imagined something larger than Castle Beaubourg, but Bryan was right: the Palace of Havenside could fit the entire village of Beaubourg inside, castle and all.

"Mary, you never told me how magnificent!"

"Oh aye, 'tis nice." Mary clucked her tongue.

"Oh aye." Anna grinned. "'Tis a mite more than nice, I think."

The carriage door swung open to Robert, standing at the ready as she climbed out. "My lady." He took her hand, dropping it the minute both her feet touched the ground.

A short, stout man dressed in the royal livery of black, blue, and gold approached, followed by four court ladies.

He bowed, reaffixing his feather cap as he spoke.

"My Lady Annelore. I am Bernard, your ladyship's master chamberman. I am here with a retinue of your ladies, to escort your ladyship through the palace to your chambers."

"Greetings, sir." She returned his bow with a curtsy.

"Ladyship needn't curtsy to me. Nor to anyone saving His Majesty."

Anna glanced back at Mary, who was tumbling out of the carriage. Robert had left the nurse to her own devices and headed into the palace. As he did so, he whispered in the ear of a beautiful, blonde woman who pursed her lips and frowned.

Robert looked back at Anna, and their eyes momentarily locked, her heart skipping a beat. Then he disappeared inside.

"Follow me, if you please," Bernard said, walking with formality toward the Great Hall.

Anna, with Mary by her side, walked behind him as the four ladies took their places to the rear. She could hear muffled giggles as she gaped up at the vaulted stone ceilings, three stories high.

"The Great Hall is through there, where His Majesty holds common court, where we feast and have revelries." He was speaking to the air, not turning to see if Anna was listening or even behind him, flicking his hands to and fro as he gave them a hasty tour.

They came to a large door flanked by guards who shot to attention at their approach. Bernard, finally checking on his charge, led them through to the throne room.

It was a long, rectangular space with an entire wall of windows to the east and a public entry three-quarters of the way down the north side wall, now closed tight, guards at attention there. A banner of deep blue, tasseled with gold, hung above the marble dais, WR, for *William, Rex*, emblazoned in its middle. Tapestries of woodland and biblical scenes hung behind an enormous throne.

His throne.

It was large enough to fit two women or one very large man. Tufted with more velvet and five feet high, it was topped on either side with gold finials in the shape of thistles with carved lion paws resting on the rug below. On either side stood two smaller chairs, one to the right decked in blood-red, the other in evergreen.

At the sight of this menacing chair Anna recalled again how fearsome the king had been to behold that June night. She could still feel those searing blue eyes on her. She caught her breath. She would not tremble.

"Bernard," she asked, turning to him suddenly, "where is the king?"

"My lady, Majesty is hunting."

"And how do you find . . . do you find His Majesty to be a good master?"

"My lady," he said, eyes widening, "what I do or do not think of His Majesty is of no significance."

Anna wished she'd held her tongue. Again. Clearly she'd posed her question to the wrong servant. She frowned and turned back to the throne, wishing she could run her hand across the velvet, as if the chair itself could give her the answers she sought—perhaps tell her if its owner was at least a merciful man.

"I can speak to His Majesty's character, for I have known him all my life." The blonde beauty Robert had spoken to curtsied before Anna.

"My lady, I am the Lady Margaux of Norwick." Margaux's voice was like a harp. "I am His Majesty's cousin." Anna took Margaux's hand in hers, allowing her to rise. Margaux smiled, searching Anna's face. So this was the Dread Duke's sister.

"Please, Lady Margaux, what do you say to His Majesty's character?"

"His Majesty is all goodness and grace," Margaux said, still holding Anna's hand in her long, elegant ones. "As children we were inseparable. And I can attest to his beauty," she added, which set the other ladies tittering. She frowned at them and leaned in to Anna. "Shall I tell my lady more, on an intimate level?" More tittering.

Was this Margaux the king's mistress? And if not, why was this fine lady not in Anna's stead?

"I think that's enough, Lady Norwick," Bernard said. Turning up his nose at Margaux, he offered Anna his arm, "shall we charge ahead to your chambers?"

He guided the ladies directly behind the throne dais and up a flight of stairs. "This wing is your ladyship and His Majesty's chambers. His Majesty's primary men of the chamber, namely the Dukes of Norwick, Cecile, Duven, Ridgeland, and Halforn, reside underneath the royal rooms when at court."

"Thank you, Bernard," Anna said, "but I daresay I could barely make my way to the Great Hall at present, let alone begin to comprehend where the men of chamber lay their heads."

For the first time that day, Bernard smiled at her. "Indeed, my lady."

They entered the middle of a thin, windowless hall lit by flaming torches. Bernard pointed to the right. "That is His Majesty's chambers. They're similar in layout to your own, except in reverse."

They headed to the left and met with four guards standing rigid against the doors, as if holding them open with their bodies. Anna, trying not to balk, walked down the open-arched entryway, peeking in between the pillars to her new rooms.

Once through, she was met with more ladies, in full curtsy in front of her, like a sea of silk and pearls. "My lady," they choroused.

Bernard released her arm with a flourish of his hands. "My lady, the queen's chambers."

Anna took a deep breath and floundered for Mary's hand. "Mary?" she whispered.

"'Tis our new home, Anna," Mary whispered back.

* * *

Robert rode out to the king's hunting party upon returning to the palace. He knew William would want to know not only that Lady Annelore had arrived safely, but also what he thought of her.

He found the group riding merrily home, with three brace of

pheasants and an eight-prong bull. Minstrels walked along beside, blowing their flutes and strumming mandolins.

"Tell me," the king said, reining his horse next to Robert's.

"That rapscallion knight made some foolhardy attempt to attack the train," Robert said. "I very nearly stuck him through."

William's face fell. "This is the first thing you tell me? That Sir Bryan was there?"

"Apologies, cuz," Robert said, sidling closer, "but he was heavy on my mind the entire ride."

"Perhaps I shouldn't have let him go so lightly."

"Those were my feelings. Should've at least locked him away until after the wedding. He followed us all the way to Kilburn, then retreated when he saw we'd stopped for the evening. I sent a patrol out and had a watch set all night. He never returned, the coward."

"Enough of him—what of my Lady Annelore?"

Robert opened his mouth, furrowed his brow, and snapped his head away from his friend as if something in the underbrush caught his eyes.

William laughed. "That bad, aye? Well, that's the last time I trust mine eyes the length of ten yards, at night, after a long, hard journey."

"No, no, Wills, she's quite striking. You're sure to be pleased on that account."

"Then not all is lost." William gave a half-hearted grin.

"I'm afraid she does carry some torch for this Sir Bryan fellow."

William raised his brows. "And how was this deduced?"

Of course he would ask. Robert sighed. "She dropped her favor from the speeding carriage as he came to free her."

William snorted. "Good Lord."

"If you ask me, I think she's ill-prepared to be queen. You'd be better off with someone who has the proper manner or air about her."

William looked sidelong at him. "Someone like your sister?"

Robert threw up his arms. Knowing he could better control Margaux, he might as well give her case one last try. "I'm the first to say my sister's a manipulative little shrew. But she knows her place and she looks the part. The country expects—"

The king flared. "I care not if the lady needs tutelage in the ways of courtly life. Perhaps she'll be a breath of fresh air rather than a stench to all our noses. Either way, the matter is settled."

"You're the king."

"Aye, Robert. Best not forget it." With that, His Majesty kicked his black mount into full canter toward the palace, his troublesome bride ensconced inside.

* * *

"As your ladyship can see, the east windows look out upon part of the yard and stables, Havenside Hills, the outskirts of the city . . ." If Bernard pointed out one more feature of Anna's chambers, she would collapse. "My lady, just a few more points of interest and I shall leave you to recover from your arduous journey."

"Thank you, Bernard—I'm feeling a bit weary."

He guided her to a plain wooden door with no lock, in the southwest corner of her bedchamber. "This door," he said, "is unique in purpose, for the only persons to come and go by it are my lady and the king. It leads directly into His Majesty's bedchamber." She clenched her jaw, staring hard at the door. He stared at her, waiting. "'Tis thy own private passageway for, well, for His Majesty's pleasure."

"I see." Anna glanced at Mary, her throat tight. She held back a shudder.

"Speaking of His Majesty . . ." Bernard said. He led her to a gigantic four-poster bed, crowned with the same thistles as the king's throne. On the headboard sprawled a dandelion, symbol of fertility, its jagged leaves becoming long tendrils that wrapped around the sides of the bed to form its rails. A golden box, three times the size of the one her father had presented her, lay in the bed's center. A scroll atop bore that same red wax seal she had seen only weeks ago.

"His Majesty bids thee welcome, my lady." Bernard extended his arm toward the gift.

"I think, Bernard, I shall open His Majesty's gift once I have restored myself." She scanned the room for something to drink.

"But of course." Bernard nodded a small bow. "I shall take my leave. Perhaps when I return we may set to the business of choosing thy last two ladies-in-waiting and appoint thy honor matron?"

With that, he performed a quick click and stamp of his heels like a little jig, bowed more fully, and left her chambers.

Anna slumped down on the bed and looked up at Mary. "This is all too much to take in."

Mary took her hand and patted it. "Tush, my sweet, let's get you some rest."

Margaux approached with the three ladies who had followed them around the palace. They all curtsied.

"My lady," Margaux said, smiling, "we're ready to make you more comfortable for leisure." She gestured at the ladies behind her. "May I present the Duchess Stefania of Duven, the Lady Brigitte of Lorve, and the Countess Amelia of Ridgeland. At your service."

Anna reluctantly rose from the bed and took each lady's hand in turn. "'Tis my hope we shall all be true friends," she said, "but now, I would dearly love a bath and some refreshment."

"But of course, my lady." Margaux arched a fine brow. "I've already had your bath started and had Countess Amelia lay out one of your gowns. You shall be right as rain in no time. I took the liberty of adding lavender oil to the bath. So much more feminine than the traditional mint, don't you think?"

She did not wait for an answer but clapped her hands, and the ladies set about their work. Within moments Duchess Stefania placed a tray brimming with pungent cheeses, fresh crusty brown bread, and bright fruit on the bedside table.

Offering a goblet filled with a light wine and a stick of cinnamon to stir it, she smiled at Anna. "A specialty of the palace in summer, my lady—chilled wine with spices and fruit."

"Thank you. It has been a long journey." The spices were bitter, but the drink was refreshing all the same. In her thirst, Anna tried not to gulp.

After she had bathed and been dressed by many gentle hands,

some shaking a bit, faces blushing at tiny mistakes, she came back to the golden box from the king. She snatched the scroll first, peeled away the enormous griffin seal, and read:

Year I, WR, 1569

Our Dear Lady Annelore Matilda of Beaubourg,

We welcome your ladyship with all warmth and gratitude to Our palace and your ladyship's new abode. We pray it is to your ladyship's liking and those ladies chosen to serve will bring thee great pleasure and comfort when We are unable. Most of all, We pray that your ladyship's kind heart will not be troubled, though it has been separated from all it holds dear. In time, We hope, thou shalt find comfort and companionship at Our side and joy in the midst of serving Troixden and Our people. As sentiment of those hopes most dear to Us, please accept this token as a symbol of Our best intentions and desire for affinity. It belonged to the late Queen Mother, one of her favorites. May it grace your ladyship's fair neck with even more brilliance.

Your Humble and Most Faithful Servant, I am,

William, Rex

P.S. We are gladdened, by the by, of thy middle name. Our Mother was very close to Our heart, and any woman named for her shall be a boon to Our soul.

Despite herself, Anna smiled. She detected no hint of undue arrogance, no tone of condescension. He had even shown some sympathy to her plight. Of course, she had no idea whether or not it was the king's hand at all. It may just as well have been his master secretary, hoping to smooth the way. Yet there was something casual amidst its formality, especially in the postscript, something that would be most unusual had the king not written it himself. Inexplicably, she felt embraced.

She walked back to the bed, rereading each line, then let the letter fall and lifted the hefty box onto her lap. Her ladies crept up around her, curious at what treasure hid inside.

With a faint creak of hinges, the box opened. Lying in a perfect circle was an emerald necklace, the center stone half the size of Anna's palm. Six more of decreasing size scooped up to the clasp.

Between each emerald lay a deep plum amethyst, again in decreasing size as they reached the close. Stunned gasps met the jewel's unveiling.

"Oh!" Anna said. "'Tis gorgeous indeed!"

"A necklace fit for a queen." Margaux stared not at the jewels, but straight at Anna.

Just then a raucous clamor met their ears from outside. Clanking armor, loud laughter, dogs barking, hooves tramping. Enthralled with the necklace, the women had not heard the hunting party's return.

"The king!" Brigitte said as the ladies ran to the east windows and pressed themselves to the leaded glass. "There he is! There he is!"

Anna shoved the golden box off her lap and leapt to the window.

"Which one is His Majesty?" She darted her head to and fro, forgetting all propriety.

"There he is," Margaux whispered in Anna's ear, and pointed to a man a head taller than the others.

He was just about to leave their view, heading down the stone wall toward a side entrance. His back was turned, but beneath his black riding cloak Anna could make out strong, broad shoulders. His hat was tucked under his arm, the sunlight striking his short-cropped hair. The sides were trim, the top combed forward in a vain attempt to tame its tendency to wave. Dark from the sweat of exertion, his hair looked like the bumpy, slick pelt of a river otter just back from a swim.

Anna bore her eyes into the back of his head, willing him to turn around. Another man approached and spoke to him. This man did turn—Robert, looking up at her with his stony glare. He guided the king quickly from view, setting off a veritable swoon among the younger ladies, the older and married among them rolling their eyes at their counterparts.

The stamp of the guard's staff outside the chamber door set Anna's heart pounding. Was it him? Already? It couldn't be.

"Master chamberman to see her ladyship," the guard said.

Bernard performed his complex little dance of a bow. "My lady, it seems best that we select at least two more ladies now. A place for everyone and everyone in her place. Ladyship must approach His Highness to have any of the original ladies dismissed, should that be thy wish."

"Of course, Bernard." Anna's head was aching after all the day's excitement. She felt her polite demeanor slipping away—surely this would be quick.

Bernard clapped his hands and the ladies arranged themselves for presentation. "Thy ladies," Bernard said, "are here to serve you in all capacities, from the stool, to dressing, to entertainment, and friendship. One lady shall sleep at the foot of your bed each night with four more in the chamber entry."

"Will they not be bored?" Anna said. *Will I not be bored? Have any of them read Augustine? Do any know the difference between fennel and dill? Who on earth will I talk to of more than court gossip?*

Bernard looked aghast. "Dear Bernard, I merely wish them to be pleased in their service, not for its sake alone, but in the pleasure of its details as well."

Bernard approached her where she sat, in an old cushioned armchair. "My lady," he said, "never forget who you are. For you shall soon be queen."

Anna nodded at him, thinking for the hundredth time how unqueen-like she was and no remedy for it.

Bernard returned to his place and clapped his hands again. "The Lady Jane of Cecile," he said.

Jane waddled up to Anna and tried her best to curtsy.

"My Lady Jane, do not strain yourself!" Anna reached to help as Jane struggled to keep her balance.

Jane gave a tiny smile. "'Twas what His Majesty said." She looked sheepishly at Anna. "They worry I may not be of much help to your ladyship in this state."

"Well, Lady Jane," Anna said, "I have been with many a woman with child and I find them lovelier company than most. I will gladly take you into my service. You shall be a boon to me, I'm sure."

Jane's face lit up. "Thank you, ladyship. I shan't disappoint thee."

"Right then." Anna smiled at them all. "I do believe we are

finished here. Ladies," she said, turning to the rest, "thank you for your willingness to serve, I am certain there will be a place for you at court if you so please."

"But your ladyship has only selected one of the four," Bernard said.

"Mary is the second, of course."

"My lady, I understand she is close to you, but—"

"But what, my lord? She has been my maid from infancy. She knows my whims, my pains, my preferences better than I do myself. There is none better in the land to serve me, if that indeed be the purpose."

"Yes," Bernard said, "but the ladies are chosen by rank as well as aptitude of service. For her to serve in such capacity would be an insult to the other ladies of court. It is simply not done."

This was the final peck on a day that had spent her to the bone. "The other ladies of court, being of rank, will have much to comfort themselves in light of this perceived slight." Bernard scowled. "Not only will Mary serve, she shall serve as honor matron."

"My lady," Bernard gasped, "you have yet to understand how matters proceed at court. Only His Majesty has the power to—"

"Did you or did you not inform me I was allowed to select my ladies?" She advanced on her horrified master of chamber, backing him to the east windows.

"I did, but—"

"And I select the Lady Jane of Cecile and Mistress Mary of Beaubourg."

"My lady, the king must—"

"Fine." She turned to the bed and returned with the necklace, thrusting the box at Bernard.

"Go to the king in all haste—take this gift with you. Tell His Majesty I would gladly accept his most thoughtful and generous token, but jewels are as nothing to me compared to human comfort."

"My lady!"

"Then tell His Majesty," she said, trying to control her now roiling rage, "that I desire and most humbly request my personal maid, the Mistress Mary, healer and friend, be appointed honor matron. You shall take Mary with you."

"There is no need—" Bernard said, taking the proffered box.

"Bernard, go!" The last of Anna's patience evaporated. "Never forget who *you* are. You are my master of the chamber—you are not the king."

* * *

The king sat in his chamber, lounging about at cards, refreshing himself after the hunt with Daniel, Robert, Gregory, and a smattering of others.

All of his senses were heightened. Simply knowing his bride was in the room next to his made his skin prickle. And knowing she was not there of her own desire made his stomach kink. So she was in love with a knave—he discarded a king of clubs—why did it matter? How many queens, including his own mother, actually loved their kings? He drew an ace of spades. He'd only known one, and she, poor thing, was met with a husband whose bed never emptied of courtiers, male and female alike. He rearranged the cards in his hand as if willing them to change their faces.

Royal marriages were not made for happiness; they were made for political expediency. Why, then, did it irk him so that Lady Annelore cared for another? Because it was rare that a woman rejected him? Because she might pull back his cloak and expose him for . . . for what?

"Bah!" He threw his hand down on the table.

"Master of her ladyship's chamber and Mistress Mary of Beaubourg to see His Highness."

William waved his assent and looked to Gregory, who shrugged, jutting out his thin lower lip.

In glided Bernard and in stumbled Mary, wide eyed. William rose to greet them, glancing at the box in Bernard's quaking hands.

"Ah, Bernard, what have we here?" William's shoulders sank. "She sends it back?"

"Your Majesty," Bernard said, "her ladyship sends her thanks for such a fine and generous gift." He opened the box. "The extraordinary beauty of the necklace—"

"I know its beauty, Bernard, I sent it," William said. "Get to the point."

"Her ladyship gratefully accepts the gift but says jewels of such beauty are nothing unless accompanied by human comfort."

Catcalls erupted from the table. Bernard winced, and Mary looked as if she might melt into the stone floor.

"Majesty," Bernard said, "her ladyship most humbly requests her personal maid, Mary of Beaubourg, be appointed matron of honor."

William looked the small, if comfortably padded, woman up and down.

"Sire," Bernard said, leaning in, "she is not even of rank."

"Mary of Beaubourg," William said. "Why do we remember that name?"

"Your Highness, if I may . . ." Mary said.

"You dare speak to His Majesty before he has addressed you?" Bernard said.

"Be still, Bernard." William held up a hand. "'Twas you." He looked intently at her. "You who came to take care of our sister, was it not?"

"Yes, Highness, 'tis she," Robert called from the table. "She wouldn't allow you into the princess's chamber."

William stepped down to her level at the chamber's entry, took both her hands in his, and kissed them.

"Our dear madam—these hands were the last to tend our beloved Princess Catherine. Sometime in the future we will bid you tell us of those days, for they have haunted us for many years."

Bernard looked from maid to king, head swiveling like an owl.

"If these same hands serve our queen, we shall all be the better for it." William released Mary and smiled at her. He then turned to Bernard.

"Tell the Lady Annelore that she shall want for nothing at our hand. We gladly appoint the Mistress Mary as her matron. And please, return the jewels with our continued good grace."

Mary curtsied, holding out her skirts. "Thank you, Your Highness. My lady will be delighted, and I as well."

"Majesty," Bernard mumbled, clicking his heels and turning to go.

"Oh, and Bernard?" William strode back to his cards, smacking Gregory's head as the duke attempted to peek at William's hand. "We need not be apprised of such trifles as these. Her ladyship's chamber is her domain. We will not stand for the airing of squabbles—we've enough of that with the French."

* * *

"Well, bravo is what I say, my lady." Margaux slid up to Anna, who was pacing in front of the fireplace. "It serves Bernard right. He puffs himself up as if he were His Majesty's right hand."

She handed Anna a glass of spiced wine. It tasted of too much anise—yet one more thing she didn't like and would have to adjust to.

"And besides," Margaux said, "how can His Majesty expect you to leave all comforts behind?"

"Bernard means well, milady," said Yvette, who had been silent most of the day. "Still, it was proper to remind him who he serves. Where the power lays."

"Power?" Anna shook her head. "I'm merely here to produce heirs, look pretty, and keep my mouth shut. All of which I fear I shall fail miserably at."

Margaux smiled. "Your ladyship couldn't help but look pretty. The other two, leave to me."

"Leave to us all," Yvette said.

Margaux blushed and returned to the matter at hand—laying out bolts of extraordinary fabrics from which Anna's first royal gowns would be fashioned. Margaux clucked at the seamstress.

"Certainly not the pale green," she said. "Just look at her ladyship's coloring! Jewel tones, madam, jewel tones."

Anna took another slow sip of wine returning to the fire. Power? All she was meant to do was pick out fabrics, wear fabulous jewelry, smile at the king's side, and bear his children. And with the bad luck this royal family seemed to have, no doubt he would require many of them . . . . Her stomach tightened. Any time her mind wandered to that particular queenly duty, she recalled the dead prostitute.

A stamp of the guard's staff harkened the return of Mary and Bernard. Anna flew to Mary's side and hugged her tight. "Tell me! What did the king say?" But of course she knew. Mary was beaming.

"His Majesty remembers your little old Mary, he does."

"Tell me."

"All's the better, dearie." Mary patted Anna's hand, looking into her face with a grin. "He said I can stay. And most gracious he was about it."

* * *

William sat at Council Table inspecting his fingernails. Today the agenda was full of frivolous tasks regarding wedding plans and other accommodations for the future queen—things he did not give a wit about. He merely wanted the lady to have what made her comfortable, and how should he know what those things might be? As for the wedding, all he wanted to do was show up at the altar, then get roaring drunk.

"Now we come to the errant knight, Sir Bryan of Beaubourg," Daniel said. William left his chair and went to lean against the giant stone hearth.

"He's a potential threat to the nuptial proceedings," Robert said. "Very unstable, as many of you observed with me." He glanced around the table to nods—except from Halforn.

"Why bother with him?" Halforn said. "The wedding will be second only to battle for number of soldiers and armed guards."

William, acknowledging the point, was silent. But the mention of Sir Bryan raised his heart rate.

"Majesty, I too observed his outburst," said Timothy, the young and lanky Earl of Ridgeland, whose lands were just beyond the southern hills of Beaubourg. "In my opinion, the young man is deranged. Perhaps the rest of Beaubourg is just as aggrieved and would not hesitate to take up arms—"

"What evidence do you have of this?" William glared at the whole lot of them. It was unseemly to be galled about such a trifle. *I'll be damned if being king turns me into James by degrees.* He took a breath. "Are you all telling us you believe this knight, fresh from that honor, would ride willingly to his swift death, bringing his countrymen with him?"

"If he be thickheaded enough to charge a speeding train of eight knights and armed noblemen, I would not put it past him to try," Ridgeland said.

William sighed. "Well, gentlemen, we are at a loss to see how this upstart could cause us, or the day, any harm."

Robert smacked the table. "I say we send an armed garrison out to scout for the knave, bring him to the yard in chains, and be done with it."

"The Grand Master General to Council Table," a guard shouted from the far door.

"Ah," William said, "just the man to put us to rights."

The general, a large, sturdy man with prematurely white hair and a wide, flat face strode into Council Table, bowed, and took his appointed seat.

"Majesty, my apologies for my tardiness—I had late report from my scouts."

"We forgive thee, Master General, and beg your counsel." William stalked back to his seat at the head of the table, with its grand view out the vast east windows. "We've been discussing whether to form a small army to fight one little knave and his theoretical peasant soldiers."

"Well, sire," the general said with his slight burr, "we may need an army, knave or no. Laureland is making to rise against your highness—egged on by our heretic neighbors to the east, no doubt."

"That is indeed grave news—and puzzling," William said. "We had hoped our journey there last month would have steadied them. Rallied them back to the fold."

"Aye, Majesty." The general scratched his resplendent beard. "It appears the Germans may use the passing over of Lady Helena for queen as argument for your fierce devotion to the Pope. 'Tis no secret they want Troixden as their own."

"What better way to conquer a country than to set it to wiping out its own people?" William said. Then, almost to himself, "What if this is all a ploy?"

"What is?" Ridgeland said. "The uprising?"

"The threat of uprising," the general said. "None have taken to arms, and there's no sign of stockpiling. Just rumors. Serious rumors, but rumors nonetheless."

"This whole thing with Sir Bryan," William said. "Could it be a ruse to draw our attention away from Laureland and the German states?"

"Doubtful," Robert said, "the Beaubourgans loathe their Laureland neighbors almost as much as they loathe Havenside. I can't imagine they'd ever join forces."

"If what Your Majesty thinks be so," the general said, "then we have much to worry on. The entire northern region armed against us? We should be gathering a force to—"

"Nay," William said. "We will not have an armed garrison slaughtering our people on our wedding day on the basis of rumors, Master General, no matter how serious."

"Aye, sire, I didn't mean to form an attack," the general said, "merely to be ready for one. The throne should never be caught unawares."

"Indeed, and that is why we have appointed you our grand master." He smiled down the table. "Gather some men to arms, but quietly. We do not want worry to spread. As for the heedless Sir Bryan, let the city wall guards keep lookout. If he's daft enough to appear, he can spend the rest of his days in Stone Yard." Robert let out a sigh, to which William gave a sharp look. Then he slapped the table. "We're off to hunt for the wedding feast. Any who want to join us had best make haste."

* * *

"I don't see why you won't let me in on your plans," Margaux said, again seated on Robert's settee. "With my proximity to the queen-in-waiting—"

"Yvette has that well in hand," he said, not looking up from his book. "Besides, it's well beyond your depth." She'd behaved herself since their spat during William's tour, but the look on her face didn't bode well.

"You know she's a heretic," Margaux said.

Robert flicked his eyes to her, then back to his reading. "That's a mighty strong accusation. Your spite may turn round and bite you."

"After reading to us from the Scriptures about Jesus healing the paralytic, she told us she'd given a dying man last rites merely because a priest wasn't at hand and the man begged her to do it. Why, Lady Jane looked ready to have her babe right then when her ladyship spoke of it."

"Hardly a case to prepare the stake, sis."

"I thought you'd be pleased." She frowned. "I'm merely trying to help you—"

He slapped the book on his thigh. "Does she make a habit of it? Does she baptize the babes she delivers? Write leaflets against the Pope?" She glared at him. "Leave theology to your betters."

"Fine," she said, clacking her strands of pearls together with fidgeting fingers. "Then I'll have to attend things of my own accord."

He gave her a dark look. "Don't muck things up. You'd be pained to cross me."

"If I don't know what you're up to," she said, "how shall I know if I'm mucking things?"

He gave a snort. "Just stay away from William. And for God's sake, don't mess with the queen."

"I will disclose my deeds when you disclose yours, brother dear." She sniffed and turned to leave. "You aren't the only Norwick who desires to change their lot."

"This is all becoming absurd," Anna said, a week after her arrival. She had just heard her slated activities for the day, all of which took place indoors while the July sun was bright outside. If the king were to leave the grounds, she might be allowed a short airing in the privy gardens with her ladies.

She pushed aside her voluminous covers, swung her feet off the edge of the bed, and scowled as her flock of ladies came forward to attend her.

"I've been cooped up in this dank, sweating palace for a week. Will Troixden truly fall to complete destruction if someone sees the back of my head from a hundred yards away? Mother of Moses, 'tis the middle of summer."

"Tush, tush," Mary said, "the wedding be only a week hence."

When she heard Margaux ask Bernard to send some letters, she looked to see if any had come in turn. But Margaux's hands were empty—again. Anna had only received one short letter from Bryan since her arrival. Much of it was smudged and he hadn't signed his name, but she recognized his cramped hand: *A, All is not lost! None will be*— she couldn't decipher the next phrase—*for me and be of good cheer.*

Was he planning to try and stop the wedding? Or did "all is not lost" mean he had found some semblance of peace back home? Whatever the case, why had he not been more forthcoming? After the debacle with the carriage, she didn't think it prudent to respond and inquire further.

"Mary," she said, "you of all people know how restless I am when I can't get out into the world. I haven't seen a living plant in days."

Margaux and Brigitte started in on her hair.

"Your ladyship is right," Margaux said, placing a pearl in a lock Brigitte pulled back. "'Tis cruel that you are shut up in chambers with no sport, no entertainment, no exercise."

"What then do you suggest, Lady Margaux?" Yvette said. "Lowering ladyship in her bed curtains from the windows in escape?"

"Nothing so dramatic." Margaux clapped her hands. "Oh, my lady, it'll be such a lark!"

"Tell me." Anna turned in her chair, disrupting her half-finished hair.

"The king has tennis with my brother this afternoon," Margaux said. "Let's go to watch! Majesty's at his finest at tennis, and no one need see us."

Yvette, who was arranging Anna's breakfast of cold grouse, fruit, and sweetbread, stopped to scowl at Margaux. "That has got to be one of the worst ideas—"

"No, 'tis perfect," Margaux said. "We shall head to the game directly after dinner. Her ladyship shall carry a large fan and not be noticed amongst all the nobles attending. It will be so diverting!"

"But how will the king not notice?" Anna said. "The prospect is enticing, but . . ."

"There are so many nobles arriving for the wedding 'tis not likely the king or any others will give us a second glance." Margaux gave Anna a knowing smile. "Besides, His Majesty will be playing the game in earnest. And when he plays, well," she leaned to Anna's ear, "he's in fine form."

Anna frowned in thought. It was true that only a few men had seen her. And if she had a large flat cap and fan . . . . But how to get around the guards?

"I agree with Yvette," Mary said. "Whether the king takes notice or not, he's given orders. He doesn't wish ye to be seen."

"Oh tush," Margaux said. "No harm will come."

"No harm indeed!" Mary shoved her way through the ladies. "Methinks you've not seen the sun enough neither, Lady Margaux, begging your pardon. The king'll be incensed."

"Now, Mary," Margaux said, "I know His Majesty, and if we're discovered, Highness will see it for the lark it is." Her smile would melt a stone, but Anna doubted it would work on Mary. "Majesty loves a good mask."

"'Tis not a mask, lady, 'tis my mistress's neck," Mary said.

"Well, not ladyship's neck, certainly," Yvette said, "but perhaps her honor."

"How is my honor to be tarnished if none but us know of it?" Anna said. "The king would barely recognize me. As you say, he and his men will be distracted by sport and the throngs of others."

"His Majesty may not marry you, for breaching orders," Yvette said.

"All the better." The room hushed. Anna couldn't help the blush that came to her cheeks, or the words that flew out of her mouth. "I'm sure His Majesty's a fine man and does me much honor, but he should have sought a bride who wanted the honor."

She looked at Margaux, who averted her eyes, and turned to Anna's toilette table.

"Dress me in more muted attire," Anna said, "and we'll tell Bernard I've taken to bed in the heat and wish not to be disturbed. As for the guards, I'll stand in the middle of you ladies who wish to attend, pretending to be one of you. With my fan up and hat down, our story well planted, I think we may just have ourselves an outing."

She glanced at Mary, whose arms were crossed over her chest.

"Don't worry, Mary. I shan't be noticed. Should I not be allowed to observe the man I'm to marry?"

"Aye, but he shan't be afforded the same," Mary said. "And he be the king."

Anna turned to Margaux and Brigitte. "Well, ladies, what say you? The dark blue?"

Margaux let out a gleeful eek while Brigitte scrambled to the wardrobe.

"I'll have no part in this," Mary said getting right up to Anna's face. "You should be ashamed of yourself, letting these girls parade ye about like a pet."

"I'm already a caged animal," Anna said. "Why not behave like one?"

"Caged or no, ye are your father's daughter, a daughter of Beaubourg—don't you forget it."

Margaux held up a flopping flat cap of crushed blue velvet and pearls. "So what shall we have you called, ladyship, if anyone asks?"

Call me Jezebel, for I am thrown to the dogs.

* * *

William entered the tennis court and began warming up, hitting his ball against the wall. A crowd had already gathered, eager to see the match between these two renowned players. Daniel was at the ready to call the play.

Robert arrived, shedding his coat, resplendent in olive green and gold striped trunks, his ruffed shirt loosed at the neck, laces flying as he began his own warm-up on the wall.

"Tell me, shall I be on the hunt for any particular lady to accompany you during the festivities tomorrow evening? As it's officially your last as a free man?" Robert grinned. "Of course, being king, you'll always be a free man."

"You're a cad, my friend," William said. "I don't think I should start this already tenuous union with the ministrations of a whore."

"Who said anything about whores?"

With a quick turn of the wrist, William sent a ball whizzing within inches of Robert's head. He ducked and William let loose a loud gut laugh, the first in days.

At the sound of the king's laughter Anna lowered her fan. He stood, wide mouth open in mirth, eyes not hostile as she remembered but sparkling, the deep blue of a calm sea. His cheeks were stubbled, there was an inviting dimple in his chin, and his shirt was light enough to see the powerful frame beneath. He wiped his brow, still grinning, and clapped Robert on the shoulder.

Whatever she was expecting, it wasn't this. He was handsome, yes, but there was something more. As she stared at him, all sound became a dull buzz. She was pricked with a thousand tiny pins all through her body. The tips of her fingers pulsed.

As the king looked in her direction she raised the fan waiting to take another peek. Anna heard a loud thwack as he served. Sure enough, the king's eyes were on his opponent now.

"Fifteen love!" Daniel called. The crowd clapped for His Majesty's point.

The king cocked a thick brow, smiled at Robert, and prepared to serve again. As he lobbed the ball into the air and attacked it, Anna lowered the fan enough to glimpse part of his broad chest flexing with a quick, practiced motion, hairs peeking out. He flung himself into the game with grace that matched his strength, moving with sure steps and small gasps of exertion to return Robert's volleys. Anna kept the fan lowered; she was concealed enough by the crowd.

The king charged the net, leaping in the air to place the ball just inside the duke's baseline. Robert dove in vain attempt to reach the ball, which had sprung, as if by magic, into Daniel's hands. The king let out a whoop and crossed the net to give his fallen friend a hand. As he rose, his keen eyes locked on to Anna's.

Her limbs liquified. Time stopped, but only for a breath. Yvette dragged her backward into the crowd. In an instant she was out of sight, back where the party of ladies had emerged, minutes before, in a flutter of giggles and shushing.

* * *

The king shoved past Robert to look through the protective nets that covered the viewing hall, searching. Robert followed his eyes only to see his sister and the back of an auburn head in hasty retreat.

What on earth could she be thinking? Did this lady have no respect for orders? For decorum? "Highness?"

The king turned to him. "I thought . . ." He chuckled. "'Tis nothing."

Robert looked through the net again, straining to see Lady Annelore and Margaux, but they were gone. He swallowed his umbrage and looked back to the king.

"You're sure?"

"Perfectly," William said. "Shall we return to the grand thumping I'm giving you?"

* * *

Anna leaned against the cold stone of a hallway, still trying to steady her breath. Margaux was at her side, doing the same. They'd practically run all the way.

"Oh, that was a lark," Margaux said. "Did you see?"

"We all saw," Yvette said, "and it was near disaster."

Yvette tugged Anna tripping down the hallway to the queen's chambers, where she delivered her to the ministrations of Mary. Then Yvette turned to Margaux and dragged her into an alcove by the ladies' beds. Anna could see the two whispering: Yvette calm, Margaux not. Yvette grabbed Margaux's wrists and shook her. Margaux jerked free—Anna thought she caught the word "*whore.*"

She turned away from them. She'd been a fool to risk the king's wrath, but she was glad for the chance to see him. His throaty laugh vibrated in her ears. Still shaky, she sipped at a goblet of wine.

This king looked nothing like the tyrant she imagined she saw in Beaubourg, but that meant little to her. At least she now understood what all the swooning was about. She had nearly swooned herself. But it wasn't just his looks—fine as they were—it was the authority he emitted, as if he sweat regality. This was what Bryan had spoken of, what danced in Mary's eyes as she returned with the box holding Matilda's jewels. There was a power in his presence that swept people toward him like an ocean's tide.

But Anna need not be caught in this wave. She refused to be. This faintness of heart she felt was only an expression of the awe the royal palace and its king naturally inspired. That was all.

The stamp of a staff at the door made her jump, spilling a bit of her wine. Would she be dragged off in shame already? She put her glass down and smoothed out her dress.

But it was only Bernard, carrying a small wooden box. "My lady," he said, face placid, "for your eyes alone."

She took the box. It bore a thin leather strap, the king's thick red seal atop, wax still warm.

As soon as Bernard took his leave, she opened it. And froze.

It was a tennis ball. Lifting it, she saw a small bit of parchment at the bottom. She opened the note.

. . .

15—all. Your service.
    ~ W

The ball dropped to the floor.

CHAPTER 6

I Shan't & I Won't

nna woke on her wedding day with a start. A slice of sunlit dust danced across her belly. She coughed. Mary thrust a chamber pot through her curtains. And while Anna's stomach constricted at the sight of it, there was nothing in her to go either direction—just acid that roiled about her insides like a serpent.

"I can't do this," she mumbled.

Mary pushed aside the curtains to reveal a room full of ladies waiting in full curtsy. "You can and you shall." Mary leaned in and lowered her voice. "Anna dear, of all the days of your lovely life, I know you're scared, but tonight when ye enter this chamber you'll be queen. And a queen daren't say, 'I can't.'"

Anna's heart stung. She had no privacy, no chance to be properly comforted by this woman who had basically been her mother. But Mary was right. She was to be a queen—no matter that she had never felt so small. She breathed deep and squared her shoulders.

"Mistress Mary," she said, affecting a louder, regal voice, "what are our appointments this morning?"

At this, her entourage rose from their knees and moved as one to the bed, each extending their daily offerings of food, drink, and undergarments.

"Milady," Mary said, taking to her duties as matron of honor with aplomb, "we are to your private mass, then to the ladies' breakfast, whence ye meet a select group of noblewomen. After, you shall change and go to the church. And after that, you're the king's business."

All Anna could manage was a nod to Mary's reassuring smile.

Yvette presented herself. "My Lady," she said as she bathed Anna's hands in rose water, "I wonder if you would allow me the privilege of preparing your toilette for the evening?"

Anna started at this hint of what the night would bring. Of course, who better than Yvette to prepare a girl for the exploits of a married woman? She managed another nod.

Next came Margaux, who handed Anna her morning wine with such force it spilled on Anna's shift sending Stefania scrambling for a fresh one.

"I'm so sorry, my lady," Margaux said, aghast, "I suppose we're all a bit anxious today."

"Certainly I am," Anna said. Margaux's face looked puffy. Had she been crying? The remaining ladies went about dressing her in the first of her gowns. This one, for her last mass as a maiden, was covered in layer upon layer of delicate cream lace and draped with hundreds of tear-shaped pearls. Her headdress was a petite tiara of gold and suspended pearls that pulled her hair up at the temples. The rest of her hair, not to be bound up until after the wedding night, was brushed to gleaming, flowing down her back like a river.

She appraised herself in the mirror. For the first time since her arrival at court, she actually felt a bit like royalty. And yet, she left her chamber and headed to privy mass with acid still churning in her stomach.

* * *

In the king's chambers jests, mead, and backslaps were passed from man to man. Robert flopped down on the royal bed and thrust his hips up and down.

"My liege, shall I warm this up for you? For it's been frigid cold for many months." Laughter erupted from the amassed crowd of friends, council members, and servants.

"Thank you for reminding me." William shoved the duke from his feathered perch and lay back, hands clasped behind his head. "Methinks I shall keep it so warm as to burn it clean through in a fortnight."

More bawdy laughter. He sat up and clapped his hands.

"But now to mass, dear friends, to mass—to repent for all our sloth and impure thoughts."

"And for all those Spanish women from last summer," Robert said.

"Touché, Norwick," Halforn said, grinning at the younger men's sport.

As William rolled off the bed, Daniel beckoned him to a diamond-paned window overlooking the countryside. Mist rose from the green hills as the climbing sun set the dew on each blade of grass to shimmering, an undulating field of emeralds.

"What a day for a royal wedding," Daniel said.

William clapped his shoulder. "Indeed it is. Let's hope the bride doesn't have to be roped and dragged to the altar."

"She'll reconcile herself when she comes to know you."

"Well, despite her ire in being here, the plan has worked. The people—save Laureland—are ecstatic."

"Yet you seem troubled, my friend. It seems to me 'tis more than wedding-day nerves."

"There you are, always getting to the heart of things." William hesitated, sighed. "Maybe this isn't right. Maybe I should be marrying Helena—or Margaux, for as much as Robert jokes, I think he expected it."

"It was expected, and I daresay by the lady most of all, if not graciously."

"Why, Daniel!" William smiled. "That's one of the most unkind things I've ever heard you say."

"Surely not the most unkind," Daniel said. "I apologize if I offend—"

William laughed. "After these many years there is very little you could say that would offend me. You've never failed in steering me aright." He draped an arm across Daniel. "And I need your wisdom once again." He squeezed his friend's shoulder, then let go. "This woman, Annelore, she doesn't want this. The crown. Me. Any of it. She's made it clear she'd rather be back in Beaubourg with her young knight and father."

"But—"

"I don't fault her." William raised his hands. "The crux of it is, as king, this should mean nothing to me." He fiddled with the gold fringe on the drapes. "She's my subject, and a woman for heaven's sake. I keep thinking how my father would have laughed at her insolence, and my brother would have done worse. But that's the way of kings, yes?"

Daniel waited.

"My mother would tell me to take pity on her, to let her go home. But my mother wasn't raising me to be a king."

"You're wrong, sire."

"'Tis William, old friend."

"Then you're wrong, *William*. Your mother did raise a king. She raised you to be a man of principle, of intellect, of faith, of wit, and of grace." Daniel hit his palm to emphasize each attribute. "If that be not the mark of a king, I don't know what is."

"So you're saying I should send Lady Annelore away?"

"Margaux is not well liked by the people, nor by you, I daresay. I do not think your mother would wish another hateful marriage upon this family."

William frowned, listening intently.

"Add to this the popularity of Lady Annelore," Daniel said. "An excitement has gripped the capital, and she hasn't even been out of her chambers."

William smiled to himself at this. Oh yes she had. Then he thought of the knight the lady preferred, and the smile vanished.

"Fret not," Daniel said. "I daresay she will come to enjoy her new status quite readily. And she will forget this boy of hers when she sees a proper grown man."

William rolled his eyes. "I'm not some youth in need of puffing up."

"Flattery it may be, my friend, but 'tis also the truth." Daniel bowed and left the chamber to queue up for mass, leaving the king to his musings.

William had been riding high on the momentum of this new adventure he had been thrust into. King! Of course it had always been a possibility—there are reasons royals have more than one child —but he'd simply never thought about becoming king, couldn't think why anyone would want the job. Yet here he was, swept up in the dramas of coronation, of rooting out the bastards from his brother's court, of presiding over legal and political policy, of nonstop feasting.

He'd viewed this whole wedding business as just that—business —never envisioning a flesh-and-blood woman who wanted nothing to do with him or his hoped-for heirs. And now, here she was, a mere thirty yards away—five if one burrowed through the walls. Breathing the same courtly air. Loathing him.

He had never felt the loathing of anyone in his life, excepting his brother James. His mother had always protected him from the fury of his father and the jealousy of his brother. Even when James was king, William was away "guarding the borders" of Troixden, their brotherly ire out of sight if not out of mind. And he'd had the time of his life. He even learned to play the lute and mandolin.

Perhaps if I compose her a sonnet? He laughed. *Ah, Wills, get ahold of yourself.*

And he left for his last mass as a bachelor with a lump of nerves lodged in his throat.

The bells of Piermont Cathedral rang loud enough to drown out the herald angels. This was Anna's cue.

She stepped from beneath the shadow of the carriage and into brilliant July sunshine, draped in veils like a shroud.

Her ladies followed, each laden with her long train as the gathered crowd of merchants, peasants, and travelers erupted in a roar, pushing against the line of palace guards ten yards away.

Bernard, dressed to the nines himself, lace cuffs dancing to his practiced movements, held Anna's hand to steady her, taking some of the gown's unwieldy weight upon himself. She smiled in thanks, though he could not see it behind the thick veil. The crowd hovered like swarming bees, jostling for position.

She remembered the small coin purse she clutched. Reaching inside, she fingered the cold outline of her future husband's imprinted profile on the coin's golden surface. Taking a few in hand, she flung them to the throng.

"Praise you, lady! God save ye, and the king!"

She turned toward the cathedral. The high gold doors were thrown wide in welcome and her party hastened inside. The organ blew, signaling her arrival to the sanctuary's occupants, an opaque glass screen serving a scant divide between the blessedly cool narthex and the guest's prying eyes. The organ pipes shook the very floors, the processional hymn keeping time with her trembling limbs.

A flood of warm air washed over her, humid and heavy in her lungs. Hundreds of candles lined her path down the wide aisle. The crowd was hushed as the hymn ended and a cappella voices rang out in Latin, clearer than any bell. Her retinue, carrying yard-high candles, moved forward.

Her skin crawled with all those eyes boring into her from every angle, trying to get a glimpse of her, forming conclusions. Whispers fluttered as she passed, and a deep blush rose on her cheeks. She walked on, focusing on keeping her balance under the burdensome dress.

Squinting through the veil, she made out the towering form of the king, standing before the altar next to the Archbishop of Bartmore. Her ladies parted in graceful curtsies as the king descended the stairs.

She curtsied, praying not to fall. The king came to her side and offered his hand. Hoping her palms weren't damp, she took it. His touch prickled—she all but pulled away at the jolt of it—as he guided her to the altar then released her.

The archbishop descended and stopped before them. He nodded his pointy-hatted head at Margaux and Brigitte, whose duty it was to remove the wreath of herbs that lay atop her veils. As the greenery left her head the cathedral itself seemed to hold its stony breath, waiting for the revelation of her face.

The king took both sides of her veiling in his hands, lifted the whole up and behind her in a swift, fluid movement, like billowing a sheet over a bed, then let it float quietly to the floor. Anna's insides threatened to follow.

His Majesty inclined his head, a slight nod of acknowledgment, then paused, searching her face. For what, she could not hope to guess. And the king's eyes—the same eyes that bore through her like arrows in Beaubourg and caught her up on the tennis court—now seared her at close range with their blue-hot flame. She knew in an instant those eyes suffered no fools. Whatever he was, King William II was not a man to be trifled with.

The archbishop, having moved through the preliminaries and satisfied himself that neither knew any impediment why they "may not be lawfully joined together in matrimony," now addressed the king as if invoking the hounds of both heaven and hell.

"Wilt thou, William Reginald Gerard Justinian, Rex, have this woman, Annelore Matilda, to be thy wedded wife—"

At the mention of her name, the king gently yet firmly took both her hands in his, casually rubbing calloused thumbs over the backs. The heat of his touch startled her, buzzing through her like a bee at her ear. She watched, mesmerized, as he stroked the blue veins so apparent through her paper-fine skin, bringing his thumb finally to rest on her knuckles.

"To live together after God's ordinance in the holy estate of matrimony? Wilt thou love her, comfort her, honor and keep her, in sickness and in health, and forsaking all others, keep thee only unto her, so long as ye both shall live?"

Without hesitation, the king smiled. "I shall and I will."

She held her breath, lips tight, mind reeling as the archbishop's voice droned on. *I shan't and I won't, I shan't and I won't.*

"Keep thee only unto him, so long as ye both shall live?"

"I shall and I will." *Dammit!*

The king squeezed her hand, then turned to the archbishop.

"Your Majesty, take her ladyship's right hand in thine own and repeat after me."

The king did so, his voice easily carrying to the far corners of the cathedral, Annelore limply following along. "I, William Reginald Gerard Justinian, Rex," he gave her an easy smile, "take thee, Annelore Matilda, to be my wedded wife. To have and to hold, from this day forward. For better, for worse. For richer, for poorer. For fairer, for fouler. In sickness and in health. To love—" He broke off, bringing his fist to his mouth, and cleared his throat. Anna thought she caught the glint of wetness in the crinkled corner of his eye. "— and to cherish, till death us do part. In loyal matrimony, according to God's holy ordinance; and thereunto I plight thee my troth."

Finished, he relaxed his grip. Anna wondered if her mouth would work. The gravity of the words she was about to speak terrified her. For with them she would bind herself irrevocably to this man, this king she feared. Blinking through tears she desperately tried to hold back, she began.

"I, Annelore Matilda, take thee, William Reginald G-gerard Justinian, Rex . . ."

No. No hiding. She would go on, tears or no. She would let him see the fear he evoked, let him feel the smallness of a man who took his wife by fiat. "To be my wedded husband. To have and to hold . . ."

The king reached out his thumb and with the lightest of touches wiped her wet cheek. Bringing thumb to mouth, he kissed it clean. She hesitated, flushed.

"I plight thee my troth."

The archbishop, apparently fearing the worst, hastily blessed the rings and readied the cord, blessed by the Pope himself, that would bind their hands together, a visual symbol of an invisible bond. The king balanced the thick gold ring upon Anna's thumb.

"With this ring I thee wed," he said, and moving it to her index finger, he continued, following the archbishop's lead. "This gold I thee give"—to the middle—"and with all my worldly goods I thee endow." Finally sliding the band smoothly down her ring finger to its base, he pressed her hand and locked his eyes on hers. "And with my body, I thee worship."

With his body? Her stomach lurched. The archbishop grabbed Annelore's free hand, turned her palm up, and placed the king's ring into it. Clumsily, she rolled it to her fingertips, swallowed hard, and touched the wider twin band to the king's thumb. She kept her eyes firmly on her work as she muttered out her promises, struggling to get the ring over his knuckle at the final vow, "With my body, I thee worship."

"Those whom God hath joined together let no man put asunder," the archbishop said.

"Amen! Amen! Amen!" the crowd chanted.

"I pronounce," a pause for dramatic flourish, "that they be man and wife together. In the name of the Father, and of the Son, and of the Holy Ghost. Amen."

"Amen! Amen! Amen!"

The archbishop looked at them, serious, and whispered, "Now go forth and give us heirs. Many, many heirs."

The king threw his head back in a laugh as Anna's gut lurched. Bartmore climbed to the top of the stairs. Turning, his blazing robe swinging out about him, he clasped his hands together.

"And now, make a final seal of your troth with a holy kiss."

In one elegant move, the king took her red cheeks in both his hands, pulling her to meet his lips—softly at first, then pressing, hers going limp beneath. It lasted only a moment, but it was long enough to wipe away all other sensation except tingling. Everywhere. This brief brush of lips gave her gooseflesh, something a long afternoon with Bryan never did. So curious, so . . . .

Her knees started to buckle, but the king was quick, catching her at the waist in his arms. A murmur of laughter bubbled through the crowd and she straightened, squaring her shoulders. Of course this would be the moment her legs failed her.

"Pardon me, lady," he whispered, breath tickling the delicate hairs by her ear, "I didn't mean to stun thee."

"Not to worry, sire." She narrowed her eyes. "'Twas just the

tangle of all these skirts." Holding her head high, she took his proffered arm. He, looking at her sidelong, gave a little snort.

The archbishop indicated they should kneel. Her ladies stretched
her discarded veil taut over the top of the couple's bowed heads.

The king leaned toward her. "We meet again, my dear. Am I so
terrible to behold at closer inspection?"

Anna continued to stare forward, watching the archbishop's deft
hands as he murmured in Latin.

"Not at all," she whispered back. "Merely impertinent to be
muttering such through the Holy Eucharist. Or doth my liege not
take succor from Our Lord's sacrifice?"

"If my lady spent as much time as I hearing the mutterings of
priests, she might tire of them herself, if not of Whom they
represent."

She stole a glance at him. "Touché, Highness."

"Lady," he said, eyes bright with mischief, "the priest cometh—
behave thyself."

As the two received the host, she mulled over their brief tête-à-
tête. Was he so informal? Perhaps—

The veil above them lifted as the archbishop beckoned the king
to rise. As he stood, he took her hand and pressed it to his lips.

"Just one more little rite, my lady."

As they had taken communion veiled in secrecy, Anna had not
seen a small throne brought in front of the wide altar. The archbishop had her turn to face the congregation, still on her knees. He
held the gold crown of queenly office aloft, hands trembling.

"In the presence of these gathered here and of God the Father,
God the Son, and God the Holy Ghost," he said, "I do crown thee,
Annelore Matilda, Queen Consort of Troixden, and do charge ye to
serve in faithful solemnity until death, with the fear of God and king
upon thy heart."

He brought the hefty crown down upon her head. Dripping with
jewels, it cast tiny beams of colored light, scattering them amongst
the congregation. And thus she was endowed with a rank only the
king could usurp.

Solemn now, the king took her hand and led her to the throne. As she sat, he took a knee before her and kissed her hand, letting his lips linger at her knuckles, their soft pressure reverberating through her body.

"I give you my fealty, Queen Annelore," he said over the top of her hand, for her ears alone. He looked her straight in the eyes. "If nothing else comes of us, I swear by God and by Troixden to give you my fealty. Please, do not disdain it."

He rose, stepping aside for her to see the people, her people, melting to the floor in obeisance before them both. As if cued by some collective intuition, the congregation rose, calling, "Long live the queen! Long live the queen!"

His Majesty, now beaming, took both her hands, raising her from throne onto wobbly feet. He offered his arm and when she took it, he laced his thick fingers up through hers, entwining them securely. Warmth spread to her toes.

The archbishop made the sign of the cross over them, blessing and charging them to "go in the peace and harmony of Christ." A light squeeze of the king's hand and the pair floated down the aisle, the king grinning in triumph, Anna holding tight to his arm. All things considered, she'd just as soon not stumble.

* * *

"Well, my queen," William said, drawing out her title, rolling it about his tongue like a fine wine. It heartened him to hear it. They had passed alone into the narthex and were headed to the stairs up to the viewing balcony. There he'd present her to the throng gathered outside.

"'Twas not so bad, methinks," Annelore said. The warmth of her spread down his arm, which she was still grasping. His fingers ached in anticipation of more. "But my liege, I can barely breathe with it all —I don't know how you manage. But of course you were born to royalty."

William glanced at her as they mounted the stairs, their minions scrambling behind to pick up her train.

"All will be well, my dear. Soon we shall sup and further our acquaintance. I promise that at least I don't bite."

"'Tis just what I feared, my liege, thank you for allaying them."

William let out a great guffaw. Perhaps she was not as dazed as he thought. He meant every word he'd vowed to her. He would honor her, keep himself only to her—hard as that might be—and try his damnedest to love her. She was beautiful, quick-tongued, but definitely frightened. And she made him laugh. All was not lost.

"Just follow my lead, and if you feel faint we'll leave forthwith." For that he got a weak smile. But then she took a deep breath, let it out, straightened her back, and lifted her chin. "Are you ready, then?"

"I am."

He nodded and the pages flung open the doors to the small stone balcony. The deafening roar of the half-drunk crowd swept over them both as they strode out, hands clasped. People tossed flowers as high as they could. William thrust Anna's hand high in the air, rousing their subjects further.

He held his other hand up, palm out, long enough to quiet the crowd. "Good people of Troixden," he said, his regal smile including them all, "may I present, our very dear and honorable . . ." He paused a few seconds for absolute silence. "Queen Annelore."

The crowd's applause and chants of "Long live Queen Annelore!" roared against the stone. They'd been so long without a proper queen, James's faithless Minerva having lost her head years ago. And now, here was their own. The people's queen. He turned to her, applauding as well, the excitement of the crowd contagious. "Indeed, my dear—long live the queen."

She stood beside him with a face gone pale. Then, a smile, small and beatific like a Madonna's in an icon, played across her face. And he knew no matter what happened between them, he would remember this moment. The moment he watched a trembling girl become a queen.

Time slowed as the wind caught a tendril of her hair, floating it across her shoulders. Sunlight glinted off the top of her crown, nearly making a halo. He was in as much awe as the lowest serf. She turned slowly to the people and moved to the edge of the balcony, leaving William behind. The crowd gave another cheer as she came further into the light, dazzling in the sun. She reached deep in the folds of her gown and flung gold coins out to them.

Then she stopped, stood silent and still, hands at her side. A hush fell over the crowd. They murmured as she spread her skirts, bent her knees and dipped her head, as low as it could go and still be in sight of the crowd below. It took them a long moment before they realized. The queen was curtsying. To them.

The silence was followed by pandemonium. William had never seen a people whipped into such frenzy, not even in battle. Daniel was right again. They had adored her sight unseen. And now, with this one graceful act, she had bound them to her irrevocably. There was more to this woman from the north than met the eye.

She lifted her head, waved to her people, turned, the picture of calm, and smiled at William, revealing pearled teeth and high cheeks that glowed like polished apples. She grabbed his hand, then thrust their arms in the air one last time, a bookend to their entry.

The echo of his people's voices still rang in William's ears as they descended the interior cathedral steps to the wedding party, quite the contrast to the happy mob outside.

"Well done, Majesty," he said to his queen. "Well, well done."

Reaching the bottom of the stairs she spun out in front of him in a curtsy, skirts flaring. "Thank you, Your Majesty," she said. A thrill of ardor washed over him.

* * *

Anna was back in her chambers awaiting the feast. She stared out the window at the sunset making Stone Yard glow, as if gilding its hideous purpose.

Yvette drew a stool up next to her. "Your Majesty?" She smiled. "It's nice to finally address you so."

Anna sighed, then gave a royal wave to make a joke of it. "I shall have to get used to hearing it."

Yvette was rubbing a small vial of deep green oil in her lap. "So then, Majesty, this evening . . ."

Anna shivered. Yvette took one of Anna's hands and stroked it like a cat. "Worry not, my queen. With a man like the king, you shall be in expert and kind hands."

"Expert?" Anna's eyes grew wide. She was worse than ill-prepared for this forced coupling. Nothing in her experiences with Bryan had ever motivated her for more than mere kisses. Though, she must admit, there were nights when she would wake in a sweat from dreams where a faceless, nameless man was doing unspeakable things, needing her fingers to wander, to rub, to release her from that ecstatic tension. But surely that wasn't what husbands were for.

Yvette's smile deepened. "He be not a rogue, Majesty. He's simply . . . let's just say as a royal he's had ample opportunity."

Anna looked back out the window. "I don't know if I'd prefer an expert or novice, for I am even less than novice myself."

Her stomach reeled. Ugh, this whole thing. What did he expect of her? Was she supposed to perform in some fashion? Just lie there? She knew it would hurt.

Yvette shook her head. "I only mean he isn't the type of man to be rough with you. It should only hurt at the beginning, if at all."

"Well, then." Anna took a steadying gulp of wine.

"To that end . . ." Yvette leaned in close, "this oil may help. It's for you. And for him."

Anna took the vial, shaking her head. "Am I to . . . surely I don't need to touch . . . I mean, I know where things ought to go . . . I think . . . but how they . . . oh, lord."

"Forgive me, Highness, but things will make themselves quite apparent. Just—follow his lead. And when he's ready, ask him to use this. He'll know what to do."

Anna sighed. "That's what I'm afraid of."

* * *

Into the Great Hall walked the royal couple, arms stretched and linked again, to more cheers and applause. The king, now in purple velvet and ivory silks, and Anna, in gold brocade and pure white, wore matching crowns of diamond and gold created for the occasion, much less weighty than the crowns of office, but no less striking.

They nodded to each upturned face as they made slow progress to their thrones. They would sit at the center of the head table, which rested above the dancing and jesting floor.

"Honored guests and friends," the king said, "we pray you make yourselves quite drunk and joyful, the better to reflect our own happiness." He took up his wine goblet and held it aloft. "To our fair Queen Annelore, may she live long and bring us peace!"

"Long live Queen Annelore!" the guests shouted.

Now the minstrels began in earnest, playing blithely on mandolins, lutes, and drums, the belled fool bounding around them like a happy puppy.

The king took another sip of his wine and turned to her.

"Did you mean that?" She said, feeling more relaxed, now that she was a bit out of the spotlight.

"Hmm?"

"You referred to our happiness. Did you mean you are happy with me?"

No matter how pleased he appeared to the crowd, no matter how many gallant remarks and smiles he sent her way, Anna needed to know if she had ruined things with her tears and sarcasm.

"Ah, my dear," he said, "you're beautiful, to be sure. I'm not entangled with a hag, nor you with a monster." She crinkled her forehead. What had he heard? The king drew her closer with a tug on her arm.

"I don't mean to tease," he said. "We know almost nothing of each other, you and I. If reports are true, then I daresay we shall at the very least live peaceably together." His eyes searched her face. He leaned closer still and she could feel his wine-warmed breath on her cheek. It smelled of oak and cinnamon.

"Let's enjoy the feast, my dear, and then? Well," he paused to smile, "we shall see."

"Yes, my liege." She flushed.

Seeing Daniel approach, the king called to him. "Dear brother, come and greet your hand-picked queen." So it was Daniel who had championed her selection.

"Your Majesties." He kissed the king's ring and bowed to her with a smile.

The king turned to her. "Madam, you will remember His Grace, Daniel, Duke of Cecile, Lord Chancellor and Master Secretary. He's my oldest and dearest friend."

Daniel took a knee before her, presenting her the top of his wiry blonde head.

"Your Grace," she said, "I am honored to reacquaint with a man so dear to the king."

He rose, took her proffered hand, and kissed her wedding band. "The honor is all mine, Highness."

"Daniel is the finest judge of character in all Troixden, my dear," the king said. "It was his wise counsel that finally convinced me to select you."

Daniel's ears reddened. "Thank you, Majesty."

"Don't stand on ceremony, my friend." He slapped Daniel's back, pushing the duke at Anna, and took his leave with a little wave.

Daniel tilted his head to the western windows, inviting Anna to walk with him. "Your Majesty," he said, "my heart is gladdened to see you here, finally wed. And how have you found the palace?"

Not wishing to repeat her performance before Robert, Anna chose her words carefully. "I have found the palace quite grand and my rooms splendid. Thank ye, Your Grace."

"Ah, good, good." They walked in silence a while, Anna nodding to unknown people about her. "And His Majesty, is he what you expected?"

She could not help but laugh at this. "Goodness, Your Grace, I hardly know what to say." He looked at her as though he really cared what she thought. "Since I expected him to be quite dastardly in manner and appearance—as he seemed to me before—I suppose His Highness is not what I expected. And at the same time, I do not know. He is . . . His Majesty is quite . . . majestic."

It was Daniel's turn to laugh. "That he is, Highness. A very politic and beguiling answer, I must say."

She relaxed, laughing with him. "That's one of the highest compliments anyone could pay me, Your Grace, as my tongue does have a habit of running on without my consent."

"You may find the king's tongue to have a similar habit," he said, smiling back. A jester bounded by her, a blur of purple and green, blowing her a kiss as he went.

"Then we shall be poor company indeed, always saying the wrong things at wrong times. I suppose His Majesty would hope his queen to bring temperance."

"You may surprise yourself, Highness, just as you were surprised by His Majesty."

Encouraged, she paused, considering. "I must admit, I had feared he was an ogre with a golden crown."

"No wonder you were frightened to come." So Daniel knew of her fight to stay home. She wondered what he might really think of her beneath his smiles and easy conversation. Perhaps she should not trust him so quickly. Perhaps he, like Robert, had an agenda.

They had reached the far western wall of the hall and made a turn down the long arm of the banquet table, small groups muttering and bobbing bows and curtsies as they passed.

"Your Grace," she said, "tell me of the king so that I may know his character the better. I wonder what a man of such stature in the king's household would advise his master's new wife."

"Majesty, I would not presume to know what a wife must be to a husband," Daniel said, blushing.

Anna bit her cheek. He had not taken to her flattery. "I only mean, what of his temperament? What of his likes and dislikes? What would he spend his time doing if at leisure?"

They had reached the table's end and now took another turn, crossing the large opening where heavy-laden servants hurried to table with platters of venison. Daniel guided her through the fray in silence. Upon reaching the other side, he stopped and turned to face her, his reddened cheeks almost crimson now.

"Majesty, it might be helpful if you remember that His Highness did not intend to be king any more than you intended to be queen."

And here came the king. "Are you so soon telling tall tales to my bride?"

Daniel bowed to them both, staring hard at Anna as if still trying to tell her something, and took his leave. The king took up her hand with a careless kiss.

"Now," he said, smile broad, "someone wishes to have an audience and I daresay you'll be pleased by the request." He guided her back to their seats where the Duke of Beaubourg waited with a smile that took over his face.

"Papa!" She ran into his outstretched arms.

"Oof, my darling girl, you must let me bow to you first!"

Anna released him but still held his arms. "Don't be ridiculous— I'm still your Anna."

The duke turned merry eyes to the amused king. "You shall always be my girl, but now you are also my queen. Give an old man the honor he so greatly desires—giving you all the honor you deserve."

"Oh, tush," she said but let her father bow before her and the king.

"Your Majesties," he said, "'tis my privilege and greatest hope to serve you with all that I am and all that I have." The king stepped forward and gave her father a squeeze on the arm.

"Your Grace, you have done quite enough for the time being in giving us a queen."

"Majesty." The duke clasped both his hands around the king's. "Hearken to our conversation. I believe in your goodness as I believe in my daughter's grace and pure heart."

"I pray we live up to your ideals, and for my part I will seek them earnestly." The duke nodded. "And as for the queen," the king looked to Anna and back to the duke, "know that I will strive to grant every wish of her heart, even before she thinks it."

The duke laughed. "Ah, Majesty, do not spoil her too much, else she will have you wrapped 'round her pretty finger as I am."

"Father," Anna said, flushing.

"I fear the process has already commenced," the king said.

Anna's cheeks were hot as embers. "I'm standing right here you both realize."

The king chuckled. "I daresay the two of you would enjoy some time together. I shall go begin the feast, lest our guests start eyeing the palace hounds."

He bowed his head in leave. Anna grabbed her father's hand, drawing him to a curtained alcove behind the royal seats.

"My darling girl," he said, "I have never been so proud of you. How regal you looked! Oh, if your mother could have seen this day."

"It all just seems a blur."

"Anna—excuse me, Majesty—"

"Papa, please don't be formal. It breaks my heart to hear you speak to me as someone so separate."

"Don't fret—you shall always be the Anna of my heart." He stroked her hand. "What I started to say was that I had an encouraging talk with the king."

"Encouraging how?"

"Nothing he said, nothing I've seen nor heard of him so far, has moved me to change my original opinion. I'm convinced he's a man of good heart—and wise. Why, with not so much as a glance from me he embraced me as friend, praised you to the heights, then invited me to court for as long as I wish to stay, saying he would immediately look to a place for me at council."

"Do you really think he will? But what happens to Beaubourg if you're here at council?"

"I'm sure he'll find me something that allows me time here and in Beaubourg. For he knows I love my countrymen, but also love my daughter. Ah, but he is a good, good man."

"As you've said."

He smiled at her, mischief in his eyes. "Have I?"

* * *

William leaned back with a slow grunt of satisfaction, his crown making a clink as it hit the high oak throne. Satiated from the twelve-course feast, his eyes were alight with candle flame and the merrymaking surrounding him.

"Well, my dear," he said, turning to look at his queen, "what say you to the gastronomy of Havenside?"

They reached for the same goblet of wine, bumping hands. She pulled hers away as if stung. William, stung himself by her reflex, moved the glass to her hand. At least she accepted it. What had he done between balcony and supper to make her so taciturn and skittish? Or was she simply shy and nervous in these circumstances so unknown to her? Heaven knows he found himself jumpy too.

"My liege," she said after taking a quick sip of the port, "I must say, 'tis more magnificence than I have ever seen. And certainly more than I deserve."

William cocked a brow. "Should not king and queen be fêted in magnificence, especially on their wedding day?"

"Sire, I did not mean . . . certainly Your Highness deserves this and more."

"My dear queen, I took no offense, only wondered why you would not think yourself worthy of such honor."

She took one more sip of port, set the glass down. "May I begin again, Majesty?"

"By all means."

"In Beaubourg, we rarely feast in elegance and when we do, our company are peasants and field hands, merchants and children. We are not afforded the company of so many people of . . . of such . . ." She glanced around at the celebrating nobles.

"Pretension?" William said.

She smirked. "I believe the word I was searching for was 'splendor.'"

"Ah, yes. That too."

"And I am unaccustomed to being treated with such deference."

"Truly? Do not your servants and serfs alike give you their honor and reverence?" In his own bandying about the world, he'd preferred to not be recognized as a prince all the time. Fraternizing with the people was more fun that way. Could a lady of peerage feel the same?

"Sire, in your many travels, 'tis a shame you have not ventured more in your own lands."

William cleared his throat. "Madam, were it not for injunctions against me, believe that I would be intimately familiar with every inch of our soil."

"Again I offend," she brought a hand to her chest. "Majesty, I myself rue my tongue and I fear you shall come to as well."

"Well, my dear, no harm. I'm a bit sensitive to my banishment. It seems my people forget that I too was victim of my brother's reign of terror."

"Yes, Majesty—certainly Beaubourg forgets. For kings come and go, but Beaubourg will remain. That has always been our thinking, begging your pardon. While we felt the iron fist of kings, we paid little heed to the intrigues of Havenside, your exile being one of them."

"'Tis good to hear my people think so little of me."

"It does take a bit of the burden off, yes?"

"Indeed." He nodded. "But you were speaking of my shirked duty in visiting my fine lands?"

"I only meant that if you had been to Beaubourg more often, you'd know that while our people certainly respect our house, we're such a small duchy and so isolated that certain formalities have been done away with out of necessity, not out of impertinence."

"Hence the lack of 'splendor' as you say?"

Before she could reply, twenty masked and costumed players tumbled in, hooting and trilling to begin their own tribute to the day.

"Ah, the mask begins." He grinned at the queen and straightened, clapping his hands, signaling the crowd to hush and the entertainment to begin. He then rested back, inclined on his forearm toward her, feeling tension in his groin at being so close to her. He glanced sidelong to find her face aglow in anticipation.

The players danced and sang, performing bawdy skits depicting the activities of the royal couple once they retired for the evening. The audience laughed—all save the queen, whose face changed from pink to red.

"Pay them no mind," he whispered, reaching out to clasp her

hand. She stiffened slightly at his touch but didn't pull away. He felt a rush of blood to his crotch again and bent closer. "'Tis their job to tease. It'll all die down tomorrow." She gave him a wary look. "My dear, to blush thus will only incite them further. Give them the countenance of that queen I spied on the balcony today."

"Sing! Sing!" a jester cried out.

"Yes, Majesty," called Robert, who had left his place at William's side to talk with a French envoy. "You must indulge us."

William looked up to see all eyes on him, eager. Robert started the guests in a chant the jesters helped spread. "Sing! Sing!" Now nobles were banging their cutlery on the table like ill-mannered peasants. "Sing! Sing!"

Annelore grasped William's forearm and gave him a bright smile "Highness, you cannot disappoint your people—nor me. Come now, your queen demands it."

William rose and faced his noisy subjects, holding up his hands in submission. "Minstrel," he said, "lend us your mandolin, for our queen demands amusement."

The audience shouted, "Long live Queen Annelore!" then quieted while he tuned the proffered instrument.

"A song for Troixden," he said. He put his left leg on his chair and started strumming. The crowd gave a cheer of pleasure at his selection, the other musicians picking up his lead. In his rich and clear tenor, he sang the merry love song to his land.

From the Truss to the Orlea, Back to Havenside's ground,
There the noblest shine That upon the world are found.
If looks and bearings fair My eyes can judge aright,
Any woman here surpasses in my sight
High-born ladies fine elsewhere!
Our fair men are nobly bred, Angels are the women of the land.
He who chides them is misled. Other truth I cannot understand.
He who doth be on his way, Seeketh virtue, loving chaste,
Come into Troixden, for there is joy to waste.

A joyous hurrah erupted from the audience. Amidst shouts of "Encore!" and Robert's whistles, he swept into the bow of an actor, coming up with a mischievous grin.

"Shall we sing now to our Lady Queen?" he called out to the crowd, stoking them further. Energized by their raptures, he turned to Annelore and gave her a wink. She had a look on her face he couldn't read. Was she impressed or thinking him a fool? Did it matter? He proceeded, orbiting around her, serenading her with the popular lover's sonnet:

Blessed be the hour when first I knew her,
Her who with heart and soul did rout me;
When all my senses were aroused to woo her,
I felt her goodness hover all about me.
And now I cannot part from her again,
Because her beauty and kindness delight me,
And her red, red mouth that laughs so brightly.
My heart and mind I have been turning
Unto the pure one, the good one, the dear one.
Ah, could I but fulfill my yearning:
I trust to her mercy that she will hear one.
All my joy on earth doth come from her,
Because her beauty and kindness delight me,
And her red, red mouth that laughs so brightly.

He ended the song on his knees before her, crooning. She pursed her red, red mouth and arched one perfect brow. Then she broke into a slow, dazzling smile.

The crowd roared. "More! More!"

William got up from his knees and handed the mandolin back to its owner. "Let us begin the dancing!"

This was met with delighted claps and murmurs as people darted to and fro, finding partners and descending to the floor. William thrust his hand to Annelore.

"My queen, will you do me the honor?" She took his hand with surprising strength.

"My liege," she said, "I would be honored and much pleased. For there is nothing I love more than dancing."

"Nothing?" he said, his mouth curling. He enjoyed teasing her.

She pursed her lips and looked at the ceiling. "I suppose I could venture to find another occupation that brings me as much joy," she said, "but at present, to dance shall suffice."

They moved to the center of the floor, other dancers creating a wide berth. There, with a flick of the wrist, he swung her out to his side, sending her skirts wide. Both bowed their heads while the minstrels awaited his request.

"A volte!" he called.

Stifled gasps arose around the room. She looked at him like a doe caught unawares by his arrow. He brought her up to face him.

"Do you not know the dance, my dear?"

"Aye," she said, "but 'tis quite an intimate selection."

"Have I scandalized you already?" he said, grinning. "And here I thought that would take me at least a month."

* * *

The king swung her away to the other side of the floor, bowing as the musicians started the sultry tune. Anna was already short of breath and they had yet to begin. A volte? Was he mocking her? It was not merely her anxiety at tripping over unfamiliar steps that had her gasping, but the thought of her body pressed against his with the eyes of all these people watching.

There was nothing she could do now. He stabbed his shoulder at her, sweeping his leg around in a jump, she following suit. They crept closer in this manner, circling, clapping, turning shoulders and heads, springing to the air, never losing eye contact, like prowling predators.

Finally reaching each other, the king snaked his arm firmly around her waist, turning her in his orbit and raised her high. She straightened her back and tensed as he thrust her aloft, his hand grasping her thigh as he lifted her. Whether it was her height in the air or the ache of his hand on her thigh—fire even through her skirts—she did not know, but her breath became shallow. Lowering her gently, he repeated the pattern.

She became dizzy with each hoist to the air. He carried her

weight with ease, letting her torso slide down his chest, their faces a hand's width apart. Her entire body pulsated with a want she'd never known. She felt his breath against her cheek, his eyes tracing her every movement. Perfect in his timing, her feet touched the stone as the final notes were played.

He kept her hand as she curtsied to him. Drawing it up to his lips, he lingered on her fingertips, blue eyes boring into her. He clasped his hand on the small of her back and drew her to him. She could not help but lean up, expectant, needing, caught in the pulse of the dance. He examined her face feature by feature, then bit his lower lip.

"My lady," he said, honoring her with a bow.

She deflated. Other dancers had joined them on the floor and were now clapping and changing partners. She looked around at the sea of pastel courtiers, as if waking from a dream. The king's eyes flicked for an instant over her shoulder.

"Our dear cuz,'" he said, turning her to a genuflecting Robert, "we give you the honor of rank and friendship. The next dance with our queen."

Without further ceremony, the king handed her into the waiting arms of the Duke of Norwick.

"Madam," he said, as a line courant dance began.

"Your Grace." She tried to look unfazed.

"Why, Highness, you look unhappy with your new partner. I cannot imagine why. Or was I . . . interrupting?" He smirked.

"As a matter of fact, my lord, I am perfectly at ease with which-ever partner His Majesty deems fit to give me to."

He frowned down at her. What was it with these courtly men and their frightening glances? She turned away, looking over his shoulder as the dance dictated.

"Tell me," he said, all pleasantness again, their heads now side by side, "what little game were you playing at the other day?"

They separated, turning in a small circle with those on their right, then rejoined in the center. Anna swallowed. So, he was going to hold Bryan's indiscretion at the carriage over her head, was he?

"I don't know what you refer to, Your Grace." Another circle.

He spoke close to her ear. "You know perfectly well what I speak of, dear queen."

"Your Grace, I don't care for your tone." She tried for authority. She did, after all, outrank him now. "I shall have to speak to the king about it."

Robert laughed in genuine amusement. "You'll tell the king how you and your ladies snuck to the tennis court, flouting his orders?"

She stared past him, focusing on one of the hall's ionic columns. Her cheeks warmed as she remembered the tennis ball the king had sent. Robert turned her with a snap, forcing her to look at him.

"Did my sister suggest your little act?"

Were these just more of the Dread Duke's schemes? Trying to turn her against her ladies?

"Ah," he said, handsome mouth a-twitch, "I see you didn't know the Lady Margaux's a slippery little eel." Another circle, this one twice round. She returned to him, composed again. "I do not believe she is the Eel of Norwick at court, Your Grace."

Robert's face lost his smile. "Since we're being candid, know that I won't let anyone, not even a queen, stand in the way of what's right for Troixden—or the king."

"And what are you playing at, Sir Duke?" she said. "I hear you've constantly thrown your sister at His Majesty. And I shan't stand for that."

The dance required her to face the king, who had returned to his seat and was talking excitedly with Daniel and Halforn.

"He is my friend; I give him what he wants."

"Sir, he is your rival."

"Watch yourself, madam," he said in her ear, heads come together for the last time. "I've been with him his life entire, and there I shall remain."

The dance ended. He bowed and left her standing alone, staring at the king. His Majesty, looking up, caught her eyes. She felt the blood drain from her body as his face turned from joy to concern. He made a move to excuse himself, but she pulled together a smile to bid him keep his place. In his stead, he sent her a goblet of wine for which she nodded her thanks.

Spying her father through the crowd, she made her way to him before another haughty noble could claim her for a dance. Upon reaching him and moving in for an embrace, she let out her breath in a sob. Drawing back, he gave her the same look of concern the king had moments before. Saying nothing, he held her, allowing her to settle in his arms like a child one last time.

* * *

"Cancel the bridal tour?" William said. "For mere rumor?"

He stood in a window alcove with Daniel, Halforn, and the grand master general, none too pleased to have been snatched away from the festivities.

"Yes, Majesty," the general said, fidgeting with his ill-fitting velvet jacket, "'tis what Cecile thinks prudent. Why take a chance, slight as it may be?"

"Come now," William said, "I've seen only seven duchies, and now I'm to stay here because there may or may not be some Laurelanders grousing about taxes and Germans?"

"I agree," Halforn said. "The bridal tour was to head west and south, well away from any danger—if there really be any."

"Majesty," Daniel said, "it seems that with rumors of unrest, leaving the capital city or the palace would not be wise at present."

"'Tis not as though I can't conduct business on the coast." He glanced to the dance floor, where he quickly spied the queen. She laughed merrily in her father's arms, skirts flying, the two galloping down the aisle of courtiers as lead couple, her auburn hair reflecting the light.

"Is not the making of heirs more important to the state?" he said, not taking his eyes from the lively, lovely scene.

"Begging Your Majesty's pardon," Daniel said, "but that can be accomplished in Havenside as easily as on the coast."

The king elbowed him in the ribs. "Have you no sense of romance about you? Besides, the same can be said for conducting wars."

"Majesty," Halforn said, "I think what your master general and

His Grace are trying to convey is that the appearance of leaving the capital unguarded is—"

"I understand that."

"'Tis but temporary," Daniel said. "Merely wait a few months until we gain more solid intelligence."

"Yes, we're in grave want of *intelligence* to be sure." He glared at them then sighed. Turning to the general, he said, "Does it not seem weak, to let them control our plans?"

"Nay, Majesty," the grand master said. "To gallivant off on a bridal tour, begging Your Majesty's pardon, suggests that ye give no care to the city's safety. By staying you give the appearance of a strong hand, ready to crush any interference."

"Crush interference?" William said. "It seems that's what I should be doing with you three."

"Majesty," Daniel said, "'tis only for a few short months. Have I steered you wrong thus far?" He nodded toward the queen. "'Tis not as though you'll be alone in the palace."

William raised his hands, palms out. "I surrender! We shall keep to the palace, but in two months we shall be away, uprising or no."

* * *

"I'm not as quick on my feet as these young men," the Duke of Beaubourg said, laughing as he and Anna finished another galliard.

"But there's no other partner I'd rather have, Father." She felt bolder as the evening wore on. When she thought back on her dance with the king, even her fear for the rest of the night diminished—a bit.

"Kind Grace," a beaming Duke of Halforn said, touching her father's shoulder, "may I? That is, if Her Majesty be willing."

She took both his hands. "But of course—it would be a pleasure, dear duke. For other than my father, I do believe I know you more than any man at court."

Another lively partner dance began, and Halforn took to the floor with surprising agility.

"I shall never forget our first meeting, Highness," he said. "Even soaked to the bone and starving, I knew you'd make a queen."

She tossed her head back in a laugh. "Oh, I must have been quite a sight."

"A sight to behold indeed," he said. "'Tis my dearest hope you find happiness here at the king's side. 'Tis one of his greatest wishes, and the wish of us all."

"Pray for us then, Your Grace. For His Highness and I are strangers to each other, and I to court. I fear I may have troubles with both."

He patted her hand. "Know that you have a friend in me, Majesty, both you and the king."

They continued in the dance, talking and laughing about the oddities of court. The dance ended and he swung her out, bowing. She looked up and caught sight of the king, back in his chair at the table, his eyes trained upon her. She nodded in acknowledgment and he smiled broadly.

She was unaware that her entire retinue of ladies had surrounded her on the floor until they bowed as one to the king, cuing music and conversation to cease. She glanced about, confused. The king rose and gestured for the ladies to follow suit.

"Go well with you, my queen," he said. "We shall see thee in short order."

And with that, the courage she had gained through dance and drink was gone. No more girlish flutters or fatherly hugs.

It was time.

Even through stone walls and wooden doors Anna could hear them making their way to her, unhurried and rowdy. She stood at the foot of the king's enormous bed, flanked by Yvette and Mary, and cloaked in a purple silk, rabbit-lined robe, nothing but her sheer shift beneath. She cringed, thinking back to Yvette's brief tutelage. In all her years of healing, she'd never seen a grown man's full nakedness. She did not know how she would muster the courage.

The vast doors swung open to reveal the king's privy chamber-men, half carrying, half shoving him into the room. Part of his jacket off, and his crown and jeweled chain of office were askew. He held a horn goblet aloft as he wrapped up the last stanza of a rather explicit pub song along with the rest of the inebriated horde.

They stopped just past the threshold, taking in the agreeable picture before them—the royal bed, a bride, two attendants, all backlit by flames leaping in the fireplace. Even Mary looked young in that light. With a roar, the men lifted the king from his feet, counted to three, then hoisted their liege onto the bed.

He sat up, toasting them as they shouted out, "Long may ye reign!" Then came more catcalls as they ambled out of the chamber: "Heirs, lots of heirs," and "Keep it up, Majesty," and Robert's, "Don't throw out thy royal back, cuz."

The king shook his head, watching the last man leave, then turned to the women, raising his cup to them. "Ladies."

Yvette and Mary curtsied to the king, who set about ridding himself of jacket, chain, and crown. The doors closed behind the ladies, and two sharp strikes of a staff outside indicated that Anna and he were shut in. Alone.

He hopped off the bed and came up to her, a smile curving his lips. "My dear wife," he said, "here we are at last."

She couldn't look at him. She could only stare at the pattern of pomegranates sewn into the rug at her feet.

He put a finger beneath her chin, raising her face to his. "Fret not, my dear."

She pulled her lips into her mouth, holding them closed, unsure what to say or do.

The attraction she felt for him had faded now that she was faced with the task at hand.

"Did you get my game winner?" he walked past her to the fire, holding his sloshing wine goblet by the rim.

She stood stock-still. "Majesty, I am deeply sorry. I knew it a fool thing once it had begun —"

"Don't worry yourself. It was wrong of me to keep you secluded for so long." He held out a goblet of spiced white wine, at the ready on a small chest in front of his fire. "You gave me quite a start. I nearly lost my game."

"Again, Majesty, it was uncalled for, I—"

"Tush. I beat Robert handily, so 'tis all no matter."

Why was he so calm? Did he not mean to punish her in some horrid way? She took a deep, trembling breath.

He sat down in a leather armchair in front of the fire, propped his legs on the chest, and looked directly into her eyes. "Seeing as our marriage will, with God's help, last a lifetime," he said, "I see no reason why we must immediately, shall we say, seal every parchment."

She gaped at him. Was he not going to demand his pleasure?

"Please," he said with a nod at the matching chair across from him, "take your leisure."

She didn't move. "Forgive me, sire, but I thought it wasn't, well, official, if we—"

He gave her a wry smile. "'Tis true, but why waste such a moment on an exhausted bride and a none-too sober groom? Besides, if I may, you look as though I'm about to crush your skull in with a mace I have somehow hid upon my person."

Too relieved to do anything but follow instructions, she sat, straight-backed, in the comfortable chair, feet planted on the floor.

He glanced from the fire to her. "Truly, my dear, you may relax. It's been a long day. I shan't molest you."

Good heavens, he was blunt. Again she obeyed, scooting back in the chair, bending her knees and perching her toes on the edge of the chest. She made sure her robe fully covered her skin so as not to cause any change of mind.

"Just this evening," she said, "the Duke of Norwick informed me of the weight of the tennis scheme. And while I don't wish to think ill of any one of my ladies, 'tis true one in particular concocted the plan."

"Ah," he said, his eyes bright with firelight, "'tis the Lady Margaux you speak of?"

"Yes, Majesty." She looked into her wine.

"William."

"I beg your pardon, sire?" She met his eyes.

"'Tis William, my dear. When we're in private, you may call me William, for there's none to hear or be offended. I daresay I much prefer it."

She remembered what Daniel had said at the feast. "Of course I shall call you William if you prefer. And you must call me Annelore. I daresay I shall prefer it."

She expected a laugh or at least a chuckle, but instead he looked long at her face.

"So be it then. Annelore," he said. "Annelore. This is my wife, Annelore. Why, good eve, Annelore—fancy meeting you here in my bedchamber." She giggled in spite of herself and he grinned back.

"So tell me then, dear Annelore, what of my fair cousin?"

Her smile turned to a grimace. "Oh, he was horrid."

"He?"

"I thought you meant the duke."

"Nay, though what did he do? I shall have his ears boxed." He took a large gulp of wine and kicked off his shoes.

"Well sire, he puffed around, admonishing me about decorum."

"'Tis William. Admonished you about decorum? That's a bit of the kettle and the pot," he said. "What then of my other cousin? It seems the pair of them haven't given you quite the welcome you deserve."

"I admit I don't know what to make of the lady. She's been such a help to me, she seems to want to be my confidante, and yet . . ."

"What you must know about Margaux is she hoped she'd be in your place. Her whole life long she assumed I'd be her husband, king or no."

"I see." But she wasn't quite sure she did. Margaux *had* been a great help to her, except for the tennis. And Anna could understand her wanting to be queen. She was so regal.

"Is it not cruel to place the lady in my service?"

"If you dislike her presence, I'll dismiss her." He waved his goblet, spilling a bit.

"Not cruel to me, cruel to her. She must now serve the person she hoped to become. I forgive her the little ploy. I feel sorry for her."

William looked at her intently. "Truly? She wishes to take your husband and your rank for herself, has been plotting to do so before you were even selected, and you have pity for her?"

"Why ever not? Desperate women may do desperate things. I should know." She looked down into the pale sweet wine again.

He sat forward, leaning toward her across the chest. "And are you desperate, Annelore?" She looked into his face, the carved mouth, the blue eyes that were kind, however intense.

"Not any longer," she said. "I daresay I've been quite ridiculous of late. Not very queenlike."

"Is that so?" he said. "Now, you've been queen for . . . eleven hours? Who could expect you to have been queenly before?"

"But I am queen now, and I don't know how to be one."

"Did you not know there's a grace period?"

"If I am to be so gently judged, then I do believe I am performing splendidly, if I say so myself." She wriggled her shoulders, stretching her neck to its hilt, playacting a regal role.

William laughed and sank back into the depths of his chair, ruffling his hair, causing the cowlicks to stand on end. "Well, my queen," he said, "I concur with your assessment. You did very well today. Despite a few tears—which I will continue to believe were due to your immense relief at my handsomeness and fine teeth—you certainly held your own."

"With some thanks to your fine teeth, of course," she said.

He chuckled, then contemplated her over the top of his goblet. "Annelore, this doesn't seem so bad after all, does it? I feel we may actually become friends."

She met his gaze, tilted her head, and gave him a sunny smile. "Aye, William. I believe we may."

* * *

They spent a companionable evening together by the fire. Then, with a featherlight kiss on her lips, he sent her back to her chambers at three in the morning. She climbed into her cold bed, falling asleep at once, barely aware of her ladies' glances and whispers.

The next morning, king and queen met again at their first mass together.

"Good morning, fair queen," William whispered, squeezing her hand in welcome once she arranged herself next to him in the royal pew. "I take it you slept well?"

"Like the dead, Majesty."

"Well that makes one of us," he said.

"Did I offend you in some way?" Her heart dropped. Were all of their pleasantries of the evening a ruse?

"Nay, wife, is more that I offended myself. Putting constraint on our marital relations has caused me some, shall we say, discomfort."

"To speak of such a thing, and at mass." Anna gulped. Relieved and horrified all at once. "That we're babbling at all during the exposition of the Holy Scriptures —"

"Oh, tush." He settled back into the pew, watching the droning priest. "I couldn't hear the man if he were two feet in front of me. Daresay he can't hear me."

"Still," she whispered, prepared to keep him from the subject of his disappointed loins, "is it not improper to show such disrespect to your churchman?"

"My lady, I fear our life may be quite dull if you refuse to speak to me in all situations in which churchmen are present."

"Then how did you ever entertain yourself before I came to take this place?" she said.

He stifled a laugh by turning it into a cough. "'Tis a good question," he said, collecting himself. "I do believe I thought on government matters, prayed, and read papers Norwick would send with me."

"Papers?"

"Aye, Madam, some of intellectual interest, some . . . not." She thrust out her hand in front of him, palm up. "Art thou my mother?"

She responded by flicking her fingers for him to relinquish the contraband. He looked uncomfortable, but in the end was no match for her determination.

"Fine," he said, digging down between his outer thigh and the high-sided pew, "but I warn you, they don't get your likeness."

She opened the sheaves as quietly as she could, grimacing when a crinkle caught the attention of the priest. The top pieces were tracts both supporting and denouncing the Lutheran heresy.

The next stopped her heart. Comic leaflets. The top one showed Anna in full wedding regalia, running to a knight with flowing hair who stood with a pansy in his hand and a bulge beneath his loin plate. The king stood to the other side, also bulging, but biting his fingernails, looking away from the scene. The next: the king alone on his bed—pouting, arms crossed, crown askew—while Annelore jumped into another bed, her knight waiting, a small tent poking up the sheets.

She felt ill. "These are horrid."

"I told you they didn't do you justice. Why, you're much taller, and those bulgy eyes? Completely off the mark."

She turned to face him, all decorum forgotten. "How can you jest about them, William?"

"Remember, my dear, 'tis not William in public. Even though none can hear, best to make a habit of it."

"Then how are you not angry, *Highness*? These are base, hurtful —an affront upon both our persons."

He was smiling at her. "I am certainly glad you disapprove of their veracity."

She blushed and looked down to her lap, ashamed to meet his face. "I have acted a fool, sire."

"Don't take it such to heart," He patted her knee. "I forget you've not been about court or town, else you would know these drawings for the daily annoyance they are. I'm used to their commentary and have learned to see the humor in them."

"I do not find them humorous." She stared down at the poison papers in her hands.

"That's because you're a pure soul," he said. "I, on the other hand, am a thick-skinned scoundrel. I shouldn't have shown them to you." He took them out of her hands and shoved them back in place.

She gave him a sheepish smile. "Well, Highness, if you take no offense to it, I shan't either."

"That's right, my girl, stiff upper lip." He took her hand and squeezed it, sending a thrill of warmth up her arm. "You'll learn the ways of gossip and slander soon enough—best to ignore it all and hold your pretty head high. At least that way, they can better capture your likeness."

* * *

William's new wife would again be relieved of duty this night, it being customary to abstain from relations on Sundays, feast days, and other high holy days. Of course, it was generally assumed that on such days, those in the oldest profession were gainfully employed, but the king, fresh with good intentions, invited Annelore to join him for another unmolested evening by the fire. Much to his groin's annoyance.

"I apologize again for offending you so at mass." He loosened the laces of his boots and kicked one toward the fire. "I didn't think, they being so commonly passed about. Will you forgive me?"

She nestled into the same chair across from him as the evening before, blowing on her mulled wine. She looked already at home there.

"'Tis I should be asking your forgiveness," she said, "considering how I acted about the betrothal, and in public—"

"Pay it no more heed."

"But William—"

"'Tis not a sin to have wanted to be with a loved one rather than a stranger. Regret it not." He struggled with his left boot. "For your sake I am sorry for it, but not for the knave's."

Tears peeped at the corner of her eyes as she stared at the fire. Having left his boots to toast, he sat on the short, thick chest in front of her and reached up to wipe the wetness with his thumbs.

"Come now, my dear, 'tis no need to shed tears over people who have nothing better to do than slander their sovereigns."

She smiled weakly. "'Tis twice now you've stopped my tears."

"If twice in two days be the pattern, then I shan't have time left to govern. Even to eat." He smiled at her and smoothed a rogue lock of hair fallen in her face, looping it with tenderness behind her ear.

She took his hand, lips caressing his fingers in quick thanks. Even this small touch sent his blood rushing in his veins. He rose to take his seat across from her, fingers tingling.

"Staying on the theme of apologies," he said, "'tis a shame we have to postpone our bridal tour. I was hoping to see more of our lands. As you so rightly pointed out, I am unfamiliar with them."

"I had hoped to get out of the palace myself," she said, "begging your pardon." Then her tiny smile changed to a frown. "If it weren't for my indiscretion and stubbornness, there would be no cause for people to draw such things."

"My dear, they would come up with something else. Believe me."

She leaned forward, her robe slipping back, revealing a creamy collarbone. "Surely, but hear me, please."

He nodded, though he did not want to have this conversation. He wanted to suck her shoulders, again verboten and all the more enticing for it.

"I have certainly not forgotten about Sir Bryan," she said. He flicked his eyes to hers. "For he was my lifelong friend. And I do not claim that in the past two days of knowing you I've suddenly lost all feeling for him."

William clenched his jaw, cheek muscles flexing. Really, did women have to get everything out in the open? "Annelore, we need not discuss—"

"But it does me good to get it off my chest."

There's a robe I'd like to get off your chest. "As you wish, but I beg you, be quick with it."

"What I'm trying to say is, I see my father was right."

"How does your father play into this?" He screwed up his face and itched his nose.

She looked desperate sitting there, brows up to her hairline, eyes big, brown bowls. He wanted to swim around in them like tubs of stout. He tried to focus on what she was saying.

"What I mean is, 'twas silly of me to play the wounded, lovesick girl when really I was just angry to be forced into a decision I didn't make of my own free will—the most important decision of all."

"Most women don't choose their spouse," he said, distracted now by the line of her neck.

"I am not most women."

"No, you are not." He took a deep swallow of wine.

"To be quite honest," she said, "'twas you I feared."

"Oh-ho, so now it's out!" He jumped to his feet and struck an absurdly threatening pose. "And am I the fearsome beast you expected?"

"Oh, aye. My tears at the altar were indeed about your teeth."

He came to sit astride the arm of her chair. "Truly, Annelore, you were afraid of me?"

"I still am, a little."

He frowned.

"Think on it," she said, looking up to him. "My origin alone tells you of my distrust of court. Add to that your family's legacy . . ."

"You were more courageous than I thought. I wouldn't have wanted to marry James either."

She smacked his knee. "Tease me not, William. You know it would be a fate worse than death."

"Well, now you're just being judgmental." He grinned at her.

She set her wine down, a smile curling her lips. "I hope you praise the Lord every day you weren't born a woman."

Looking down upon her, he spied a hint of cleavage beneath her sassy face. "Aye, Annelore, every blessed day."

CHAPTER 7

Consummation

It was no secret the marriage had yet to be sealed. Already people were talking, and the leaflets were so bold Robert refused to show them to the king. Robert, of course, had his own ways of knowing what had—and hadn't—happened: a bribed laundress, a smug Margaux. He also knew he couldn't be sure until he observed the couple with his own eyes. He would know a change in William's countenance, no matter how subtle.

In swept the queen on Monday morning, stunning in emerald silk and the late Queen Mother Matilda's necklace. Her hair was pulled back in the custom of properly married women. The king rose from his throne, met his queen at the bottom of the dais, and lifted her from her curtsy.

"Majesty, you look remarkably well this morning." He leaned in and whispered something that made her smile, then blush.

Robert could all but see the sparks of tension flashing as William escorted her to her seat and the two continued to whisper. Tension in the morning did not suggest fulfillment the night before.

After council, Daniel pulled Robert aside.

"Robert, what are we to do? Does he not realize the gravity of the situation? Of course, yesterday was Sunday—"

"Sunday be damned," he said. "William doesn't give a wit about such things."

He had watched in council as the respect poor Daniel had fought for while championing Annelore eroded in the light of the royal couple's celibacy.

"I'd say he doesn't want to force her," Robert said. "'Tis that damned notion of gallantry he's always had." They walked toward the Great Hall for dinner. "Let's go to him together. He'll take it better coming from us both."

Daniel grimaced. "If he takes it at all."

* * *

"Friends, welcome!" William embraced Robert and Daniel in turn as they entered his chamber, glad to have them share in his good mood. "It seems too long since we've met alone together."

"Majesty, 'tis good to see you in such high spirits," Daniel said.

"You needn't be so formal," William said, smile fading.

"Apologies," Daniel said, "but we've come to speak to you about something rather delicate." Daniel glanced at Robert, who nodded.

"Well, out with it then," William said.

"We recognize that you're hoping to build, let's say, an alliance with the queen." Daniel wasn't meeting his eyes. "You do not want to push her into anything . . . uncomfortable at this juncture."

William raised a brow. "Go on."

"For God's sake, Wills," Robert said. "You need to bed the queen."

"I can always count on you to get right to the point, cuz."

"Well then?" Robert said. "Now that we're at the point, what say you?"

"Daniel's right," William said. "I don't wish to force her. It feels not only disrespectful but a sorry way to start an alliance, as you call it."

Daniel cleared his throat. "The issue is the legality of your marriage, not the comfort of the queen, bonny as she is—"

"Enough!" He turned to shuffle papers on his desk. "Everything you've said I already know."

"What are your plans to remedy the situation, then?" Robert said.

William jerked his head up. "And why are you so eager to hear them? I know damn well what needs to be done."

"Then take the bull by the horns!"

"Dammit, Robert," William strode round the desk to him, fists clenched, "you can't speak to me like that anymore."

"Well, someone needs to." Robert made to step closer, but Daniel slipped between them, a hand on William's shoulder.

"Look, we know this is a delicate subject. We have no wish to pull back your bed curtains, my friend."

"Apparently not all of you." He glared at Robert, who scowled.

"I know the burden these last few months have placed on you," Daniel said. "And I know this situation only adds weight—"

A swift stamp of the staff outside the chamber door drew their attention as Halforn entered, out of breath.

"Majesty, you must come with me," the duke said, "with all haste. We must be there by break of day tomorrow, else we miss the whole thing."

The three friends looked at each other, puzzled. William called to a page. "Send for the queen after we've done with the Duke of Halforn." He then turned back to the most rotund of the assembled dukes, thankful for the interruption. "How may we be at your service, Your Grace?"

His queen stood before him in his chamber. "Dear Annelore."

She looked pretty enough to devour right there, in a green damask gown, large emeralds dangling, drawing the eye down to her bosom.

"Sadly, I must leave directly after supper this evening," he said. "I promised Halforn I'd witness the wedding of his eldest daughter, and with the excitement of our own nuptials, it completely slipped my mind. The date was set well before our own, I assure you."

She nodded. He continued. "The duchy's only a half-day's ride, but as the wedding is just after dawn, I must ride today."

"I shall miss your company, William."

"And I yours—in more ways than one." He paced, then stopped, looking directly into her face. "After all, my dear, we have yet to, ah, legalize our covenant."

"I see." She spoke to the floor.

"Whilst I know it brings you some trepidation, 'tis my dearest wish that when I return on the morrow we may remedy the oversight."

"I see."

"Do you?" He looked at her intently. "I haven't forced you—and don't wish to."

"And I thank you for it." She finally looked up.

"But I must insist," he said. "Tomorrow night, we settle the matter."

"I shall be ready."

"Truly, you must be." He walked to her, lifted her taut chin. "Please promise me."

"I cannot promise I won't still be uneasy, but I will try to live up to your expectations."

He cupped her supple cheek in his hand and moved to kiss her forehead, but stopped. He tilted her head further back, meeting her lips instead in a languid kiss. If only he had the power to stop time, to sink into her lips. Opening his mouth, she responded, her tongue tentatively tasting his and his body burned. He needed this. And what's more, standing there, his cock stiffening against her thigh, he realized it wasn't simply the sex he needed. He needed her.

It took all he had to break away from her yielding yet eager mouth, forehead resting on hers, still cupping her warm, reddened cheeks.

"You see," he whispered, "'tis not so horrible after all."

He watched her chest heave below him, desperately wishing he could take her then and there.

She licked her lips and took hold of his forearms. "I daresay I shall await your return most eagerly."

He moved to kiss her once more, only to be interrupted by that blasted pounding staff, heralding unwanted duty once more.

She smiled at him. "I hope to not be the death of your reputation, William."

"Worry not, my dear, for it hasn't far to fall."

* * *

William rode back double time the next day, all the more eager for having watched another pair of newlyweds stare sappily at each other. Once ensconced in his chamber, he called for the queen.

She appeared in a robe, cinched tight around her waist, hand clutching the fabric together at her neck. She merely bowed and remained silent. Swallowing his rising lust, he knew he must be patient, gentle, instructional even. What his body ached for must heel. For now. Later . . . .

He led her to the wine poured at his desk, window open behind to let in the fresh summer air. She trembled as he offered her a goblet with a smile. Watching her fumble with the glass for a moment, he took it from her without a word, set it down, and engulfed her small shaking hands in his.

"Annelore." She did not look at him. He opened his arms, drawing her in. "Come here."

He felt her rapid breath against his chest as she burrowed her head into his shirt, trembling like the rabbits he hunted as a boy, so scared, so soft under his hands. He gave a gentle kiss to the top of her head.

"Come now, dear, 'tis not that bad." He heard a tiny snuffle in his shirt and bit back a sigh. This was not going to be quite the night he had envisioned.

"Best to get it over and done with right?" he said lightly.

She reared back and shoved him away. "Over and done with?"

His smile fell and he rolled his eyes. "I was jesting. But you did realize it was part and parcel of the whole marriage business, yes?"

"So I'm just to be used at will? Like a whore?"

"Whoa, whoa, whoa!" He held up his hands. "We're supposed to be securing the throne. Whores would actually make the situation worse, as my own father could illustrate."

She released a shuddering breath. "I'm sorry. I'm quite touchy on the subject."

I hadn't noticed. "You must know by now I wouldn't hurt you. In fact," he sauntered to her, "I've found women can be quite pleased with the whole of it."

Her tight face sent him back on his heels.

"Some of us," she said, "are not so familiar with the practice."

He chortled. "Are you choosing now of all times to give me a lecture on virtue?"

"I care not you are no virgin, but being one myself I can't help but worry what you shall do to me. I've spent many an hour at the bedsides of birthing women —"

"You don't really think I mean to ravish you, get you with child, and send you packing? You'll have the best in the land to attend you —"

"Enough." She downed her wine in one long gulp and strode to the bed, disrobing as she walked. "We might as well get it over with, as you say." She climbed onto the bed, drawing her knees to her chest, a scowl on her face, her body shaking beneath her thin shift.

He looked up at her with good-humored disbelief. "If you say so." Indeed, not how he had planned, not how he'd imagined, but if the deed must be done, he could still help her to relax. He drained his own wine and walked to the other side of the bed. He reached over to gently straighten her body, then pulled his hand back. Her cheeks were soaked with silent tears as she stared straight out the tall window and into the gardens and looming hills.

"Oh Lord, please don't cry," he said, sitting next to her. "I can't stand to see you cry."

She looked at him, eyes wet. "I can't do it."

He took her hand gently and kissed her palm. Slowly, he moved up to her wrist. He felt her soften ever so slightly under his lips.

That's all this needed. Softness. Patience. But when he got to her forearm, she let out a little yelp and yanked her arm away.

He drew a deep breath. "Don't play games with me, Annelore. I have an entire court who plays games with me—I won't brook it in a wife."

She crossed her arms over her chest, scooting away from him. "I don't wish to fool with you," she said, tears wiped away. "I'm sorry, I'm just not ready."

"You don't mean to fool with me, aye?" He rolled off the bed and came to stand, looking down at her both body and mind riled by this whiplash. "Do you know what kind of agony I was in last night? And the two nights before that?" She scowled and looked away. "I've kept myself pure for you since our betrothal," he said, hitting his chest for emphasis, "not a very kingly thing to do, I might add."

She narrowed her eyes at him. "I'm not trying to torture you—"

"Have I not proven I am not my predecessors?"

"Yes, but—"

"Any other king—any other man—would have turned you over on our wedding night and had his way with you."

"But I—"

"At the very least he'd have a more willing woman to his bed by now!"

"Are you threatening me with a mistress?"

He let out a groan and clutched his head in his hands. "You know that's not what I mean!" She scampered out of bed and grabbed her robe. He followed close behind. "I've told you I would be kind, but there are greater considerations here." He reached to take the robe from her hands. Why couldn't she see sense?

"Two nights before I came here," she said, eyes slits, "I held a dying girl in my arms as she gave birth."

His face softened. He tugged on the robe to bring her to him. She yanked back. "Surely you don't think—"

"Not to mention my own mother died in the act of birthing my brother, after she'd come all the way to this very court to try and save your sister."

Well, dammit. He let go his pull on the robe and leaned to her, hand outstretched, an olive branch. "I am so sorry, Annelore—"

"Don't touch me."

"If I'd known—"

"You'd what?" she said, jerking up. "You'd still demand your pleasure from me."

He closed his eyes. He did not deserve this. "The process of getting with child certainly doesn't kill a woman." She glowered at him even more. "I'm sorry for all you've spoken of, but it doesn't change the matter at hand. You must—"

"I will not be forced. You said you wouldn't!"

He let out a heavy sigh. "I ask you to do it willingly."

"And if I refuse?"

This was the last straw. The audacity of the woman. He was her husband—her king! He'd shown more restraint than either of those titles demanded. He leaned right into her face. "Then someone else will gladly take up this cross you find so repugnant."

He left her, picked up his wine goblet, and flung it at the fire.

She burst into fresh tears and flew down the stairs to the hall, covering her face with her hands. As she ran toward the safety of her chamber, he hollered for Robert.

* * *

"He'll banish you to a nunnery," Yvette said when Anna finished telling her and Mary the tearful story. "What were you thinking?"

What indeed? Anna sat on her bed, exhausted, sniffling, shaking her head. "I don't know what to do."

"Do you want to be sent away?" Mary said. "For if you do, it won't be into Bryan's arms. Besides, seems to me you've taken a bit of liking to His Majesty."

Anna nodded, woebegone. "But he was so cruel—"

"I don't blame him," Yvette said.

Annelore looked up, startled. "But I wasn't toying with him. I have dreamt of dying from childbirth most nights since arriving—"

"Majesty." Yvette took hold of Anna's shoulders. "Whether you die or no, you cannot refuse the king. No one refuses the king."

Anna shook her head. "'Tis nothing to be done now."

"There certainly is," Yvette said, "for he may well be about to bed another as we speak."

Anna stared, agape. He wouldn't, surely? She'd be damned if some strumpet took her place. But hadn't she all along been hoping for this—hoping to be left alone, perhaps even sent home while he pleasured himself elsewhere? Where was this sudden, stabbing jealousy coming from? And she knew as she sat there, it was not her fear of dying that held her back. It was the fear of caring—really caring—for this supposed monster of a man who was no monster at all. Even now, all she felt was the panic of losing him. She could not let that happen.

"Help me." She grabbed Yvette's hands.

"I shall, Majesty." Yvette looked to the alcove where the ladies were gathered, sewing and gossiping. "Where's Margaux?"

Brigitte answered, tittering. "She said she'd been called away by her brother. She gave the post to me, then left." Yvette spun around to Anna.

"We've less time than I thought, Highness. All haste now."

Anna jumped off the bed.

"Warm the bath!" Yvette called to the room. "And for God's sake someone fetch Bernard!"

"What?" William didn't look up when he heard the banging staff at his door.

He sat behind his desk, glaring out the open window. It annoyed him to see the clouds so cheery in their triumph of late sunset when he was so disgruntled below.

"You asked for refreshment," came a silken voice.

He turned, surprised, and rose when he saw the lady bearing a tray laden with a pitcher and two goblets.

"Lady Margaux, to what do I owe the honor?" She placed the tray on his wide desk.

"Majesty, I've merely brought what you requested."

"Always at my service, hmm?" He couldn't help the rush of blood that surged through him at her nearness, her feminine fragrance. He was already hard.

"Highness, you know if there is ever anything you might need . . ."

Relieved of her delivery, she dropped to a full curtsy. She remained folded to the floor, looking up at him, her cleavage on full display. "Majesty, I hear you may be desirous of companionship this eventide."

He walked to her but made no move to help her rise, his lascivious mind enjoying her there on her knees. "Whatever do you mean, my lady?"

She rose bit by bit from the floor. His heat rising with her, his breath shallowing.

"My liege," she said, standing close now, "your bed hath been cold these many nights. A man," she paused, holding his eyes, "nay, a king should not be treated thus."

She drew a line down his chest with a fingernail, careful not to let it tangle in the laces of his loosened shirt. He grabbed her finger, stopping her progress before she reached his lower abdomen, his faculties barely acquiescent to his higher mind.

"Margaux," he said, "you insult your mistress."

"'Tis you I ultimately serve, sire, and it seems to me my mistress has insulted you." She stepped forward until her chest brushed his.

"Ah," he said, "so you're offering me your singular service. Of companionship, is it?"

She licked her lips, arched a blonde brow. "Whatever you desire, Majesty." She brought her hand up to cup his cheek, rubbing her thumb against his stubble.

God that hand felt like heaven, the touch of a lustful woman. And a woman unafraid of that lust, emboldened by it even. And she was, after all, of royal blood. She'd be in line for the throne in her own right if not for her sex. He took a long breath, inhaling her scent of silk and lilies. Blood rushed to his loins. He grabbed her wrist, pulling her closer. So what if she wasn't his wife? He was the king. Concessions could be made. He deserved this. She wanted this. He closed his eyes —

And saw Annelore. Sitting by the fire on their wedding night, her sweet face so earnest, so trusting as she begged compassion for this woman. Dammit! He took a steadying, deep breath and opened his eyes.

"What I desire, dear cuz," he said, hovering centimeters above her face, "is for you to serve your queen with all fealty."

She startled, smile still plastered to her face. He tightened his grip on her wrist.

"She has done nothing to you but extend friendship," he said low into her ear, pulling her closer against him. "She has even defended you to me. And this is how you would repay her?"

"But sire . . ." She had reaffixed a sultry look to her face, yet he could smell her fear. "If she's not to please you as a wife should, certainly someone must."

"That may be the case, my lady, but it will not be you."

"Begging your pardon, Highness," she said, smiling as she slipped a hand between his legs, "but your manhood doth make you a liar."

With a chortle, he pushed her away. "A man's unquenched member may respond thus to a rutting hog." She stumbled backward, tripping over her skirts.

"Majesty! To be treated such —"

"Nay, Margaux, you're treated far better than you deserve. If you come to me with such treachery again, I'll have you thrown from court and into a convent, cousin or no."

"But William —"

"Enough!" he shouted. "I am your king, Margaux. I haven't been your playmate for many years. You will show me respect and your queen allegiance. Get out of my sight."

She made a hasty curtsy and an even hastier exit.

"Guards!" he called, exhausted with all the theatrics of the day. "Let no one enter. No one. I am done with foolishness for the night."

And with that he walked to the fire and slumped into his thick chair, cock angry and head in his hands. No wonder kings raged so.

* * *

Anna watched His Majesty's guards stamp their staffs upon her arrival, heard the king's angry voice through the doors.

"Didn't I tell you no visitors?"

"Her Royal Highness," the guards shouted back.

There was no response.

Anna stood outside the barred doors with something close to stage fright, Mary and Yvette flanking her as they had on her wedding night. Yvette flicked her hands at the doors as if entreating them to open of themselves.

Anna sucked in her breath with as much queenly dignity as she could muster. "Open these doors, sirs."

"But—" The guard gestured, eyes wide, to the still-silent chamber.

"That was not a request," she said. "'Twas an order. From your sovereign."

The four guards standing post looked askance at each other. With conflicting orders, of course the king's took priority over the queen's.

"His Majesty specifically requested me, sirs," Annelore said. "Now open this door."

The ranking guard flinched but shook his head. Anna looked at Yvette in desperation.

"Quick!" Yvette grabbed Anna's hand, and they all but ran back to the queen's chambers.

"Will we bid him come to me?"

"No, Majesty," Yvette whispered between breaths. "The door. The king's passage."

Of course! How could she have forgotten the little door that led into the king's chambers? Surely it was unlocked at his end as well.

They tore through Anna's chamber, ignoring the gasps of her other ladies. Once to the other side, Yvette pushed the king's door open, hinges creaky with lack of use.

And there he stood, hands on hips, backlit by the blazing fire, blinking down at them. Her knees threatened to go.

* * *

William stared at the tableau before him. The queen stood, state crown upon her head, cloaked in the purple and ermine of royal office, eyes focused on his chest. Mary and Yvette were behind her, bowing their heads and bending in half curtsy. He was too tired in head and heart to even speak.

"Your Royal Highness." Annelore's voice carried like a flute, soft but clear. All at once she melted to the floor, a plum waterfall. Her hair, darker in this light, splayed about her. "Majesty," she said, face to the stone, "I most humbly beg your mercy and forgiveness."

Yvette and Mary snapped to attention at this cue. In no time the maids had relieved the queen of her crown and cloak and returned to their former places. Then the queen rose, standing before him, wearing nothing but a gossamer nightdress. He was barely able to focus on her face.

He took a few steps and with a flick of his hand sent the maids away. He leaned on the bedpost, arms folded. Annelore's voice was steady.

"Majesty, I have been a discredit to myself, my people, and to you. I have been utterly selfish, petulant, and unfeeling. I know 'tis my duty to be thy wife in all ways, and as queen, my most important role is to bring thee children. Fear hath stopped me, but no longer. If I am to die in carrying out my duty then so be it, for 'tis my honor to do so."

She stopped, having come to the end of her script. He crept closer, exhaustion forgotten.

"Please, William. Please forgive me. I'm begging you. Please say you'll keep me. Here. With you. I won't repel you again."

He slid his right hand under her chin, bringing her face up, feeling that same astonishment as at the cathedral balcony. The glorious audacity of this woman . . . .

"'Tis beneath the dignity of a queen of Troixden to beg. Even of her king." He took her hand and drew her to him. "But 'tis good of you to have come."

"Then you forgive me?"

"I should be begging forgiveness as well, for I was rude and ungentleman-like."

"Ah, but I drove you to it."

"Well then, I suppose we're even." He walked her over to his desk and poured out a glass of the untouched wine. "You see, I hoped . . ." He poured the second. "I hoped I hadn't driven you away for good."

"Your words did sting," she said. "But I will say, introducing the possibility of some competition settled my mind rather quickly."

He laughed. "Oh-ho, so 'twas not merely my good teeth that brought you back?"

She smiled and touched his arm. "Pride cometh before the fall, William."

He offered her a goblet, then toasted her with his own and took a sip, swirling it around in his mouth. His heart was near bursting. Perhaps this night could actually be what he'd hoped for all along, and even if not, he knew they'd at least made peace. And it put him to rights in a way he didn't think possible.

Waving off her drink, Anna looked at him with all seriousness. "I came back because whatever kind of king you really are, monster or saint, you've been kinder to me than I deserve. And the thought of your looking at another woman the way you sometimes look at me . . ." Her pale cheeks turned scarlet. "Well, it troubled me more than the thought of . . . of anything else."

He put down his glass, took her hand, and led her to the foot of the bed. "Annelore, I couldn't look at another woman the way I look at you, even if I tried."

He slid his hand up her arm, thrilling as each of her hairs stood up in response. Daring to move his other hand to her mouth, his finger traced its outline until she released a tiny sigh. He didn't realize he'd been holding his breath, hoping, waiting for signs of her willing surrender. Moving his hand to her warm cheek, he brushed it with his thumb.

"I don't know how, but my hope is we two can rise above our stations and the fray of court and be true companions." He was bending to her now, voice rough with want and tinged with some long slumbering emotion awakening itself in him. This was more than mere lust. This was something new. Something more. Something threatening to overwhelm him. "Will you help me, Annelore?"

She nodded, seemingly entranced. He opened his mouth to speak again, but instead leaned in and took her lips. They yielded, taking him, offering him an absolution he didn't know he needed. He laced his fingers through her hair, cradling the back of her head and pressed in to her, sinking in to her mouth, she now returning his pressure. He lingered there, lost to everything but the pillow of her lips, her whispered, stuttering breath. She tasted of mint tea and salted tears.

He felt her rise to him as he parted his lips, tongue daring to slip in and tease hers. She responded with a sigh, wrapping her arms around his back, unconsciously pulling him closer, urging him on, lapping his tongue, sucking his lower lip.

He smiled against her and drew away, watching a tiny frown knit her brow. He wondered if she made that face when she came. He desperately wanted to find out. Unfastening his trunks in a quick, practiced motion, his shirttails were left hanging, his cock heavy, yearning, against his thigh. But he must slow down. Savor this. More importantly, let her savor this, for it would set in motion all their future couplings. And by God he would make sure she was sated.

Moving to her again, he untied the blue ribbon cinching the scoop neck of her thin shift. Once loosed, the nightgown hung tenuously on the tips of her shoulders. He stood back so he might take her all in, imprint this picture of her in his mind, roll it around time and again.

He shook his head at his luck: here she was, femininity itself, ripe, firm. Breasts creamed and glowing in the firelight, a small pouch at her belly, and round hips crying out to bear children. And she was his. How he'd managed it, he didn't know and he didn't care. All he knew was he'd been smiled upon by a greater power than his own and he would relish it.

Stepping to her, hands on her shoulders, he kissed her again. Harder this time, deeper, but only for brief seconds. She stood on tiptoes, clearly wanting more, but he let her lips go, painfully slowly.

He walked behind her, prowling, dragging his hand lightly across her collarbone, delighting in the fluid feel of her. Sliding his hand down her arm, he took the nightdress with it, hand coming to rest on her full hip. It filled his palm, plump and perfect. She took a sharp breath but remained stock-still. Grinning to himself, wolflike, he drew back the curtain of her silken hair, exposing her neck.

"With my body," he murmured, sending a probing hand up her front and kissing her luxuriously, almost idly, his breath caressing the base of her neck, "I thee worship."

She moaned, throwing her head back on his shoulder, allowing him greater access. He cupped a breast, marveling in its weight, its warmth, shutting his eyes so he could focus on each nerve surging with blood, focus on her precise heft, her precise smoothness, focus on each tiny pucker of gooseflesh spreading across her body as he tenderly devoured her.

Rolling the nipple, it immediately hardened under his touch. Her responsiveness astounded him, especially given her vehement protests and abject fear. But her quiet whimpers, the wriggling of her round buttocks against his cock, her tightening breasts, told a story of open desire, a secret wantonness. Lord, he thought teasing her with words was enjoyable, but teasing her now, with his hands, his lips, his flesh, was something he'd never tire of.

He lifted her, cradling her in his arms, hers thrown about his neck as they continued to sup on each other's mouths, tongues dancing, sucking, never parting until he laid her carefully on the bed.

"I just need to look at you," he said, covering her with his eyes as he wished to shortly do with his body. Laying there she was radiant. Finally full bared to him, hair splayed on his pillow, breasts lilting to the sides, hips rounded even more, and the dark shielded nook nestled atop her thighs beckoning—how he screamed to delve deep there, losing himself as if in a forest, bringing them both to that ecstatic brink.

She gazed back at him, open, smile relaxed, eyes dancing, and he realized he should afford her the same contemplation. He shed his shirt. She gave a little gasp of alarm upon seeing his bulging nakedness, but meeting his eyes, her smiled widened.

"I just need to look at you, too."

He grinned at her. "I promised I wouldn't hurt you."

She nodded, bit her lower lip, her eyes caressing his dips and domes. "I know."

He climbed on the bed, gently spreading her legs to kneel between them. Still biting her lip, she kept her eyes on his face. He leaned to hover over her then lowered himself, inch by scorching inch, cock hardening, balls aching, heart thumping, her warm skin melding to his, coiling with his body.

His senses had not been taken to these heights of delight in, well . . . perhaps ever. Certainly his earliest sexual experiences had been stunning in their ferocious explosiveness, but they had been quick, means to ends, nothing like this. He was sinking into her like a warm bath after a cold hunt or a raw battle. Soaking in her scent, her skin, her light arms embracing his back.

He moved to taste her eager mouth, cradling her head again in one hand, the other more than filled with her breast. The way she pressed up against him, met his desire kiss for kiss, moan for moan, merely stoked his fire for her.

Leaving her lips he said, "Not so horrible after all, is it?"

She shook her head and gave him the most glorious smile. "I don't know why you didn't tell me." She reached her arms up, clasping her hands behind his neck.

"Tell you what?"

"What this feels like, the deliciousness, the feeling free, alive — like riding out at full cantor in open fields in summer."

"Admittedly I did try to tell you," he said, tracing her lips. "And yet." He paused, searching her face, knowing what she described: being one with your horse, with your body, with the wind, with the pure joy of being alive, all the while speeding through the air, that added potential injury heightening your senses. "I couldn't have told you. Not really."

"I had to experience it?"

"Yes, but also," he furrowed his brow, barely understanding his own words, but knowing they were true, "I couldn't have told you because I've never felt this before either."

She started to laugh, surely not believing a man of his standing and age could say such a thing, but he cupped her face, stilling her. He'd slept with more women than he could remember, some superb in the art, others drab, most simply unremarkable, so of course she'd think he was teasing her or trying to make her feel, what? Complimented? But he was in earnest. This was no mere fucking.

"I mean it, Annelore. It's . . . it's not normally this, this . . ." He floundered, searching for the right word.

"Hungry?" She supplied, then pressed his face to her cleavage. And all need to find this right word was gone. He took each breast in his mouth, kneading their softness, lost to their blatant femaleness, relishing each nipple, gorging on the taste of her skin. She was like sweet rolls, salt, and something floral he couldn't place. She tasted like home.

Hands drifting to her bottom, he didn't know how much longer he could wait, how much longer he could moderate his pace, no matter how much he wanted to make sure this night would entice her for years of nights to come. He nipped a nipple and she swore.

He snapped up, afraid he'd hurt her, but she shook her head. "More," she whispered.

And he could not stand it anymore. Sucking two of his fingers, he brought them to her groin, his immediately responding with impatience.

God she was soft, already wet and wanting. Her whole body flexed at his touch, her eyes shot wide, breath stopped. He couldn't help grinning at her, these guileless reactions, like a child's first taste of sweets.

He pushed himself up to kneeling, fingers never leaving her slick folds.

"I want you," she said, desire pulsing off her in waves. "I don't even completely know what I mean by that, but I need you. Desperately."

He gave her a lopsided grin. "Don't worry, my queen, I know exactly what you need."

He nodded to the side table at a small green vile. "Be so kind as to hand me the oil."

Her eyes widened again as she obeyed. "Yvette told me you would know what to do with this."

He raised a brow. "Intelligent woman." Maybe Yvette would tell her even more things and wouldn't that be a boon.

She watched him intently as he uncorked the bottle and poured a bit on his warmed fingers. Then he watched her watch him wrap his hand around his marble-hard girth, shuddering with his own touch. He would show her now how much he needed her as well.

Guiding himself to her opening, he kept his eyes locked on hers. "This may hurt, may pinch, but I will strive to move at your pace, just tell me."

She nodded and he notched himself between her lips pressing gently. She gasped again, but he could tell it was in pleasure. Her hands found his bottom, helping him to modulate his depth. He went deeper, her warm walls clenching, pulling him further until he felt her maidenhead. Leaning down to her breasts, he sucked one, twirling the nipple with his tongue. She groaned and thrust her hips up to him. All at once he broke through and she winced, crying out. He stilled, she exhaled. They paused, breathing together. Then, rocking ever so slightly in and out, he reached down to press his thumb to the pebble above her opening, and felt her relax, her whole body opening to him. She groaned, deep in her throat while he undulated into her hips, her divine darkness grabbing hold of him, dragging him deeper, deeper. Digging her fingers into his buttocks, she slammed his hips to hers, embedding him flush against her pelvic bone.

"Yes, this is what I wanted," she said. No, not said, positively growled. Then she smiled, laughed, and sought his mouth with hers, seeking his as he moved inside her, thrilling with every pulse.

Finally, he let himself go.

* * *

The next morning, William sat in his ebony calfskin desk chair, half dressed, one leg tossed over its arm. He ate an apple and smiled, watching his wife sleep. She lay on her belly, sheets cutting a perfect angle from shoulder to hip. One arm curled up under her, chin almost resting upon her loose fist. She was snoring, ever so slightly.

He sighed with satisfaction as he recalled the previous night. He was surprised at how singular the encounter had been. Perhaps it was because he was now a king and not casting about looking to sow oats. Perhaps it was because she was so tentative and sweet and shy at first. Or perhaps it was watching her come, feeling the whole of her pulse against him again and again, hearing her scream out his name, senseless to anything else but her pleasure, seeing her face contort and release in bliss, amazement fill her eyes. How she demanded more, her hands gripping his ass, driving him in to her, all bashfulness banished in passion, his own—first—orgasm so violent, so loud he thought he heard his guards flinch. Whatever the reason, he awaited their next tryst with impatience.

She stirred, making little grunts as if pained by the natural rhythm of waking. Her eyes flashed open and her whole body balked as she looked around, startled eyes finally resting upon him, sitting like a boy, grinning in his chair, chomping happily on his green apple. She yanked the sheets to her face.

"Why, good morning, my dear." He bounded out of his seat and offered a bite. She remained under the sheets. "Ah, don't be shy." He sat down on the bed, arm balancing his weight on the other side of her torso. "Methinks we're well past that now."

"Aye, my lord," she said, her voice grainy, "but I'd like a sip of wine."

"Of course."

He reached to the side table and handed her a half-drunk goblet, left there the night before in the midst of their revelry. She swished it around in her mouth and swallowed.

"That's better," she said. "I had the most wretched taste in my mouth."

"Ah, *mon amour*, what pretty sentiments after our official wedding night." He popped the last bit of apple in his mouth.

She rearranged herself upon the numerous pillows. "Can you do better then, sir?"

"A challenge?" He prowled over her, panther-like, finally lighting on an exposed shoulder, which he sucked, reveling again in her singular flavor.

"William!" She laughed.

"Hmm?" He looked up at her, all innocence.

She swatted him with a free pillow. He grabbed both her arms, pinning them to the bed. "Now I have you, my queen."

She bucked against him. "Move . . . off!"

"That's not what you said last night." Her cheeks reddened. "Oh, Annelore." He laughed, releasing his captive. "Be not abashed now, my dear." He kissed her turned cheek and proceeded down her neck. "Although 'tis rather enchanting, this shy side of you."

She grabbed his head, pulled him in, and near bit his lip. "And what of this side?"

"Mmm." He released his weight down upon her, moving his mouth on hers as he spoke. "Yes, this side is quite a happy surprise." He licked her lower lip. "Who would have thought a young maid from the north would be so enthusiastic?"

She drew his head back. "I'm full of surprises."

"I daresay." He laughed and propped himself up on an elbow.

This time the pillow hit him square in the jaw and he rolled off her onto his feet.

"Alas, my dear, no more languishing about. On your feet, Majesty! Time for mass." She let out a groan, stuffing the pillow over her head.

"What's this, Highness?" he said "Is it not improper to show such disrespect to your churchman?"

She removed her pillow and gave him an exaggerated pout. "Can we not this one day skip mass? We only went thrice a week in Beaubourg."

"I'm appalled, my dear, appalled, at your lack of devotion."

"At the moment I doth believe my soul will be the more ministered to in receiving sleep than communion."

"And where might we find that in the Scriptures?"

"The Lord has appeared to all number of people in dreams."

William jumped back on the bed and rolled to her side. "And I do believe there was wrestling involved, at least once."

She looked down at him. "The wrestling you speak of and the wrestling of Jacob aren't quite the same thing."

"No harm in testing the theory." He took her arm and worked his way up it with his mouth. She giggled and turned in to him, but the sound of a staff interrupted.

"Blast!" He groaned then shouted toward the door. "No visitors!"

"Your Highness's dressers," the guard shouted back, "and breakfast."

"Does no one in this palace heed my instructions?" He sighed.

"I did," she said. "Though it took me a while."

He pinched her bottom. "That you did, my dear." He rolled out of bed to bid them enter.

"William!" Annelore said, eyes wide, "I'm not fit to be seen."

"I beg to differ, darling—"

"You know what I mean," she said, attempting to sit up and hold sheets over her nakedness.

He came to her aid. Pulling off the sheet and holding it taut, he feigned looking away as she clambered out of bed.

"Send for the queen's ladies first!" he called to the waiting attendants. "I'll take breakfast in the dining chambers." He enveloped her in the white sheet, still warm from her body, then hugged her to him.

"Wait here for your ladies," he said, smiling at her upturned face. "I'll eat first, then finish dressing—keep you from the gaping eyes of my manservants." He nibbled on her right earlobe. "Although you are tasty enough—why I should need to eat anything else is beyond me."

He ignored the doors, which opened with a whining creak as Yvette, Mary, Stefania, and Brigitte passed through, averting their eyes.

William gave his wife a last, lingering kiss, then took all three stairs in one bound. "*Adieu, mon cherie.* Until mass." He paused at the door and raised a brow at the women.

"Ladies," he said, doffing an imaginary cap. Then he was gone, the door shutting behind him.

* * *

Anna could barely contain herself. The minute William left her she wanted him back again. It was not only the physical desire, which astonished her in its continued intensity, but the desire for his companionship: his look, his voice, his wit. She simply wanted to be near him. Now.

To be sure, she'd adored Bryan and had always enjoyed spending an afternoon in his company, yet when they parted, she did not yearn for him to return, did not pine for his presence.

God in heaven what William had done to her that night. Just the feel of his lips on her mouth, on her skin, his exploring hands, she could be content for hours with that alone, but then. Oh, then . . . . She knew men bandied about insinuating the size of their manhood as if it were some great accomplishment. And as the only member she'd ever seen was eight-year-old Bryan's as he'd peed in the snow, she assumed they probably equated to finger size—the more well endowed perhaps the length and breadth of the middle finger. Was she ever, utterly, wrong.

She smiled to herself remembering him taking off his shirt, her breath catching at the expanse of his muscled chest, his taut stomach, and then, why it was the size of a bratwurst. And that puzzling contradiction of fear—for it surely was too large to go anywhere inside of her—and animal desire, that need to consume him whole and be consumed by him. She was both repelled and pulled.

And when he'd entered her, how patient he'd been, how tender, how skilled. Once she passed that initial shock of sting, the fullness she felt, the desperate want, was voracious. When he took her breast to his mouth, his hand circling her most tender of places, his cock swallowed inside her, she'd literally seen stars. They exploded behind her eyes as her body was showered in a burst of light. She'd lost all sense of time, of reality, of herself. When she came to, all she wanted was to feel that utter bliss again.

Yvette, Mary, Stephania, and Amelia came forward to attend her, all demure smiles and adverted eyes.

"Yvette," she said, grabbing the woman's forearms, her own eyes wide.

Yvette quirked a brow. "And are you pleased, Majesty?"

Anna continued to stare, gobsmacked. "Yvette."

Her maid swallowed a smirk. "So I was right, then?"

"Remind me to believe everything you say," Anna said, shaking the poor woman.

Yvette gave a rare laugh. "I shall hold you to that, Majesty."

Anna pictured William right before he left, happy and spent yet still wanting her. She felt as though some vital internal organ had left her body when those doors closed after him and it took all of her sense not to scurry after him. She had never been so impatient to see anyone in her life—and someone she'd just seen moments before.

Eventually she finished bathing and dressing and after a hurried breakfast, scurried to mass. The king was already at the altar, kneeling, and just the sight of him buckled her knees and warmed her groin. He glanced over his shoulder when the rustle of genuflecting skirts announced her arrival. As she took her place beside him, hands held together in hasty prayer, he cleared his throat.

"A tad tardy, are we?"

"I daresay," she whispered through her teeth, "I was left quite unceremoniously in disarray this morning."

William made a little grunt sending her nerves on fire. How was she going to function like this? "I wouldn't have called our time together unceremonious, Majesty."

The priest lifted the host high above his head before breaking it and intoning in Latin, either unaware of the queen's late arrival or tactfully ignoring it.

Anna stole a quick glance at the king in his golden silks, sunbeams kissing the top of his head. He glowed like an archangel and she had to swallow to keep from swooning.

"Whatever it was," she said, "it left me quite unfit for public appearance."

The priest was now approaching them with the Eucharist. As each partook, he prayed a blessing over them and, Anna thought, gave the king a little wink. When he turned his back, William leaned toward her.

"Now 'tis official, my queen. With this shared Eucharist, we are truly united body and soul."

He took hold of her hand and squeezed it. Her body responded as if he'd kissed her — she was wet, ready, and frustratingly unable to do anything about it. He helped her to rise, glancing at her sideways as they walked, still holding hands, past the pews of bowing courtiers, those of highest rank trailing in their wake.

"My queen, since we have a few moments before privy court, we could show you the difference in masonry techniques we spoke of yesterday." He nodded at a passage away from the Great Hall.

"Is that so?" She had no idea what he was up to, but would play along.

"As a matter of fact," he said, guiding her down the hall, their entourage following this curious detour, "the library has a unique example, found nowhere else in the palace."

Upon reaching the doors, he turned to their attendants. "You will excuse us, please. The queen feels," he looked at her, not breaking character, "rather shy about her lack of architectural knowledge. We will only be a few minutes."

"Thank you, Majesty," Anna said with a small curtsy.

They slipped through the doors alone, puzzled looks shut away behind them.

The library was a long, thin room with an enormous hearth and shelves of books, floor to ceiling, on three walls. The view was the same as from the king's chambers, made more dramatic by a fourth wall of leaded glass windows that looked out on the private gardens and the low western hills beyond.

William strode across to the matching pair of doors on the far wall and rattled the handles. "Excellent!" he said. "Locked."

On his way back to Anna he stopped mid-room at a small, square table. He rattled it, squinting, then shook his head.

"William," she said in a loud whisper, "what exactly are we

doing?" She had started to investigate the room herself and was standing under an unlit torch beside the gaping fireplace.

"Annelore," he shout-whispered back, "why are you whispering?"

He sauntered toward her, hands clasped behind his back, forcing her into the wall. He let out a long breath, examining her at length. The heat he evoked in her could have lit that torch over her head. Then, quick as a cat, he grabbed her waist, pulling her to him, meeting her mouth with ferocity.

"Here?" she said, breathless.

"Do you have a better idea?" He moved his hands around her bodice, searching for purchase. "I swear, if I had to wait one minute longer—" he interrupted himself by kissing her again, ravenous. Her only reply was a guttural sigh, her body relaxing into his, a willing sacrifice to whatever he meant to do.

His hands now moved to her skirts, flying about trying to gain entry, she just as impatient. He pulled back from her, screwing up his face. "Good Lord, all this damned fabric."

"Well, it does take four ladies to dress me—" And beneath all that fabric her body pulsed for him, warmth alighting between her thighs, dampness blooming.

"Ah-ha!" He finally found a bare thigh. "Hold still now," he said, dropping to his knees in front of her. She felt his hands glide up her legs and she nearly collapsed to the floor. He looked up at her, all mischief. "I learned this in France," he said, and popped under her skirts.

He urged her legs apart and she felt his breath on the delicate curling hairs nestled at the crest. And then, sweet Jesus what was that softness, that divine pressure . . . . She melted against the stone, hands clenching the masonry, his grip against her thighs the only thing holding her upright. Her yelp echoed in the empty room as she felt him kissing her folds the same way he kissed her lips, tongue exploring, probing, imbibing on her. Stuffing a fist in her mouth to stifle her screams, she knew her legs would surely give as waves of ecstasy built in her body, demanding release, demanding more of him. But he held her hips fast to the wall, those hands of his digging into her skin as she helplessly bucked against his mouth again and again.

"I can't," she breathed, her groin throbbing, wet from his mouth and her own multiples of pleasure, "too much . . ."

He gave her one last lick and she collapsed in his arms, he chuckling all the way.

* * *

"So you see, Highness," the king said, a bit too loudly, leading the queen through the library doors fifteen minutes later, "how one must use different instruments, indeed, different techniques, when carving marble versus limestone."

Robert's keen eyes took in the pair: the queen's flushed cheeks, her diadem crooked, the king's chain of office off kilter, hair mussed. He nudged Daniel.

"I see, Majesty," the queen said. "I particularly appreciated the techniques applied by our French neighbors. They do delicate, exquisite work."

William coughed to cover a smile. "Indeed, they are masters at the art."

"Your Majesty," Daniel said, keeping pace with the king, "I do not mean to interrupt the, ah, art history lesson, but we must make haste to privy court, as council shall take most of the day afterward. We have troubling word from the north to discuss."

All trace of levity left the king's face. He thanked Daniel, then turned to the queen with a small bow. "Your Royal Highness, I eagerly await your arrival at privy court."

"Indeed, my liege," she said with a curtsy.

Daniel waited for the king to sweep past him toward the throne room, then grabbed Robert's arm to hold him back as the parties of gentlemen and ladies went their separate ways. Walking at the tail end of the king's retinue, he gave Robert a look.

"I'd say the rumors are true," Robert said. "They've done the deed."

"Most likely." Daniel frowned. "Although the king looks half-crazed."

Robert laughed. "My friend, your celibacy hath muddled your mind."

"My proclivities have nothing to do with this conversation."

"They do if they make ye blind," Robert said. "A man may behave like the king when he's, well, in heat. To be quite blunt."

"I know he's our friend," Daniel said, "but he's still the king. I do not think it appropriate to use such terms. Or to patronize me in the process."

"You brought it up." Robert clapped his red-faced friend on the back, which sent him tripping into the throne room. There, privy court passed uneventfully, save a Solomon-esque dispute over chickens, which had the chessboard-marble floor covered in white feathers before it was over. All three enthroned men were distracted, all three waiting for the same woman—one waiting to touch her, two waiting to observe.

Their impatience was rewarded a half-hour later when the queen swept into the room. At mass she had been wearing olive green velvet, now she glowed like a precious stone in royal purple taffeta with ivory slashed sleeves, a diamond and pearl tiara on her head and Queen Matilda's emeralds about her neck.

The king all but ran down the stairs to meet her. As always, he took her hand in his, lifting her from her curtsy.

"Majesty, you look radiant," he said, bringing her hand to his lips. He kissed her knuckles as if he would like to consume them. Daniel shifted in his chair and glanced at Robert, who flashed him a grin.

No more proof needed. She was, in every way, William's queen.

Suffer the Little Children

W
eeks later, a frail, balding man stumbled into the throne room, shackled by heavy chains, accompanied by guards. His body shook head to toe. Anna watched the Archbishop of Bartmore sweep past him to the foot of the throne dais and give a perfunctory nod to the king. He held a thick, leather-bound book to his chest, face smug.

The prisoner's face was puffed with bruises and swollen red cuts. His mouth quivered, his wrists raw and bleeding. One of the guards handed Daniel the charges.

"A Mr. Fitzroy Mason," Daniel said, "charged with two counts of heresy, Majesty." He handed the papers to the king, who scanned them.

The little man's milky eyes moved from Daniel to William to Robert, then landed on Anna. He was even older than her father.

"These charges are grave," William said. "Ownership of a Luther Bible, desecration of the host. What say you?"

The man limped forward, favoring his left leg. Perhaps his hip was out of joint. Or maybe his back. Anna wished to rush forward and tend to him.

"All rags an' bones he was, little thing," the old man said. "He come to the church starving, looking for somethin' to eat, and there warn't nothing but—"

"You fed an urchin boy the consecrated host?" Daniel said.

"You see?" the archbishop said. "He admits it. Sign the death warrant."

"N-no—no, Majesty, please—he would've died!" The man's legs threatened to give. "I was working on the pillars and he saw the bread to the side there. How could I not—"

Bartmore made to start again, but the king cut him off with the slice of his hand. "That is the problem, sir." William leaned forward. "It is bread no longer, but the body of our Lord and Savior. Or do you not believe it?"

The man looked confused and William let out a deep sigh.

Anna squirmed in her throne. How could a poor stonemason confronted with a starving child be expected to understand transubstantiation?

She rose, breezed past Bartmore, smiled into the man's desperate face, and took his gnarled hand in hers. "Sir, did you know this boy?"

Bartmore huffed. "How is this at all—"

"Silence, Eminence," William said.

Anna gave the mason a nod to continue.

"Y-yes, Your Majesty. He's my neighbor's boy, left orphan by the plague this spring. I didn't think the Lord would want—"

"'Tis not your place to think on such matters at all!" Bartmore said.

"And 'tis not your place to speak," William said, "until given leave."

Bartmore turned to Robert, but the duke was watching Anna.

"'Suffer the little children,'" Robert said.

"'Suffer little children to come unto me,'" Anna said, "'and forbid them not: for of such is the kingdom of God.'"

"'Verily I say unto you,'" William continued, with a hint of a smile, "'Whosoever shall not receive the kingdom of God as a little child shall in no wise enter therein.'"

Robert grunted and cracked his knuckles.

"Sir," William said, "while it pains us to hear of the desecration, it was our Lord Himself who rebuked the Pharisees when He and His disciples picked and ate grain on the Sabbath."

"Majesty—" the archbishop said.

"As to the second charge," William said, "give the book to Her Majesty, Eminence." William sank back, elbows on the throne arms.

Anna looked at the prisoner, who shook his head. No mason would ever have the money for such an extravagance as a book, let alone a contraband Bible. And yet when he saw it, tears sprang to his eyes.

"M-my wife. Please don't hurt my Gerte—"

"Your wife?" William leaned forward. "'Tis your wife's book?"

"She be half German—from Laureland, Majesty," he said. "The book was her dowry. We didn't know what it was, I swears it! Just that it were a book and worth a pretty penny—we never touched it, I swear!"

"Swear all you want," Bartmore said, "it was found in your possession. Ye are condemned."

"Need we remind you, Eminence," William said, "that we are the one who has the authority of condemnation in this land. You may charge him a heretic, but we have the final word."

"The Lord has the final word, Majesty." Bartmore said, curling his lips.

"Since He be not here, the duty falls to us."

Robert coughed to cover a laugh.

The archbishop handed the hefty tome to Anna with a grunt of distaste. She opened the front cover and read. "*Biblia das ist. Die gantze heilige Schrifft: Deudtch. D. Mart. Luth. Wittemberg.* This is the Holy Bible, in German."

Bartmore crossed himself and turned to William. "The man—and his wife—must burn."

The mason fell to the floor, arms outstretched for mercy at Bartmore's feet. "I didn't know, I swears it—"

"*Sprechen Sie Deutsch, alter Mann?*" William said.

The old man looked bewildered.

Anna handed the Bible to Bartmore, who again clutched it to his chest. She came back to the dais to sit by William. He took her hand and kissed it.

"As the man is illiterate and does not speak the tongue," William said, "we see no reason why he should be punished for something he did not understand."

Bartmore swung around, face purple as his robes. "My liege, we cannot overlook such a breech—nor have such filth as this book in our realm."

William pushed himself up, walked down the dais, and came to a stop inches from the archbishop.

"This is the last time we will remind you who is king, Your Eminence. You may have manipulated our brother and father, but we will not bend so easy."

"But the heretic—"

"Do not think we are unconcerned about the heretical influence in our realm. But this man," William gestured to the mason, "is no heretic. Confused, perhaps, but no Protestant."

William turned from Bartmore and started back up the dais. "In fact, Your Eminence, we had hoped you would be of better use in ferreting out true agitators in our midst. And here you bring us this man—as if burning him would stop a war."

"But the book—"

William threw his hands in the air. "Burn it. 'Tis so large we could roast a few pheasants while we're at it."

Daniel got up, but Robert stopped him, rising himself. "Give it to me, Highness—I'll take care of it. With pleasure."

"Suit yourself."

Robert pried the book away from the archbishop, as William returned to his throne and took Anna's hand. "Release the prisoner."

The guards moved to unlock the man, who looked at the royal couple in utter amazement. Anna smiled.

"Sir mason," William said, smiling as well, "keep thy peace about ye. For we do not wish to see you next week with some story about your bad leg and the communion wine."

* * *

Later that evening William found himself standing in front of the queen in her chambers, hardly knowing how he got there, but certainly knowing why. Loins tingling and fingers aching, he stared at her, sitting prim in lilac silks, working a needle with her ladies spread about her like some opulent fruit plate. He could tell she was trying not to grin at him, the corners of her mouth twitching just so.

"I—ah," William said, "was hoping to speak about court today."

She nodded, stuck her needle to her work and looked up. He could swear he saw her shudder as she met his gaze.

"Of course." She raised her voice. "Ladies, you are free for the evening."

"The whole evening is it?" He said, jumping his brows. That got him a glare while her ladies tucked away their work and floated out in to court.

She stayed where she was, sitting in his mother's tufted chair, watching him. And a sudden panic hit. Was she angry at him for some reason? Somehow soured with his company, bored with his ministrations? Dammit this woman! She had him in knots.

She held his eyes. "You don't need to make up excuses to see me."

"Excuses?"

She rose, slow, casting her needlework aside. "By the look of you, I dare say you don't wish to speak about court."

She stepped toward him. He would let her come. He would make sure this was what she wanted. He shrugged. "It was the first time you'd interjected, and I thought—" With each step she took, his heat rose and he grew stiff beneath his shorts.

She brandished a finger at him, a smile finally gracing her. "See? Excuses." She stopped a mere hand's width in front of him. He felt her look him up and down. Accessing. Her voice was throaty, quiet. "You don't need an excuse to bed me, William. For I am always at your service."

And that was all he needed to hear. He grabbed her waist and thrust her to him, capturing her mouth with his, hard, hungry, she meeting him with equal fury, her tongue wrestling, fingers buried in his hair pulling his head to her, urging him with her soft moans.

Still entwined, he walked her backward to her bed. Reveling in the feel of her bottom, he hoisted her up to sitting as she wrapped her legs around him, pulling his hips to hers, clamping on like a crab. He thrilled at this entrapment, at this small act of claiming she made to him. She wanted him, every part of her, even unconsciously. It roused him even more, made him want to show her how much he desired her, needed her, in return.

He gently laid her back then knelt, feeling his way up her calves along the smooth silk of her stockings to find the ribbons at her thighs. Shoving up her skirts with his shoulders, he bent to the ribbon ties, undoing them with his teeth, letting his tongue tickle her inner thigh at will, luxuriating in her scent of salt, roses, and sunned grass. She gasped, muscles tightening, her buttocks instinctively clenching. He chuckled against her warm milk skin, drew her hose down, then went to repeat the process.

But while he was there, why not just . . . he trailed his fingers up, up, finding her sex. He brushed her lips with his fingers and caught a whiff of her want as she gasped again.

"Please, William," she groaned.

"Please what, Annelore?" He swirled his fingers against her, devilishly delighting in their slickness.

"You wretched man, you know what!" She groaned again and laughed, wriggling her bottom to coax his fingers.

"That I do," he said, teasing her outer lips up and down, weaving through soft hairs, his own need solid and demanding to be handled. "But I still want you to say it."

He dipped a finger just inside her and felt her clamp around him, helplessly trying to pull him deeper. He couldn't help his growl.

"Gah!" She thrust again. His other hand was already undoing his shorts. "Will—iam! I can't—" She thrashed her head from side to side.

"Can't what?" And he pushed into her, two fingers all the way to the hilt. She hissed.

"I need you inside me—I can't stand it." Her face was scrunched up, eyes shut, grabbing for that elusive release as he slithered his fingers in and out, thumb stroking, coaxing.

"Do you not enjoy my digits?" He smiled at her, toying and loving it. "I can take them out." He began to pull them out but she grabbed his arm.

"No! I mean yes—I mean, they feel divine, I just—"

"You'd enjoy something with more substance perhaps?"

Her eyes flew open and she narrowed starving brows, temporarily stopping his own breath. "If you do not fill me again, right now, I will . . ."

He'd kept his middle finger inside her and now flexed it up, tickling her from within. "You will . . ." He grinned at her, knowing he'd made her beyond speech.

Finally withdrawing, he grasped her hips and pulled them to the edge of the bed, her sex prone before him. He ripped off the rest of his clothes as she quietly whimpered to herself. He knew he must finish her now.

He notched his cock, looked her straight in the eyes and shoved into her, not playing anymore. The feel of her walls enveloping him evoked his own moans and nearly sent him fainting. She yelped and thrashed as he plunged, fast, hard, his tip hitting up against the end of her over and over.

He couldn't hold much longer. He needed her to come now, or he would. She let out a squeal, the pitch so high it lofted into a silent wail, her body trembling around his, and he was lost to all reason, all thought, the feel of her around him and through him and with a final thrust he exploded.

He collapsed on top of her, head pillowed between her still encased breasts, blissfully spent.

She lifted her chin and patted the top of his head. "Again?"

* * *

Later, both surely satiated, William leaned on Annelore's bent bare legs and watched candlelight play off the burnt copper in her hair.

"Every night you came here?" she said. "Just thinking of you—the little prince nestled with his sister in his mother's arms, saying prayers and listening to stories."

"And soon," he said, "we shall have the same pretty picture, I hope. Certainly our full efforts have been put to the task." He grinned at her. "And you, my dear, *were* superb today—I truly did want to speak of it—I should want you defending me when my neck is on the line."

"He was no threat, " she said, batting the compliment away with a hand. "You saw that in an instant."

"I should allow you more entrée into state affairs." He drew a finger across her clavicle, entranced by its pearl-like smoothness.

"Truly?" she said, face alight. "You know I'd love to help however I may."

"Just like my mother." He grinned and she chortled. "Wait, that didn't sound good—"

"Do you know," she said, "all this talk of your mother reminds me —we've met before, you and I."

"We have?" He stroked her shoulder absently. His cock twitched as deliciously lewd images of her forcing his head to her crotch flashed in his mind. How could he still be so easily aroused after that marathon session? "How's that?"

"I was at the parade—James's realm review, after his corona-tion." He sat up now, all attention. "I've been so preoccupied, and 'twas so long ago, it slipped my mind until just now."

"So what was I doing? Pouting at James's pomp?" He climbed under the bedclothes, bringing her head to rest on his chest.

"My mother so wanted to see the parade," she said, "but she was in the middle of helping a birth. So she sent me with a bundle of wildflowers, with sprigs of lavender—the queen mother's favorite, she told me."

"Reminded her of her homeland," he said, a lump rising in his throat. "Cate and I spent many an afternoon gathering bouquets for her."

She kissed his fingers and pressed them to her cheek. "So there I was, wreath of lavender in my hair, dragging Mary behind me. I found my way to the front just as the first of the knights passed."

"Why, you must have been—how old?" he said. "Eight?"

"Five."

"Good Lord, am I as old as all that?"

"Yes, dear heart, you're quite ancient." She patted his chest. "But let me finish."

"By all means, for I love to hear about myself. Whatever did I do that made you so terrified of me near twenty years later?"

"I had my flowers, ready to hand to the queen, but everyone was screaming to King James and there were so many knights and guards I could barely see. Then I saw the canopy of her litter. I started to jump up and down and scream and wave." She was excited now, sitting up to face him, acting it out. "All my commotion must have spooked James's horse, for the next thing I knew, his mount reared and the crowd moved back. He was angry, glaring down at me. I don't even remember what he said, but he leaned down, spat at my feet, and swatted my flowers away into a pile of manure."

He imagined her there, so small, so innocent. "I'd call my brother a bastard, but that would insult my mother."

She waved this away. "Dearest, 'twas years ago."

"I would kill him right now if he weren't already dead, knowing he caused you even a moment's grief." He sat up, engulfing her whole to his chest.

"But I haven't got to the best part," she said, muffled by his muscles.

"Then I shall hold my murderous tongue." He reclined back, taking her with him.

"The queen mother must have seen, for I started to cry. She bid you come to her, spoke to you and handed you a nosegay. Princess Catherine's head lay in her lap and the queen was stroking her hair."

The lone candle flame at the bedside table fluttered, as if those ghosts had gathered to hear their own tale.

"You dismounted, walked to me, bowed rather stiffly, handed me the flowers and said, 'My lady, with Her Majesty's compliments and mine.' Then, gallant as ever, you swung up on your horse right in front of me, smiled down like the sun itself, and galloped off to have words with your brother."

"Quite the little gentlemen, if I do say so myself."

"Yes," she said, rising to an elbow, facing him, "yes, you were. 'Tis a shame I forgot. Why is that?"

William traced a finger from her chin to the base of a breast, thrilling again at their heft. "The mind is mysterious, my dear. Perhaps it's the heat that recalls it now."

She slid on top of him, brushing his eyebrows with her thumbs. "Whatever the reason, oh king of mine, I do thank ye. 'Twas a noble thing to do."

"Apparently 'twas my mother's idea." He tilted his chin down so he could nibble hers.

"She the inspiration, but the valor all your own," she said. "I'm feeling greatly under your debt, Majesty. However shall I repay you?"

He rolled her over. Not caring the whys and hows of his unquenchable libido, just damned thankful for it. "I'm sure I can think of something." Then he buried his face in her neck.

* * *

Diagonally down from the queen's chambers, Yvette lay resplendently nude on Robert's bearskin rug, eating grapes, and feeding him hard cheese with a knife. The palace was quiet, save for the changing of guards. It was well into the early morning.

"So the queen intervened on his behalf?" Yvette said, curling voluminous lips at her lover.

"Even I was stunned into silence," Robert said.

"A rare thing indeed."

He leaned to bite her nipple and rolled onto his back. "And how doth she go in chambers? And what of Margaux? Is my sister behaving?"

Yvette sighed and edged next to him on her belly. "Apparently the queen is naturally gifted in the art of love."

Robert let out a little snort. "Perhaps that knight of hers wasn't so pure after all."

Yvette rolled her almond eyes at him. "Perhaps 'tis the king, with all of his travels, who is her instructor in these matters."

Robert sat up on an elbow and dragged a finger along the curve of her back, watching tiny, translucent hairs rise in response.

"I prefer you not think of the king in such a way."

"You're the one who told me to get her into his bed and keep her there. You can't now question my methods," she said, a grape squirting its juice onto his shoulder as she bit it whole.

"And my sister—what of her schemes?"

"Your sister licks her wounds. Every time the queen returns ravaged and glowing from the king, she seems more and more sullen. She barely sews, just sits and scribbles and chatters with Brigitte. I think she's taken to drink. She's always about the wine."

"Serves her right." He tore off a leg of cold chicken from their shared platter.

"And what of her once the king cools to the queen?" Yvette said as he attacked the drumstick. "For 'tis bound to happen. No man stays loyal to the same woman for long."

Robert jabbed at his chest with the leg bone. "Ah, but this wild beast hath been tamed."

"I don't believe your wife would agree." She took his thumb to her mouth, sucking off the chicken grease.

Robert laughed. "All right, besides my wife. I haven't strayed from you these many years."

She released his captive thumb with a pop, the tingle winding it's way to his groin. "Three years is many, is it?"

"For a man's cock—mine own in particular—three years is an eternity."

She frowned. He collapsed on his back with a groan, tossed the gnawed leg at the fire, and clasped his hands behind his head.

"It makes me ponder what this will all come to. When I speak to you, it all seems so simple, and yet the queen is a wild card. I can't get my mind around her. Is she, or is she not, sympathetic to the cause?"

"I very much doubt the matter has even crossed her mind," Yvette said.

"But what of that lover of hers, the knave? Is he not a resource we can utilize somehow?"

"It would appear that under the king's ministrations, she has forgotten all about her girlish love affair. As should you."

With that, she straddled him, clearly finished with the conversation. Her ripe buttocks fell between his thighs, knees bent next to his. Licking her palm, she wrapped it around his cock, gliding her hand up and down as he grew and tightened under her practiced ministrations. He moaned deep in his throat.

Pulling down, she revealed the head, red, hard, and already slick with his anticipation. He remembered how, when they first came together, she could make him spurt in his trunks with just a look. She made him no less eager now.

Bending over, she took him in her warm mouth, circling her tongue around him like he was a dish of cream and she wanted the last drop.

He would give her what she wanted.

He flexed into her, rubbing the roof of her mouth, his tip tickling the back of her throat, her soft gags only urging him on. His blood, his juices, all of him was surging now, but she wouldn't let him come.

Pulling away with a wicked smile, she mounted him, drawing his cock inside her, sitting on him like he was her God-given throne. *Long may she reign.*

Undulating her hips, he couldn't help but thrust himself, seeking, needing more of her, her globe breasts bouncing as she moaned out her own rising pleasure. He flexed his ass, giving her the firmness he knew she needed, watching that tell of her brow creasing, a silent scream forming on her lips. It was ecstatic just looking at her. He could play this image in his head during those long hours at council, or those dark, echoing nights she was with the queen. That it was his body inside her only roused him that much more. Her bronzed neck strained, black lashes closed against her sharp cheeks, pink mouth just parted. The fire dancing off her arms, her nipples, her belly.

Her fingers were like talons on his shoulders as she drove him, used him, pounded herself into him, he desperately holding back his own release, watching, waiting, savoring.

Then she threw her head back, her entire body rigid, hips shuddering, and all at once she melted, flowing off him onto the bearskin.

After a long exhale, she turned her face to look at him, eyes dazzling in the dim light.

"My turn?" he said, member still stick straight. A smile broke her face and she had the audacity to chuckle at him.

"Maybe," she said, "what will you give me?"

He grinned back. "Turn over and find out."

* * *

It was Anna's first official visit to Council Table. She had no power, being only queen consort, but as William promised, he obliged her with the offer to attend. That he valued her opinion warmed her, and she resolved to make sure he'd not regret the invitation.

As she passed the king's throne they exchanged polite smiles, having agreed to comport themselves with propriety in public. But that didn't stop the surge of heat that passed between them, urging her to straddle him right then and there.

Off to the side was her throne-like chair, facing the half-full table and conversation hushed as she made her way to her seat. *What on earth do they talk about that the delicate ears of a female can't hear?*

Daniel called the council to order. There were brief debates about whether the emperor or just the zealous Lutherans were the ultimate cause of trouble in the northeast. Apparently, Daniel and the master general had been a bit hasty in recommending the royal couple abort their wedding trip, for the rumors were simply the saber-rattling of one lord railing about taxes on his considerable holdings. Still, the threat of the Laurelanders' secession—or worse, assault on the throne—still loomed. But with an heir . . . .

The men stole glances at Anna. Was it so soon that a child would be demanded of her?

"Cecile," William said, "was there not something you wanted to speak upon?"

"Yes, sire," Daniel said. "It seems we must revisit some of our outer lands to re-evaluate their revenues in respect to the crown's income." Anna shot up straight.

"King James, God rest his soul," Daniel said, "levied much

higher taxes percentage wise, but his financial management put the crown in debt. Some of that has been alleviated by a thorough going-over of the books, but if we need to build an army anytime soon, we must remedy the situation. Higher taxes, for a time, are the only solution."

Various suggestions arose as to how much taxes might be raised.

"Begging your pardon, my lords, Highness," Anna said. All eyes turned to her, all but the king's amazed.

"Is there something you would like to contribute, Majesty?" the king said.

Anna chose her words carefully."Yes, Majesty, my lords. The taxes levied upon the people are overly burdensome already. I would think any move to raise them would merely add fuel to the fire—especially that of these Laurelanders."

Daniel looked at William, then at her, smiling, polite.

"Your Highness," he said, "I can understand how you might see it that way, but under the improved management of funds all should benefit in the long run."

"My lords, none of our people will see it that way." The councilors fidgeted in their chairs. "All they see is more money from their pockets, less and less for their families. If the funds be well managed, could we not cut back here at court for a time? I often did the same at Castle Beaubourg and the duchy in such times."

"With all due respect, Highness," Daniel said, keeping to his calm tone, "if we are thrust into combat, the people will require defense, and only the crown can protect and provide for the whole of the country, no matter how frugal thy royal household."

He was not listening. "Your Grace, I am not saying people should not be taxed their fair share, especially those who have gone without paying under King James's favor. But with the burden already so great—why even in Beaubourg, despite our efforts, we have seen villagers starving."

The king turned his eyes to Robert, who sat pale and stony. Why did he always look to these two? Especially Robert, who only wanted what was good for Robert?

"Majesty . . ." The king glanced at her, then back to the gathered men. "We thank you for reminding us of the plight of the poor, for they are indeed always with us." He turned from her to Daniel. "But we agree with Cecile. We must investigate ways to gather funds quickly. We cannot be left defenseless."

"Hear, hear," Robert said. "King James, rest in peace, etc., frittered everything away on whores and feasts. We cannot keep depending on the good graces of country lords for arms and men."

For what purpose had William invited her? To sit and listen to councilmen ignore her concerns about the lives of people she knew and loved? Was she not the people's queen? Perhaps she had overstepped decorum, but she was in the right and had a mind as keen as any of these puffed-up men.

The council moved to other topics. When William glanced at her, she stared black-death back. He dropped his eyes and frowned.

Any heat she'd felt before had turned to white hot rage now. She seethed for another hour until he came to escort her out. She refused to look at him, head held high all the way to her chambers, then snatched her hand away as she took her leave. She caught blue eyes rolling as he went his way.

* * *

The two met again five hours later to sup in the king's dining chambers with the last remaining dignitary from the wedding, the elderly Viscount de Alba of Spain. While only the king, queen, and viscount dined, the room was packed with servants and courtiers, standing to the sides, observing the delicate game of diplomacy. Their countries were allies, but Anna knew such alliances were fluid.

"Majesties," the Spaniard said, "what a marvelous diversion this trip has been. We pride ourselves on festivals of amor, but your small country has bested even us." He raised his glass to the couple.

"Thank you, my lord," William said. "I have always enjoyed the riches of Spanish culture as well."

Anna narrowed her eyes at him. Spanish culture indeed.

William turned to her. "Is that not so, Majesty?"

"Since I have only read of the joys of Spain in books," she said, smiling so hard her cheeks hurt, "I will have to take both your words for it. Majesty."

De Alba chuckled. "Ah, Queen Annelore, let me take this opportunity to invite you personally to our fair land. You shall be a celebrated beauty!" He raised his glass to her again.

The rest of the meal continued, with the two men recalling their various voyages through Spain. William attempted to draw Anna into the conversation to no avail. The audience ended just after eleven, and Anna, weary, had the duty of walking the viscount to his accommodations.

"Your Highness," he said, wrapping her arm around his and patting her hand like a doting grandfather, "I must congratulate you again on your nuptials."

"Thank you, my lord."

"'Tis not often a royal match, or any match, is made whence the two parties are so well suited." He smiled knowingly. "Just give His Majesty a bit of grace."

Anna started at this. He nodded and winked at her. "Yes, I have watched you both with keen eyes for over a month now. He is yet learning to be a king—and a husband. He needs your mercy, and your help, though he does not know it."

Having absolutely no idea what to say, she remained silent.

"At the very least," he said with a chuckle, "your Spanish is better than his."

They had reached the end of the hall. He took both her hands in his, squeezing gently.

"Please excuse my boldness, Majesty, but I am a man who loves love. I can't help myself. 'Tis in my blood and an old man's last comfort."

She gave him a wan smile. She'd managed to hold on to her hurt all evening and did not want a romantic old Spaniard undoing it all.

"One thing I do know," he said, "is that he adores you absolutely. And you him. And this, my dear lady, is more rare than the crown gracing your stunning head."

"My dear viscount, he is peevish." She could not help but smile. "And so am I."

He chortled. "Ah, sweet queen. I know not what he has done to deserve your wrath, but do not punish him for too much longer."

* * *

Anna was surprised to find William in her chambers, standing by her sputtering fire in all his official splendor, fidgeting with his chain of office.

She looked about for her ladies, but he had apparently banished them. Blast the man. She just wanted to go to bed and pity herself to sleep. Never mind how the cleft between her thighs wakened at his presence. She nearly swore.

"Holy Scripture tells us," he said, "that one must not let the sun go down upon one's anger."

"If I wanted a homily I'd have sought out my almoner." She turned her back to him, advanced to her toilette table, and began to undo her headdress with trembling fingers. "Besides, the sun has been set many hours."

"It appears you won't make this easy on me."

"Oh, I don't see why you should trouble yourself, my liege." She ripped at her hair, unweaving the plaits. "My thoughts aren't of national import, after all."

He sighed. "Why must you jump to such overwrought conclusions?"

She turned on him, brandishing a golden brush. "Well, what am I to think? You play the part of doting husband very well in private, but in public 'tis 'Wives should be seen and not heard.'"

"That's not what I said."

"You didn't need to say it—your meaning was clear." She turned back to her mirror to remove her jewelry.

"Having you at council at all was unprecedented to begin with—"

"But why bring me if I'm only to sit there?" Her fingers fumbled with her earbob. In the mirror she spied him coming closer, rubbing stubble. She could not help the quiver that shot through her, remembering how those whiskers felt against her neck, her cheeks, her thighs. *Dammit!*

"Because that's what you wanted," he said, now less than five feet behind, approaching her as one would a squirrel, "you wanted to know more about the wheels of government."

"So I'm to sit quietly and learn, but none can learn from me?" She snapped the earbob box shut. "You've only been king a handful of weeks longer than I've been queen."

"True enough." He put his hands on his hips. "But my life entire has been spent in observation of the governance of other lands. And those few weeks you speak of were not spent in idle pursuits."

"And my life entire," she said, glowering at him in the mirror, "has been spent in observation of the governance of *this* land and how such governance affected the daily lives of its people."

"Touché." He reached to her shoulder to help untie a sleeve. She jerked away with a scowl. He held up his hands in surrender.

"Annelore, I don't doubt your keen mind, for I've been its companion these many days and nights. But you must understand how outrageous it is for those gathered men to not only have you present but expressing an opinion!"

She spun around to face him. She knew he was right, but her ire would not be soothed. "But Daniel was wrong. And you sided with him!"

"First of all," he said, "Daniel is rarely wrong. Second, there were no sides to be taken. He was merely suggesting we look into the matter —"

"So you agree with him simply because he is rarely wrong?" she said. "You're the king!"

"Ah!" He raised a finger. "But I'm not a king — rather, I wasn't supposed to be." He sighed and sat in the high-back chair she used for sewing.

"Nor is Daniel, no matter how wise and kind and well placed," she said.

"And now here we both are, my dear. Neither of us what we were supposed to be."

She sighed too and sat on a tuffet next to him, one sleeve hanging half untied. "I shouldn't pounce upon every imagined misstep,

William. I'm sorry. I just—when you've seen your people go without for so long, 'tis hard to hear they must suffer further."

"I wouldn't hamper your passion for our people for anything. But there's a time and place—"

"But isn't that time and place council?"

"Not for a woman—certainly not a vehement one. But I am sorry I cut you off. You did have a point, which I could have acknowledged."

"Which I could have made less *vehemently*." She rolled her eyes.

"You must have patience. God knows I must as well." He turned his head toward her. "Forgive me?"

She rose, took his cheeks in her hands, and gave him a light kiss. "Yes, Highness, I forgive you. And I ask it of you as well. I just got so angry I couldn't help myself."

He grabbed her waist and pulled her down on him. "I've noticed that trait about you." He smiled. "Now. Shall we see about getting you out of these clothes?"

CHAPTER 9

Some days later, William left Anna outside her chambers with a kiss to her knuckles and a sparkle in his eyes. She entered to find Margaux grabbing a bundle of papers out of Bernard's hands.

"I will see that Her Majesty receives them, sir," she said with a final tug.

Bernard rocked back on his heels as the letters left his hands. Immediately Margaux began to sort them into neat piles on a little silver tray.

"Milady, it is highly unusual—oh!" Bernard turned crimson at the sight of Anna and performed his little jig-bow. Anna smiled as she recalled William's attempt at imitating this particular obeisance. As light on his feet as he was, he'd tripped over his bearskin's head and landed in her lap. Of course, he might well have fallen in her lap on purpose.

Margaux fell into a curtsy, a dazzling smile on her face. "Majesty, you've arrived just after the post," she said. "I've taken the liberty of sorting it."

"Thank you, Margaux," Anna said, moving toward the table. Margaux held out two letters, keeping the rest close to her chest.

"If that will be all, Majesty," Bernard said. As he bowed, he bumped Margaux's elbow. Three of the letters she'd been holding fluttered to the floor.

Margaux scowled as she bent to pick them up. Reflexively, Anna bent to the floor as well. The last letter was addressed only to "Her Majesty."

Anna's heart stopped. She knew that writing.

"Goodness," Margaux said, "I must have missed that one. Apologies, Majesty." She shrugged her shoulders, and rose from the floor.

Anna rose as well, trying to look indifferent. "Thank you, Lady Margaux."

Margaux looked at the letter again, now held against Anna's chest. Her eyebrow gave the faintest of flicks as she curtsied and turned to the rest of the ladies. Had she seen Anna flinch when she saw the letter? Even so, surely Margaux wouldn't know who it was from—it was only the second to arrive from him since she came to court. And why did it matter anyway? Could she not receive a letter from an old friend?

Anna swept her chambers with a glance to make sure she was alone, then ran her finger under the small blue wax seal of a fish.

Sweet Anna,

I have your latest and await with eagerness the Festival of Harvest. My gift will aid and comfort you, 'tis my hope. Fear not and forbear! You know I shall always be,

Your very dearest and constant love,

B

What in God's name was he talking about? Would he really be so bold as to appear at the annual Festival of Harvest? Of course she may not even see him there, with all five regions of Troixden gathered at court presenting gifts and being blessed by the king. And "latest"—latest what? She hadn't written to him. Was it the extra stores she had set aside for his mother?

Whatever he meant, it certainly did not sound as though Bryan was living content back in Beaubourg.

* * *

There were two more letters: one confirming her order of herbs for the privy garden and one from Daniel. He asked, ever so politely, if she would join him in his meeting chambers that afternoon.

She found him standing behind his large desk, papers stacked in neat piles, a quill in his hand.

"Highness," he said with a swift bow. "Please make yourself at home."

She took the arm he extended. He led her to a chair in front of his desk and he took the one next to it. "I have sent for some refreshment," he said. "My secretary will be taking notes."

"Notes?" She gripped a fold of her skirt.

"Yes," Daniel said, his cheeks coloring just a bit. "I want to make sure to take down precisely what you say."

She laughed, but couldn't help a flicker of unease as Bryan's letter leapt to mind. "Am I being examined?" She tried to smile naturally.

Daniel folded his thin, white fingers in his lap. "After the last council—well, I hoped we could explore some ideas together about taxation."

"Indeed?" Anna gave an inadvertent snort.

"His Majesty tells me you understand these matters from the people's perspective . . ."

She didn't know what she had expected, but it wasn't this. "Your Grace, you need not humor me on the king's command."

"The king did not put me up to anything, Majesty." He knit his brows. "I merely wish to hear how the people might be roused to support the crown in their hearts, not just with their funds." He grabbed a parchment from his desk.

"Well, certainly in Beaubourg my duties went well beyond needlepoint."

He startled, then relaxed when he saw her smile. She reached out to touch his arm. "Come now, Daniel. The king trusts and adores you, and I trust and adore him. Surely we two can be at ease together?"

"I'd very much like that, Highness." He flicked his eyes from her fingers to her face.

"Now let's talk about taxes," she said. "I do understand that armies require funds, you know."

A tray of wine, fruits, and cheese were brought and Anna took a glass of the spiced white wine gratefully. It tasted fresh and sweeter than her own—apparently Daniel had his own stores.

"Medicinals, Majesty. The taxes associated with doctoring." Daniel motioned to his secretary, who sat up at his own little desk in the corner, quill at the ready.

"I daresay I know a lot about that," she said.

"Indeed you do, Majesty. Now let's see what scheme might avoid starving the people without leaving them defenseless."

* * *

It wasn't until late that evening that William had his queen to himself. He leaned back, shirtless, in his deep leather chair, which was now positioned by the open window. She was nestled between his thighs, resting on his chest, her hair spread over his shoulder, feet on the windowsill. The soft breeze kept catching her thin silk shift, billowing it about, distracting him from their lazy conversation.

"An interesting day, my dear?" he said, brushing an errant tendril of her hair out of his mouth.

"Indeed," she said. "But I've a question for you." She poked his belly with a finger. "Did you put Daniel up to it?"

"*Moi?*"

She pulled back to look in his eyes.

"No, my dear," he said. "I rarely need to put Daniel up to anything. He sees and knows more than anyone in the realm."

"Ah," she said. "I wasn't sure I believed him." She looked back out the window.

He kissed the top of her head and hugged her to him, inhaling her scent of roses, the faintest salt of her sweat, almonds . . . what else today? He took a deep breath into her hair and relaxed. Thyme.

"He was reluctant to say much about your conference," William said, "but he seems to think you came up with a fine solution. From the little he told me of it, I agree."

She searched his face, thoughtful. "Thank you, Majesty," she said. "I do have some ideas of merit that men may learn from, no?"

He chortled. "Indeed, that little head of yours does a mite bit more than look pretty." She gave him a swat. He laughed, then sobered.

"And what news of home?" He studied her face, waiting.

She met his eyes. "Does Daniel lower himself to reading my mail in defense of thy royal cause?"

"Daniel's not the only little bird at court, to be sure," he said, "if less pernicious." He kept his eyes to hers. Their gaiety was gone, but he couldn't read them further.

She closed them for a moment then looked up at him again. "William, do you doubt my fealty to you?"

He gave a harrumph. "The last I heard of your knight he was trying to wrench you from the royal carriage. And you were throwing him your favor."

"I would think subsequent events might have calmed your mind."

He gave another snort and looked out the window.

She returned it. "Is it a crime to receive letters, uninvited?"

Well, he had to bring it up. It had been on his mind all day since he overheard Margaux and Brigitte not so subtly talking of it in the hall. *So this is what I'm reduced to now? Heeding idle court gossip?*

"William, he's had no word from me." She cocked her head at him, eyes wide and sweet. "And 'tis only the second I've had from him, both letters rather clipped and bizarre besides. Something about a gift for the Festival of Harvest."

"I'll make sure no rolling horse statues arrive." He said. "And I suppose I need have no fear of losing your attentions to a crazed knight, then?"

She started flicking his chest hairs, sending a pleasant tickling trickling downward. He'd need to finish this conversation soon.

"Oh, Bryan's not mad. Though he has been acting a bit irrational of late. You should pity him, not be jealous—"

"Me, jealous?"

She looked up at him. Taking his face in her hands she kissed him till they were both breathless. "Does His Majesty need a bit more convincing?"

He cupped her cheek in his hand, fingers lacing through her hair, and brought her to his lips. He could feel her humor fall away, replaced by a rising urgency.

"What was it we were talking about again?" he said.

A slow smile broke upon her face. She crossed her arms in front of her, lifted off her shift, tossed it behind his head, revealing her perfect, perky breasts. She rolled down his chest, every inch of his skin singing as hers made contact. Finally coming to a stop, she traced his lips with her forefinger.

"Nothing of any importance," she said. He still couldn't believe his luck in finding her. That she could be intelligent, witty, delightful company, stunning, *and* an eager lover—he wasn't sure what he'd done to deserve such a life, but he would revel in every moment.

And in *this* moment, she had reached between her thighs and unbuckled him, one brow cocked, lower lip tucked in her teeth.

"Let me help you," he breathed, taking up an earlobe, his breath caressing her neck, his hands sliding down her butter-smooth back.

In answer, she slipped her hand into his shorts. Unconsciously, he flexed himself into her waiting palm and it was warm, beckoning. She curved her hips up, those beautiful breasts pressed hard against his chest, and eased him into her, slipping down his length as slowly as she'd unfurled on his body.

He shuddered, and a grunt of willing surrender passed his lips.

"I am at your service," he sighed, and lost himself in her, gloriously, once again.

* * *

One of the king's speckled spaniels yelped in delight, frolicking among the close-trimmed shrubbery, happening upon a fat, brown toad shading itself from the late-summer heat. The three-tiered fountain bubbled as the queen and her ladies strolled along the manicured lanes of the royal privy garden. Anna was deciding where to plant her personal garden, one that could be overgrown and unencumbered, with medicinal herbs and other such plants as she might fancy. William told her she could take over the royal gardens entire if she wanted, but she was content to have a small patch of land to call her own. Somewhere she could come and be with her own thoughts, even if it was in the company of a trail of ladies.

"So," Mary said, coming alongside her, winded by the exercise, "is it to be every night now I'm kept waiting up for you without a how-you-please? Ye can't romp at a decent hour?"

"Mary!" Anna turned and saw her maid grinning wide.

"And you thought ye wouldn't like him, dearie."

Anna took Mary's arm, beaming. "I'm not ashamed to say I was wrong. He truly is the wittiest, most handsome, the kindest, the —"

"Seems you've been bit by the bug."

"Shall I go on, then?" She smiled at Mary's breach of etiquette in interrupting her sovereign. The habit was hard for the woman to break, and Anna didn't try to. Their easy banter reminded her of a simpler time.

"We've all seen the man — we be knowing his fine qualities," Mary said.

"I couldn't have imagined he would actually be someone I would respect, let alone enjoy." And dear lord above did she enjoy him. She shivered remembering the evening before, how he coaxed her to climax over and over with his tongue, his hands, his —

"None of us knew for sure," Mary said, "but, dearie, I'm so glad of it. It near broke my heart seeing how poorly ye took the situation. And to see you and your father so upset with each other? 'Twasn't right."

They walked on a ways in companionable silence, breathing in the early afternoon warmth, smelling cut greens and roses in full bloom. She laughed to herself remembering how recalcitrant she'd been, how hell bound to escape. Had she gotten her way she never would have know this . . . this need. Overwhelming, all-encompassing need to be near him. Not just his body, but his essence, the whole of him. Every moment without him was just a pitch darker. Even when he enraged her, she'd rather be in his presence and livid than without him and sanguine. So was this love? Surely something like it.

"And what of your knight?" Mary asked, lowering her voice. "Is he fair forgot, then?"

Anna sighed. "Not forgot. 'Tis just, well . . ."

She realized she had yet to come up with words for her feelings. She knew Bryan to be part of her past, a past that seemed years, not weeks, behind her. But there was tenderness in her heart for the first boy who held her hand, held her in warm embrace, kissed her lips. Even with his recent lapses in sense.

"You know I've always treasured him, Mary," she said, watching the bounding spaniel, red ears flapping about, chasing something or other. "But Bryan, well, he's a boy. The king is a man."

"And you're the queen, and that's the end of it? My, my." Mary whistled. "And what of the Festival of Harvest next week? And St. Crispin's tournament next month? Will you see him?"

"I suppose I shall have to in some capacity. And who knows if the king will even allow that."

"Why would he worry himself about it?" Mary stopped to sit on the wide stone lip of the fountain, fanning herself with her skirts, ignoring all propriety.

"You're right," Anna said, "why would he hesitate to welcome Bryan back to court? The king has nothing to fear."

She bent to pluck an errant daisy. She was in complete thrall to the king. And while a part of her balked to be at his mercy, she also didn't mind it, as long as he was hers.

"My lady!" came a shout from the second floor of the palace.

They looked up and spied the king himself leaning over the open arched hallway, wind catching the corner of his short cape, billowing it out like a sail in salutation, her heart sailing to the skies with it.

"Come, join us at council!"

* * *

He watched her rise from the fountain, shielding her eyes from the sun, drooping wildflowers in her hand. "Is council so dignified it cannot meet out of doors, sire?" she said. "'Tis such a glorious day!"

He laughed, his deep tones carrying on the breeze. "Nay, wife. They be quite a boring bunch. Who knows what sunshine might startle them into?"

She was near the foot of the wall now, the palace's shadow covering her as she smiled up at him. And his heart was full.

"And I suppose it would not be king-like for you to miss such a meeting to romp amongst the lilies and the ladies?"

He swung a leg over the ledge making as if to jump. "'Tis the best offer I've heard all day."

"Nay!" She laughed. "Don't leap to your death, Majesty. I shall be in presently." She blew him a kiss and turned back to her rambling gaggle of maids and dogs, looking like blooms them-selves from his vantage point. He watched her clap to the spaniels and take flowers from her hair. The scene seemed from a dream—if he blinked the garden would be gray and empty, he still a lonely bachelor surrounded by grasping men and false women. He warmed to see her so blithe, so lovely in the sunshine. With a sigh, he headed to the somber faces awaiting him at Council Table, counting the minutes until she would appear.

* * *

"So that brings us to the matter of taxable goods, specifically medicinals," Daniel said.

It had been a fortnight since Anna's last, fateful attendance at council, and those who could flick their eyes to the queen without moving their heads did so. Daniel paused for a second, then continued.

"It has come to our attention that medicinals are currently taxed at a flat rate, yet the apothecaries and doctors who dispense them charge wildly different rates throughout the land."

The king looked to Anna, stood up, and moved to stand behind his chair.

"Her Majesty, I believe, would be better suited to explain the matter," Daniel said.

"Is that really necessary?" she heard someone whisper. William shot a dark look down the table.

"Indeed it is," Daniel said. "She and I have talked privately as well. Highness?"

Anna's heart pounded, but she gave him a polite nod. "Thank you, Your Grace. My lords, medicines vary in price according to their rarity. A physician or healer, depending on where he lives, will have put much personal cost into obtaining them. The current policy of taxing these precious resources makes many too expensive for people to use and physicians to dispense."

"With all due respect," Timothy of Ridgeland said, "is this not something a man in the position ought to address?"

"Her Highness," Daniel said, "and Her Highness's matron of honor are experienced, indeed renowned in the field—"

"Yes, yes, Cecile," Timothy said with a wave, "but come now. Let us not make council into some plaything for the—"

"It will not go well with you to finish that sentence," William said. Silence followed.

Anna frowned down at her hands. This was not going to be as easy as defending a falsely accused mason.

Robert cleared his throat. "Are there not apothecaries whose very business is obtaining these to dispense amongst the population, Your Majesty?" he said, addressing her. "Should not that cost be built into their business already? Surely you are not suggesting we simply not tax?"

Was he trying to make her sound like a fool? She pursed her lips at him. "No, Your Grace, but kindly let me explain. Many who have no access to apothecaries depend upon their local healers and physicians. Some people travel miles on foot for items others could pick in their own gardens. Mistress Mary and I have traveled days to find medicines and bring relief to those stranded."

The men glanced about the table at each other.

"So what is being suggested?" Robert said, looking at Daniel.

"I suggest we not tax medicine—" Anna started.

181

"Ridiculous!" and other one-word negatives erupted from the table. William frowned at them. She raised her voice to be heard over the fray.

"Services rendered should be taxed, like all others, but not the medicine." The men quieted to only grumbles now. "It encumbers the practice of healing and is detrimental to the health of our people. Besides which, there is no way to keep track of all the home gardens that grow simple things like peppermint, which can be used for food or medicine."

"Very true," Halforn said. She could have run over and kissed his balding head. "It does seem wrong to deny help in time of need because of cost or location, especially when others may receive it so easily."

"And," Daniel said, "if our people know their king is for them and not against them, it will do much to stabilize the realm."

"Thank you, Cecile," she said, "my point exactly. If we—"

"Excuse me, Highness, Your Grace," the archbishop said, "but 'tis the church who dispenses many of these medicines."

"Of course, Eminence," the king said, "no one takes issue with the church's ministry."

"And yet 'tis the church who receives the funds from this tax in particular—as well as the crown. Unlike physicians, we are unable to charge a fee for our services, and these medicines, as Her Majesty says, are dear in cost."

"I never charged a fee either, Eminence," Anna said, "and yet I managed to keep our castle and duchy healthy. The church, I daresay, is much better positioned."

"Majesty," he said, refusing to even look at her, "with all due respect, I believe I can better speak to the positioning of the church."

"How have you managed in the past?" the king said.

"Well, sire," he said, "we manage. But of course we could do more, with more funds."

"I don't doubt it," the king said. "In fact, we believe that is always the case." A few councilors chuckled.

"My lady," the archbishop said, rising to finally address her directly. "I understand you read the Holy Scriptures to your ladies each day." He looked down is nose at her like a tutor. "So uncommon for a woman—yet perhaps they will remind you that 'tis our duty— the church's duty—to care for the poor."

"I do not begrudge the church their tithe," she said, leaning forward in her throne, "but I daresay creating a cycle of servitude by taxing already poor congregants is not what our Lord meant when He said the poor shall always be with us."

"We are called to servitude—we must carry Christ's cross."

"And yet," she said, "we are admonished in St. Matthew twenty-five that the Lord will not know us if we refuse to help the weak. By this teaching, we are not allowed to let the responsibility of care fall solely to the church."

Bartmore flushed a deep red. "I hardly think I need a lesson in theology from a woman, sovereign or no—"

"That's enough," William said.

"Majesty." Bartmore turned to the king with a forced smile. "We are not here to debate the Scriptures. The queen has had her fun— now let us get down to business."

"Your Eminence," William said, "'tis you who brought Scripture into the business we have been discussing."

Uncomfortable chuckles, guarded glances, and unmistakable tension rose from around the table.

"We believe the queen has a valid point," William continued. Bartmore sat back down with a huff. "We also believe the Lord called all men to love his neighbor as himself, not to simply have the church love his neighbor in his stead." He glanced at Anna, whose heart froze for a moment. It was a jab, albeit a very subtle one, at the practice of indulgences, one of Luther's chief complaints.

She caught Robert's flicker of a smile.

"And in light of that," the king said, "we agree with Cecile and Her Majesty. We shall not tax medicinals." A few grunts of protest rumbled about. "Yet we shall not ignore the church—should an urgent and specific need arise, we will find funds even if our own person be inconvenienced."

With that, he took Anna's hand in his and gave a nod to the men.

"The matter is settled. I believe a bit of sunshine is called for, my lords. Her Majesty and I find the air in here stagnant."

* * *

"How dare she?" Bartmore said as Robert gathered up his papers to join the foray into the gardens. "How dare the king?"

Robert sighed. The man was not a thorn in William's side only. "The king shall do as is his pleasure, Your Eminence, and his pleasure did not turn toward you today."

"When does it ever?" The archbishop slapped his papers into the arms of his page. "Methinks the king takes his pleasure elsewhere a bit too much of late. And with no results."

"Bartmore, methinks any pleasure a man takes with a woman is too much according to your lights. Yet the lack of results, as you say, be all the more reason for his pleasure-taking."

The archbishop glared at him. "I have been offended enough for one day, sir! Remember, 'twas I who found the king's father with a knife in his back, from all his pleasure. This king would do well to remember the sins of that father."

Robert grabbed Bartmore's arm and thrust his face right up to the churchman's nose. "Are you threatening the king?"

Bartmore jerked free. "Nay, I merely fear the queen will be his downfall. As King Solomon says, 'A virtuous woman is a crown to her husband: but she that maketh him ashamed is as rottenness in his bones.'"

CHAPTER 10

Fraternization & Foolishness

Anna was beginning to regret her insistence on being part of Council Table. While she did not attend each of the near-daily meetings, she quickly came to see why William disdained them so. The wheels of government turned slowly, thanks to thick skulls lodged in the gears.

For diversion, she thought of the delayed wedding tour, now scheduled to happen in a fortnight. She'd never been far from Beaubourg and was eager to see the south, though she desperately missed home. She was stirred from her daydreams by the entrance of Bernard, who did his customary jig of a bow to the king.

William waved him over to Anna.

"Majesty," he whispered, "you wished me to inform you when the Lady Jane's time had come."

Anna shot out of her chair to the startled looks of the few councilors still left that day, made a hasty curtsy to an amused William, and half-dragged Bernard through the doors, and into the throne room. Once there she grabbed his arm.

"How long has it been?" she said.

"I just received word, Majesty."

"Then let us make haste. Send to the laundress for my stores of sheets—Lady Jane shouldn't have to dirty her own. And send Brigitte to find my old linen gown."

"You cannot mean to attend upon her yourself, Majesty?"

Anna clucked her tongue at him as she continued down the hall to her chambers. He trotted behind her. "Majesty, 'tis beneath thy dignity! Good heavens—"

"Mary!" she called.

Mary was already dressed down, a box of tinctures under her arm. "I'm just waiting for a few more things from the kitchens, Highness."

"Good. I'll need my linen gown as well."

Mary let out a heavy sigh. "I thought if I could get away before you came—"

"Nonsense! I would move heaven and earth to help Lady Jane at her birth. Decorum be damned." This last she addressed to Bernard, who stood scowling in the doorway.

"If Majesty is obliged," Yvette said with a bow, "I would attend with you."

"By all means, Lady Yvette," Anna said, "we could use more hands. Lady Margaux, who is the best midwife about? Who attends the ladies at court?"

Margaux had a peculiar smile on her face. "Why, I can hardly—"

"The best midwife in Havenside," Yvette said, "doesn't attend the ladies at court."

"Why ever not?" Anna said as she shed her voluminous silks.

"Mistress Rebekah?" Margaux said. "She's a Jewess." She glanced from Yvette to Anna. "Hardly better than a heretic."

"Send for her."

"As you wish, Majesty," Margaux said. Under her breath she added, "but don't say I didn't warn you."

* * *

"Majesty, you came!" Little Lady Jane sat enthroned in pillows, her bottom hanging off her bed, legs on the arms of the birthing chair, tendrils of her hair stuck to her reddened face. She let out a loud groan.

"Excuse me, Highness, I—"

Anna rushed to her, grabbed her hand, and squeezed it. "Jane, I'm not Your Highness now. In the birthing room, you are queen." Jane gave a weak smile. "I mean it, Jane, no demurring for my benefit. We're here to keep you and your babe healthy—nothing more, nothing less."

The other maids and nurses made a wide berth for Anna's party. And as Rebekah the midwife entered the room, several other ladies took their leave.

"Good riddance," Yvette said.

"Come along," Mary said with only a moment's hesitation. Neither she nor Anna had ever seen a Jew before. She was short, lithe, and carried herself like a courtier.

Jane flinched as Mary reached inside her. "This one's coming fast," Mary said with a frown.

"My lady," Rebekah said, "is this is your first birth?" Jane nodded then let out a loud moan. Rebekah turned to Mary. "Strange then, that the babe be coming so quickly."

"Aye, mistress," Mary said. "We'd best massage her to avoid a tear."

Rebekah nodded and opened her own store of tinctures, pulling out a yellow-hued oil. From then on, the two midwives worked and murmured together as though they'd known one another their lives entire.

Anna gave Jane an encouraging smile and rubbed her shoulders. "It won't be long, dear Jane. It may be hard, but you have a stout, strong heart. And you have the best in the land to help you."

Jane nodded, then arched and yowled at another contraction. Anna pulled Yvette aside to prepare a draught.

"Now I recall why you weren't so eager for the king's bed," Yvette whispered.

Anna let out a quiet snort. "And for nothing so far, it seems." She blushed. "Though 'tis certainly not for lack of trying."

"Worry not, Majesty—it's only been two months." Yvette considered Anna for a moment. "The position I taught you, when you feel particularly amorous of the king, make sure and—"

A scream to shatter glass cut her off.

"Anna!" Mary yelled.

* * *

William sat in his hearth chair, a cool glass of mead balanced on his chest, fingers drumming.

The little wooden door by his bed creaked. He glanced up to see the sheepish face of his bride peeping at him. He pursed his lips to try and hide his smile. She tiptoed in, her high cheeks rosy, face glowing.

"Apparently," she said, with a little curtsy just beyond the door, "I'm to seek your forgiveness and accept your censure."

He took his feet from the chest and placed his drink down with a deliberate plunk. "Oh?"

"Yes, Majesty." She bit her lip.

He got up, adjusted his trunks, and leaned on the hearth. "Because you helped bring about the safe and blessed delivery of another bouncing baby boy of Troixden?"

A wide grin broke on her face. "It wasn't just me."

He went to her, lifted her up in his arms and kissed her. "What am I going to do with you?"

He put her down and she moved her hands up his chest to hang on his neck. "You always think of something."

He let out a laugh and patted her perfect bottom. "I won't say it didn't raise a few eyebrows—Her Royal Highness, midwifing for one of her own ladies-in-waiting. And with a Jewess, no less." He led her back to his chair, easing her into his lap.

"I'm sure that's an understatement," she said.

"Anyone that matters thinks the better of you for it."

"Ah, so no one at court, then."

"I wouldn't say no one. There's me, after all, and I daresay my opinion should hold some weight."

"All the weight in the world, O king." She kissed him, tickling the hair at the back of his neck with her fingers.

"Are you trying to distract me from telling you how uncouth you've been?"

"Not trying," she said, mouth on his earlobe.

He slid his hands down her back. "You'd do a better job of it if you didn't always come to me in all these prohibitive outfits."

She got up and thrust out a hand to him, eyes alight. "Come then, my liege. Teach me a lesson."

* * *

The king and queen sat enthroned on the dais of the Great Hall, their ladies and chambermen flanking them down the steps, all turned out in silks of gold and cream for the harvest festival. The queen held a large bouquet of wheat across her lap. She pursed her lips as each region's representatives entered. William could tell she was looking for someone—her father, surely.

A long table behind the throne was already dripping with gifts representing each region of the realm. Giant pies of smoked boar and delicate, woven tapestries from the midlands; lavender honey, berry wine, and delicate sweetbreads from the southeast; smoked fish and a ten-prong elk from the southwest. As each group of five made its way through the crowded court, Archbishop Bartmore anointed them with oil and prayed to God for a bountiful harvest, after which William blessed them and invited them to stay for the feast that would be prepared from the gifts.

The royal cooks hated the festival. Each region seemed bent on outdoing its neighbor in creativity. It was a tall order to come up with a meal, let alone one that was palatable, from all the queer concoctions people brought. Luckily, the people seemed to have tempered themselves somewhat this year.

William's stomach clenched from hunger and nerves. Mercifully, there were only two more regions to bless. "Representing the northeast: His Grace the Earl of Laureland; the Lady Helena; Mr. George

Strauss, blacksmith; Mr. Bartholomew Witt, butcher; and Mr. Jonathan Beark, printer."

A murmur passed through the crowd as the delegation from Laureland approached the throne. William saw Annelore look at him sidelong. Thank God he'd listened to Daniel and not married Helena. He reached out to take the queen's hand but stopped mid-squeeze.

The earl walked in, head high, the partially veiled Helena behind him. The three other men carried their gift between them: a long gold box looking every bit like a child's casket. The little party gingerly laid the box at the feet of the dais with a soft thud and knelt to receive oil and blessing.

"Majesty," the earl said, rising and doffing his feathered hat, "we humbly present ourselves for your blessing in all we set to."

The three men opened the box to reveal a broadsword, hilt of gold and leather, fat blade of iron. While too big to be used in battle, it was not embellished as a sword of ceremony. This was a not-so-subtle hint to show him they were ready to come against the throne if need be.

He heard angry gasps and heated whispers from the crowd swirling around him. He saw Robert's hand come to rest on the hilt of his own sword. All eyes, anxious, were upon the king. How would he react to the gift at his feet?

"Exquisite handiwork," he said. He looked to the blacksmith. "Is this your doing, Herr Strauss?"

The brawny tradesman startled at being so addressed. His hands clenched at his sides, but he looked straight at William.

"Yes, Majesty," he said, voice scratched and tinged with a guttural German accent. Seeming to remember his place, he gave a little bow.

"It's the finest workmanship we've seen—even better than that of our neighbors to the east," William said. "A true honor, sir."

Strauss's face turned red and he bowed again.

"As fine a gift as this is, though," he looked now to the earl, "we must admit we were dearly hoping for some of Laureland's famed sausages."

A titter ran through the court.

"Yes, Majesty," the earl said, faced pinched. "We have already left them with the palace cooks, for they are in delicate condition."

The rotund little butcher dabbed his forehead with a hand-kerchief.

"What a perfect gift, then," William said with a broad smile. "Sausages and a knife to cut them with." Now the court erupted in laughter, all save the frowning earl. "And you even brought a printer to help circulate the tale. You've thought of everything, Your Grace."

William saw Annelore smile down at her bundle of wheat. Catching the eye of Helena, he nodded her forward, rose, and descended the dais to take her hand.

"Dear lady," he said, "we hope you know what a pleasant and peaceful time we had under your hospitality in June."

She curtsied. "Thank you, Your Majesty."

"It shall be my pleasure to finally find you a match worthy of your gentle heart, for we fear ours is too calloused for your sweet hands."

He could see the tops of her cheeks redden.

"And I, Majesty," she said, barely above a whisper, "am pleased to hear that the queen has brought you much joy."

"News travels fast." He kissed Helena's hand and led her to the queen. "May we present Her Royal Highness, Queen Annelore."

Helena bowed low. The queen worked free a sprig of wheat and extended it to her. "My lady, may you and your peoples be blessed," she said.

William handed Helena back to her father and walked to his throne, stopping to whisper in his queen's ear. "Well done, my dear."

"And you."

"Representing the northwest!" the caller shouted. Annelore sat up straighter. "His Grace, Duke Stephen of Beaubourg."

A fresh buzz whipped through the crowd.

The queen's father wore a smile to break stones and had eyes for none but Annelore, and she for none but him. William's stomach uncoiled. Thank God the duke was alone.

"Majesties." The duke swept his arms wide in a bow. "My peoples have already given and had blessed the highest treasure we possess. But we would be remiss not to bring some trifles both Your Majesties may appreciate."

He swung his arm toward the entry, and in trotted a snow-white filly followed by a dappled gray stallion. The crowd responded with gasps and applause.

"'Tis not fair, Your Grace, for you know our hearts too well," William said. The duke gave a bow of a nod.

"Shall I, ah, anoint the beasts, Majesty?" the archbishop said.

A bout of laughter erupted and the presentations thus ended as they should have, in merriment. Leave it to the Duke of Beaubourg to help William get exactly what he needed. Again.

* * *

The next morning broke bright and clear, a perfect day for the picnic and ride the king had planned. Anna near gulped her breakfast in anticipation. Her favorite horse Bess to ride again and the entire day to spend with William—there was almost nothing better.

Her mind turned to Bryan's queer note. My gift shall aid and comfort you. Certainly her reunion with her horse would comfort her, but aid her? And surely her father had no part in Bryan's schemes.

Her troubling thoughts left her when she turned into the stable yard and beheld William, dashing in his riding clothes, a jaunty grin on his face. She all but skipped to him. He swung her once around in his arms and gave her a chaste kiss.

"I can't believe my father gave you Fitzsimmons!" she said. "It's his favorite dappled gray." William kissed her hand. "Come, my dear." He drew her next to Bess, ready to help her mount.

"Just a moment, Highness," she said. She removed her riding glove and stretched out her hand to stroke the mare's cloud-white neck, in return for which she got a shiver of pleasure and a happy whinny. "Oh Bess, I've missed you too."

She nuzzled her face into the filly's neck. Reaching up to scratch Bess's ears, her sleeve caught on something attached to the bridle, dangling behind a purple tassel. It was a little leather pouch.

"And what's this?" She glanced at William, who looked puzzled. Her smile faded. "You didn't put this here?" He shook his head, frowning, and came to her side. She handed the pouch to him. "It must be from father." But even as she said it, she knew.

William opened the pouch and dug out a note and a gold ring set with a small sapphire. His frown deepened.

"My love," he read, "when you ride out on Bess, wear my mother's ring." He looked up at her, eyes hard. "I shall see and know, and come for you. – B."

Anna's face went white. William, staring at her, raised his hand in the air. "Leave us," he said. "And take the horses." The stable hands melted away with their charges.

William closed in on her. "Do you think I'm an idiot?"

"William — "

"Do not address me so familiar now."

"You think me so low and foul and false as to be plotting all this time?"

He didn't move, his eyes still scorching her. "I . . . you claim to know nothing of this?"

"Claim? You must think me an idiot, *Your Highness*, for only an idiot would hand her husband her supposed lover's declarations without a second thought!"

William looked down at his feet. "You have a point."

"I have more than just a point." She took a step forward and grabbed his arm. "I am in just as much ignorance as you."

He watched her face for a long moment. Then clasped her to him, holding her as if clinging to life itself. "God damn that knave! How in the hell could he know we ride out today?"

"I have no idea," she said, "but he can't think I would just run off with him."

"I'll have the guards search our route." William drew her back, taking her face in his hands. "You keep saying he's harmless. But my dear, nothing I've yet seen of him has proved him so."

She wanted to come to Bryan's defense — to assure William that her childhood friend would never do anything so foolish. Her throat tightened.

"I'm beginning to think you're right," she said.

* * *

"It was a flat-out declaration of war," the grand master general said. "Presenting Your Highness with a sword—they could not have been more obvious if they arrived with a battalion of armed men!"

"And a butcher to boot," Gregory of Duven said, "as if they needed to spell it out any further."

William gave a grim smile to his gathered men. "Spelling things out was the printer's job, no?"

"Indeed," Robert said, giving a little snort and rubbing his goatee. "They did a fine job of making their feelings plain."

"I believe," Halforn said, "Your Majesty did a fine job rebuking them. You certainly made them look the fool—killing them with kindness."

"Maybe a bit too kind," Robert said under his breath. William shot him a look that paled his cousin's face.

"Do you call us coward, cuz?"

Robert took a moment to answer. "Majesty, you know I only wish to protect your person and the realm. And usurpers must be dealt with."

"There is more than one way to handle usurpers," Daniel said. "The sword being one, artful diplomacy another."

"We've tried diplomacy," the general said. "Obviously it's failed."

"Hear, hear," Timothy of Ridgeland said. "And I'm as convinced now as I ever was, this Sir Bryan is in league with the Laurelanders, ready to kidnap the queen for their cause. We must to arms."

William had sent Bryan's ring back in its leather pouch, closed to dripping with the king's royal seal. And the queen had written him a letter telling him to clear off, then sent a separate note to her father asking him to speak with the boy.

"The knave acts alone—we are convinced of it," William said, leaning back in his chair. "He's a separate threat, one much more easily dispatched."

"How can you be so sure," Ridgeland said, "begging Your Majesty's pardon?"

"The queen believes it and so do we," William said. "That is the end of it, Your Grace."

Ridgeland frowned and flicked his eyes to Robert, who in turn gave a slight shake of his head.

"Be that as it may, sire," the general said, "Laureland must be taught a lesson."

"We shall not teach it to them in blood." William slammed the table with his fist. "The last thing our people need is another warmongering tyrant. Then they shall have not just a reason, but a right, to revolt."

"But when they threaten ye outright, sire!" the general said, face blotchy.

"Their gifts were indeed inflammatory," William said, "but they have not taken to arms. And even if they plan to do so, we are heading into harvest. They would not fight until next year's thaw. More than enough time to ease their minds and ours."

"We stake a great deal on these crazed northmen seeing sense, Majesty," the general said.

"Nay," William said, "we stake much on our powers of persuasion. And if that fails, then we shall seek a remedy. Do not misunderstand us: if they take up arms, so shall we."

* * *

A week later William flung open the doors of the queen's chamber to find her seated at the window opened wide to the warm September breeze and an occasional fat bumblebee.

"My lady?"

"Majesty," she said, rising for a curtsy. She looked like the stamen of an iris, standing there in bright yellow brocade, surrounded by the folding petals of her ladies. "Whatever is the matter?"

"That's what I'm here to ask you," he said, perplexed.

"Why, Highness," she said, placing her sewing aside, "nothing at all is the matter."

"But you sent for me in haste," he said. "And thus I have come, leaving council in the midst of a briefing on, well, the price of bacon to be precise."

"A most pressing issue indeed," she said. "But Highness, I did not send for you."

The king snapped his fingers to one of her ushers, who stepped forward at once and knelt. "Repeat what you said to me, sir."

The young steward quaked. "Majesty, I said the queen would like a private audience to discuss a matter of grave import."

William swept his arms out and raised his brows.

"Sire, I did not mean immediately—simply at some point in your schedule." She shook her head at the usher. "And I do not believe I said 'grave import.'"

William relaxed and took her hands, kissing them each in turn. "So you are not in duress? You gave me a fright, my dear. In the future, send Bernard. He's far more seasoned in these details."

"I'm sorry to have alarmed you," she said. "Please, don't hesitate to return to your pork."

"The men or the bacon?"

"Take your pick, sire." She walked to the nearest window, leaning out to inhale the thick air.

"Well . . ." He came up behind and embraced her about the waist, resting his chin on her shoulder. "Since I've already left and the subject only makes me hungry, perhaps we should have that audience after all, hmm?"

He nibbled on her neck, but she turned in his arms to face him. "Be forewarned, sire—I did actually mean to speak with you."

"If it's of more interest than pig parts, I'm all ears." He turned from the window. "Ladies, gentlemen, please amuse yourselves elsewhere. For the queen and I have grave matters to discuss."

As their entourages took their leave, he helped himself to a drink and settled himself on the window seat. He took off his chain and jacket and loosened the neck of his shirt, catching the breeze.

"How can I be of service, my lady?" he said, head against the frame, a rivulet of sweat rolling down his neck. She sat opposite, picked up one of his feet, removed his boot, and proceeded to expertly knead.

"Lord, you'll put me right to sleep, wife," he said. Half closing his eyes, he wiggled his foot to encourage her not to stop.

"I've been thinking," she said.

He lifted a finger. "'Tis a dangerous pastime."

"William, don't tease—I'm trying to be serious."

"I shan't interrupt if you shan't interrupt the work of your hands."

"It's Robert." She moved her knuckles up the spine of his foot. "He just . . . it seems to me that he hasn't your best interests at heart."

William gave a grunt. "I know you've not had the best introduction to him, but he has never strayed in his fealty to me, even as a child."

"But he's no longer a child. And he has something up his sleeve."

William thought for a moment, then exhaled. "'Tis the lot of kings to be surrounded by people with agendas."

"But Margaux said—"

"Margaux?" He sat up, taking her hands in his. "Margaux is about as trustworthy as the serpent in Eden. And less shrewd."

Annelore looked down at their interlocked hands and began to stroke his. "I just don't know what I would do if . . . well, if something were to happen to you."

He lifted her hand to his mouth, kissed it, then closed his fingers over it again.

"If anything happens, it won't be at the hands of Robert. But it does my heart good to hear you worry for me, my dear."

"You're sure? Because his sister insists—"

"Your trusting heart is but one of the reasons you are so dear to me, but you must remember that not everyone looks out for your best interests. A queen is no different from a king in that respect."

Her face clouded and she took a moment to choose her words. "I hope you know I have absolutely no agenda, no ambitions, beyond your company."

"That's one of the things I take most solace in."

"I want us to be William and Anna to each other," she said, "not King William the Just and his Queen Annelore of Beaubourg."

"William the Just, am I?"

She threw up her hands. "I don't know what they call ye, William —I made it up. 'Tis beside the point."

He got up from his seat, pulling her up and close to his chest. "I don't mean to tease, Annelore. Or is it Anna now?"

"It is," she said.

"Then you won't ply your arts to bend me to your will, like my fair cousins?"

"I couldn't be false with you if I tried," she said. "Just know, when you need a place to take off your mantle I shall be that place for you. I'll never betray your trust. As I know you won't betray mine."

"Mercy, Anna," he said, "you knock me clean out of my boots."

He drew her face to his and kissed her deeply. Stooping down, not loosing her lips, he lifted her into his arms. He laid her on the bed—then stopped, struck.

"We must celebrate!"

She sat up on her elbows with an exaggerated pout. "I thought that's what we were about to do."

"Nay, I mean, we must go on our wedding journey." He felt like a child stealing sweets from the kitchen.

"We're to go to the south coast in a week, are we not?" she said.

"Yes, but let's leave now. And let's go to Beaubourg."

"Truly?" She bounded out of bed. "Nothing would give me more pleasure!"

Oh, the look on her face—priceless. And the trip would be perfect. His scouts could nose about this knight and make sure he was sedate, and he could make sure the Laurelanders' ill sport hadn't traveled to the west. And Anna could see her home, her father.

"But what of our scheduled tour?" she said. "Surely people will be disappointed?"

"They'll get over it, and we shall go soon enough." He grinned at her. "I say we go to Beaubourg in secret, surprise your father. Take only a few attendants. Leave the rest of court to their own devices."

Anna jumped to his arms. He swung her around, feet off the ground, dancing on air. "You wonderful, wonderful man," she said, running her fingers through his cowlicks.

"I told you I was at your service. Now," he said, bringing her back to earth, "as much as it pains me to say this, my just-Anna, we must part, for there is much to be done before the morrow."

* * *

After the minimal royal entourage was settled within the Castle Beaubourg's walls, well fed and merry at their homey reception, the king dismissed all to bed and he, his queen, and her father sat in high-back, tapestried chairs before an enormous fire, sipping castle-made spiced cider.

"Your Grace," William said, "I see again why Her Majesty was reluctant to leave this place."

The duke nodded and smiled at the king. "Although it cannot compare to the splendor of court, Majesty. I had said as much to our lady in encouragement for her to attend upon thee."

"I am sitting right here," Anna said, wrinkling her nose at them. The king squeezed her hand and drew it to his lips. "My dear, you aren't so soon forgotten."

The duke touched his hand to his heart. "To me, you are here even when gone. My, how you have changed, even in these few months. Your mother would be so proud to see you thus."

"The queen tells me stories of the late duchess, may she rest in peace," William said. "To hear her tell it, you and she are the stuff of legends. Eyes meeting across the church at King James's baptism, a hasty flight back to Beaubourg . . ."

The duke chuckled. "I was so afraid your father wouldn't allow the match, begging your pardon, sire."

"Oh, I'm sure my father was in a right fine mood to allow such a woman to pass out of his grasp," William said. "You're a lucky man,

Your Grace, to have loved two of the finest women Troixden has known."

"And you as well, Majesty."

Anna got up, stretched her arms and yawned. "If you two are to spend the evening swooning about your women, then this lady shall take her leave, else she nod off in your noble midst."

Both men rose. She gave her father a kiss on the forehead and smiled upon him. "'Tis truly made my joy complete, being here and seeing you, Papa."

"'Tis truly made my joy complete," he said, "to hear you say you've joy in your present circumstances."

"Well," she turned to William with a wry smile, "just look at the man."

William laughed, his deep bellow echoing off the castle walls so the hall itself joined in his mirth. "She only likes me for my teeth, Your Grace."

Leaving her father she sauntered to William, entwining him about the neck. "And they're such very fine teeth, Majesty."

"Shall I escort milady to her chamber?" he said, voice lowered.

"Thank you, my liege," she said, brushing her lips on his whiskers, "but as I've lived here my life entire, I do believe I can manage."

"You're all sass tonight." He kissed her well, but not so well as to risk making her father uncomfortable.

"Good night, sweet king." She made a little curtsy and left the two men who loved her best to end the night together.

* * *

"When can we be alone?" William whispered in Anna's ear, his stubble rubbing her cheek. He'd caught her by the waist after the following morning's chapel, pulling her into an empty hallway, the rest of their retinue trailing into her father's hall for breakfast.

"It took all the strength within me to pass by your chamber and into mine own last night." He drew his lips down her jaw line and back again, his hands traveling up her bodice. She made a little grunt of pleasure, heart racing.

"Wills," she whispered, nervously glancing past his head. "I must admit my discomfort in taking our pleasure under my father's roof."

He drew back from her, hands caging her ribs, frowning. "Seriously?"

"Queen or no, I'm still his little girl."

"And I'm his king and you're my wife," William eyed her hungrily. "Would he not be proud to know his grandson was conceived in his own castle?"

"No man wishes to think of his daughter doing what's required to get with a grandson."

"Anna, do you truly expect me not to take liberties on our own wedding tour?"

She spotted Daniel, who guided Halforn away by pointing out a fine tapestry on the opposite wall. She looked back at the king, shook her head. She sighed and roped her arms around his waist, pulling him back to her. "Wait until after breakfast. I know the perfect place."

"We're to see the duke's lands after breakfast," he said, almost pouting.

"Worry not," She grabbed his chin in thumb and forefinger and brought his face close to hers. "For they're my lands too."

* * *

"I told you 'twas perfect," Anna said, smiling with self-satisfaction, king and queen's horses nibbling the last of the summer's green that edged the wide meadow.

They had ridden about the duke's lands with Daniel, Halforn, and her father in tow, admiring the varied topography of the acreage. As the rest of the party made ready for a picnic under the willow by the creek, Anna led William away, back to the western forest, guards following at a respectful distance, finally arriving at this meadow, surrounded by a stand of magnificent old trees at the edge of a bluff, offering the privacy she wanted.

"Remind me not to doubt you," William said, swinging off his cloak and spreading it on the ground.

He strode back to Anna and took her hand, then called for his manservant to lay out their own picnic. He leaned to her ear, his breath tickling and sweet. "Though I'm not sure if eating actual food is front of mind for me." He nipped her earlobe sending a thrill of anticipation winging through her body.

Instantly back to kingly comportment, he thanked his man with a hearty handshake and a question about the health of his young boy, who, apparently, was a strapping, lively lad.

"May it always be," William said, sending the man on his way. Anna marveled at how nimbly he could change his demeanor, how easy he made it seem to one second be sending her delicates aflame, and the next, genuinely interested in the welfare of this man's child. He was a marvel. And when he turned to her with that predatory grin of his, she wondered how she ever thought she could resist him, or why she would ever want to.

He stood next to his cloak, raking her with his eyes, hands on those narrow, deadly hips of his, grin growing. He didn't need to speak. She knew what he wanted. Her.

The delicious thrum that raced in her veins sent her too him. But she liked to tease just as much as he did. She stopped a foot above him on the sloping grass. She mirrored his stance, arms akimbo, and cocked her head. "I like this. Being as tall as you."

His eyes continued to rove her. "So you can boss me about?"

"I didn't think of that, but yes." She stuck out a forefinger and stabbed him in the sternum, making him rock ever so slightly. Smiling, she said, "'Tis quite nice to send you back on your heels."

He grabbed her finger. "My queen, you do that just walking into a room." He took her finger to his mouth, his lips curling around it, his tongue flicking the tip. Unheeded, her eyes rolled back, her breath caught.

"What I meant to say," she said when she regained consciousness, "was that I like looking you straight in the eyes." And she did so, holding them, falling into their blue depths, flecks of robin's egg and ocean winking at her in the sun.

He did not avert his gaze when he said, "I know a better way of accomplishing that goal." He closed the distance between them clasping her to him, her breasts pushed up and aching, his desire clear against her upper thigh, even through her skirts. "But it involves you in a very different position."

He bent slowly to her neck and inhaled, his lips so close her skin sparked with anticipation. He hummed deep in his throat. "Rosemary. Today you smell of rosemary and lavender." She couldn't help but go slack in his arms at his worshipful tone, and when he finally, tenderly pressed his lips to her neck, she moaned. He nuzzled her and whispered, "turn around."

Quite willing to oblige, she twisted beneath his splayed fingers, trying, and failing, to calm her breath, her speeding heart. This man did things to her she never imagined all those late nights in her girlhood bed, wondering what drew two people together, wondering why, when she touched her most tender places she wouldn't see Bryan, but rather some faceless, powerful man covering her with his body, showering her with kisses.

But those imagined kisses were nothing like this, nothing like the carnal, sumptuous, slow devouring William did to her. How her body reacted now, alert to every minuscule movement, the sigh of his breath across the back of her neck as he swept her hair aside, the nimble flicks and pulls of his fingers as he undid her laces, the way his lips lingered at her nape with every freed length of silk. She simply had not known such pleasure existed to be able to fantasize about it.

"I've been pondering all morning how I might take you today," he said, leaning in again to whisper in her ear.

Take you. Lord, she was undone with that phrase alone. Her heart thrummed and she swallowed. "Is that so?" she managed to squeak out.

"Mmmm." He slipped off her bodice and sleeves, but not before generously sucking on each shoulder. "It's been so long —"

"It's been something like eighteen hours," she said, surprised she could formulate words let alone calculate time.

"What I did to you in the carriage on the way up here doesn't count." He went to work on her skirts, untying the various cinches, letting each layer fall to the earth. "I'll admit, most of the time I was nodding to this morning's conversations I was in truth nodding my assent to the visions I had of you in my head. Say, a hay loft, or some absent courtier's room, or up against the side castle wall . . ."

He trailed off as he trailed his hands down the length of her legs, taking her stockings with him, stopping at her boots. The heat that shot to her groin with him crouched below her could start a grass fire. She swayed, but somehow kept upright.

"All of these were fast and sweaty, yet all the more enjoyable due to their speed and clandestine nature." He spoke of his conquerings as if he were reviewing court for the day, with absolutely no heed to how his words were rousing her, pummeling her as he'd wished to do to her body. She whimpered, he chuckled.

Finished with his task, he smoothed his hands back up her legs, his body unfurling behind her. His fingertips caressed the sides of her breasts, sending her nipples to points as he continued up to her shift. "But being in this peaceful, beautiful place . . ." Gliding his warm, rough hands from her shoulders to the top of her breasts, he untangled the last of her ribbons, the one holding her silk shift. "I thought it would be a travesty"—as on her wedding night, he pulled her shift down, and, hands at her hips, he turned her to face him and he took a step back, feasting upon her with his eyes—"to waste this view."

Despite all the pleasures they'd taken together, this wonder he had in her still made her blush. She made to move to him but he stilled her with a shake of his head. "Please," he said, almost to himself. "Please, just let me look."

She closed her eyes, took a cleansing breath of sea-salted air, straightened her back and watched him watch her. She noted where he lingered, each part singing with the focused attention: the curve of her left hip, the sharp tip of her right nipple, the shadow of her left breast, the dips of her clavicle and belly button, her mound of soft hair below. Her fingers, her neck, her lips, and eventually back again to her eyes.

He brought his hands to his trunks, unbuckling them. "I'm just noting every place I want to taste you." Her eyes widened, mouth parted in a gasp, flesh aching for him to live up to his word.

But now it was her turn to watch him. How the muscles of his back strained through his white shirt as he yanked off his boots, how his brows furrowed as he worked his trunks and hose over his knees, the way his stomach flexed when he pulled his shirt over his head, his sex uncovered and well ahead of his desired pace. She took him in, this hardened, slightly bronzed, mountain of a man, and shook her head in continued disbelief of his existence, let alone the fact he was hers and hers alone. And she understood what he meant about going slowly, for she too wanted to worship every inch of him — wanted to trip her fingers over his arms, sup her way down his back, rub her chest against his, feel the sparse hairs at his nipples tickle her own, to kiss him from tip to tail.

He took a step toward her then fell to his knees. Cupping her hips, he drew her to him, his tongue lazy on her inner thigh as she gripped his hair as much in pleasure as for balance.

"And you taste," he said between licks, "inexplicably of oranges and sugar." He paused, then lashed her folds with the precision of a portrait painter.

"Ah, God, Wills—" She threw her head back, digging her fingers further in his hair. He nosed his way up her front, hands in his wake, seeking, stroking. "I can't—" But he stopped her desperate protests with his mouth as he scooped her up.

Lying her gently on his cloak, careful not to splay her on the cold roast, he feasted on her. Cupping her breasts in both hands he molded them, sucked them, rubbed his stubbled cheeks against them, sending soft groans tripping out of her. She was deaf and blind to all but the tumbling sensations of his generous attentions.

Every now and again his cock would brush against her thigh, her hip, her stomach, and her body clenched wanting him. He meandered his way with his mouth, swirling around her stomach, down to her groin, blowing on her hairs and soft folds, his breeze cooling her wet heat, sending shivers up her spine.

He bent to her, humming to himself, then latched on to her feminine lips. "I could gorge on you for hours," he said with a wide lap of his tongue. Her only reply was to press her hips into him, forcing him back to his delicate, skilled business. She managed a glance down, through her breasts, over her belly, and caught him staring up at her, tongue never ceasing. His eyes slashed into her skull, his desire bursting from them, pinning her in place. Then they crinkled at the edges and she could feel his smile in her crotch as he pinpointed her nub and churned it like butter. She screamed, birds alighted, her thighs clamped around his ears, her torso mindlessly jerking up and down as the lightning of her orgasm shot through her body and out the top of her spine. Senseless and yet awakened to every cell as they crackled under and over her skin.

Finally opening her eyes, she saw he'd sat up, her legs spread around him, his cock hard in his hand. He grinned at her. "Oh I'm not finished with you just yet."

She was too weak to reply. Pulling her hips up his thighs, he rubbed himself through her wetness, sending her into mild convulsions again, making her whimper with renewed want. How could he do this to her? Where did he learn this? She immediately wiped that question from her mind. She didn't want to know. She preferred to pretend he just came about it naturally, like his wit and charm and jawline.

He drew her into him, his length gliding inside, filling her with that familiar aching stretch. She wanted him to stay like that forever. Enveloped in her, physically, mentally, longed to see him yearning for this, for her, always. Becoming one, together. But as he stroked in and out, his rhythm building, features furrowing, she could focus only on how every thrust drove her higher and higher, that delicious wave coming to wash her out to this sea of ecstasy. They shouted in unison as together they came hard and long.

He leaned back on his arms, gulping air, staying inside her as if he'd somehow understood her longing to remain joined. And when he finally, reluctantly, pulled back, she nearly wept at the vacancy. As if it left a hole in her very soul.

But then, this man, this dear husband of hers, this supposed tyrant king, cupped her cheek, looked deep into her eyes and said. "With all that I am, and all that I have, Anna."

* * *

Anna lay naked in William's arms. Blades of grass scratched against her skin, as she lay her head on his bare chest, snuggling under his beaver-lined riding cloak.

"I used to come here as a girl, to be alone," she said, staring off to the horizon. "When my mother died, I'd come here to talk to her about all manner of things. What I had for supper, what Mary was growing, what horse Papa had bought. Or how unjust it all was when I got in trouble."

"Which I'm sure was rare in the extreme," he said, all false seriousness.

She swatted him. "When I was older, I'd tell her who was sick in town, believing if I listened hard enough I could hear her tell me which medicines would be best."

"And did she answer?"

"In a way, I think." She turned, resting on her elbows to look at him. "And of course I came here to seek her help about you."

"Did you ask her to smite me?"

"I thought that might be treason, even in heaven." She settled back down again. "I do wish she could have met you."

"Ah, but she did—when I was fifteen. We met, rather briefly, before my unofficial exile. Or rather, I should say, I screamed vitriol at her through Cate's doors."

She gave a little laugh. "You're the first person I've brought here. Even Mary hasn't been. I could always hear her holler from the back garden. Somehow she knew not to come find me."

"Not even your knight knows of it?"

"Nay," she said, feeling him tense. "'Tis my very own place."

"So why bring me?" He looked about at the giant trees, silent guards of her girlhood secrets.

"I wanted to introduce you to my mother." She shrugged, attempting indifference.

He looked down at her and paused. Untangling himself, he pulled on his trunks and shirt in silence, then bent to his knees for the second time that afternoon, eyes turned to the sky.

"My Lady Julia, Duchess of Beaubourg," he said to the clouds, "dear friend of my mother. I am William. We met once. I was much aggrieved, but your response was grace and mercy, which I humbly ask for again."

Anna sat up, hugged her knees. Yanking his cloak up to her chin, she took in its musky smell mingled with his scent: cloves, sweat, firewood, and the barest hint of their coupling.

"I have come with your devoted daughter to ask your blessing upon us. We are wed, she and I, by strange circumstance. But I ask by the love you bear her, please bless us in our union. Smile upon us, dear lady." He dropped his arms and twisted back to look at Anna, the wind billowing out his shirt like a standard. "Do you think she approves?" he said.

Anna rose and knelt in front of him. Glad tears trickled down her wind-whipped cheeks. And she knew he didn't need to be physically inside her to be joined with her. She took his face in her hands, thumbs rubbing the stubble. "Aye, she approves. For what woman in heaven or earth can resist you?"

* * *

"'Tis the God's honest truth," said Jeffrey, the Duke of Beaubourg's horse master. "That horse could fight a war on its own."

"Ye be lying, Jeffy," Old Thom said. He scratched his bum and spit through his missing front teeth to the straw-strewn tavern floor. "The king's 'orse couldn't be that big."

Grunts of agreement circled the small table as a plate of bread, cheese, and sausage landed in its center.

"Well," Mrs. Cleaves said, slamming down a jug of ale next to the platter, "if his horse be that big, I'd like t' take a looksee at the rest of him!"

The bar erupted in laughter, patrons raising their mugs. The pub was packed, everyone hoping to catch a snippet of gossip on their local royal.

The old tavern's door swung open with a thud, revealing two

royal guards, stamping attention. Mrs. Cleaves turned to wipe down a fresh table

"And these the size of his men at arms?" She whistled. "Well, if wee Anna don't like him so much, perhaps she'll let me have a shot at him!" She grabbed her crotch.

"You will have to ask her yourself, madam," came a calm, deep voice two feet behind. "For our part, the offer is tempting, but we'll pass."

Mrs. Cleaves turned, inch by inch. She dropped a pitcher of ale, sending it sloshing over His Majesty's calfskin boots.

She fell at his feet. "Oh, Your Royalness, I beg your mercy!" She bobbed up and down, kissing his beer-stained boot. Once her penitence died out, the tiny tavern was silent. Everyone gaped, so stunned by the king's sudden appearance they barely noticed Anna at his side.

"Dear mistress," the king said with a sunny smile, "do not let us interrupt the evening's entertainment." She looked up at him, mouth open like a trout. He threw his arms wide. "We wish to join in, for we are parched."

She made no move to rise.

"As far as your spilled merchandise," he said, removing his cap, "let not your heart be troubled, for 'tis on the crown." He swept the room with his hand. "The entire house is on the crown. For we have come to celebrate."

A rumble of appreciation, starting low but rapidly building in volume, met this pronouncement. Mrs. Cleaves scurried behind the bar. William bent his head to Anna, who whispered in his ear, then marched straight up to the bar and confronted his cowering subject.

"Your very best ale, Madam Cleaves, for king and queen. A stout for the stout man, and a cider for the thin. Keep coming whatever your patrons want—and send a pint to my men in front. They deserve a wee respite."

"Y-y-yes, Your Highness."

"And one more thing," he said, leaning over the bar. A breathless pause from the cowering Mrs. Cleaves. "My horse really is that big."

He winked at her and turned back to his party, leaving the barmaid too busy to faint dead away.

* * *

The long center table had been cleared for them: Halforn, Daniel, Mary, the queen, and two lower chambermen, one the royal taster. People inched closer, unsure how to behave. No one spoke above a whisper. For a king to pop into the pub for a pint was simply unheard of.

The king sat astride a bench facing Anna, leaning an arm on the sticky table. "Perhaps we're taking this 'friend of the people' business too far," he whispered to her. "They look as if I shall smite them at any moment."

Anna clucked her tongue. "'Tis but a matter of their getting used to the idea, sire." Spotting Jeffrey in the crowd, she called, "Why Jeffrey, shall we have some music?"

Jeffrey pulled out his flute to begin a jig. A fiddler and mandolin joined in. Mumbled conversations at other tables soon resumed.

Daniel relaxed and raised his cider to Anna. "Majesty, again you charm us all."

"Here, here!" Halforn said, clanking his stout to the king's ale. "I must say, Majesty, I'm honored to return to your homestead. Your father is the essence of hospitality." He took in his surroundings with wide eyes. "Very, ah, rustic in the pub, but what better way to know the people we serve. Aye, Majesty?"

The king laughed. "And Cecile, does this not remind you of our time in Siena? Especially that one taverna behind the piazza . . ." Daniel's face turned pink. "And the barmaid, who shared the sentiments of our patroness but lacked the age? And the wart?"

"Humph," Anna said, "I don't know if I like the idea of you tramping through taverns, my liege."

Daniel's eyes met William's.

"Indeed, my lady," the king said, "such tales are not for your delicate ears." He leaned in for a quick kiss to her earlobe. "Alas, the signorina preferred blondes." Daniel's blush deepened.

The king kept an arm loose about Anna's waist as he and Daniel began to recall their youthful adventures abroad, much to Halforn's delight. Anna turned to Mary, who was sitting beside her.

"Don't feel as though you must be stuck to me. Circulate! Greet your friends and hear all the news."

"Well, you're the news," Mary said, throwing up a hand, "and I feel funny in all these fancy clothes. They'll think I'm putting on airs."

"And I feel funny with a tiara on my head," Anna said. "You're the matron of honor to the Queen of Troixden, but you're also the same Mary and I the same Anna. These are our people. Our friends."

Mary shook her head. "You're most definitely not the same Anna, and so much's the better." She squeezed Anna's arm. "But if ye insist . . ." And the famed healer of Beaubourg scooted away to her old companions.

Anna turned back to the table to find the king halfway across the room, having shed his cape and jacket, holding a mandolin. Halforn stood behind him, egging him on.

"I surrender," William said, "but only if you dance."

He began a lively tune while two men, father and son, poured their hearts into their flying feet, the crowd clapping in time.

Anna beamed at her husband, knowing he'd win the crowd even as he had won her. She sighed, content, and scanned the room. There was Caroline the milkmaid, whose foot she and Mary had mended, blushing under the flirtations of a stable hand, and George the cobbler, telling one of his tall tales.

Then she saw him.

In the back corner booth, scowling into his beer. His elder brother Thomas sat next to him, stealing glances at the royal table and talking out the side of his mouth. Bryan looked up straight into her eyes.

Oh, how she wished she could comfort him, help him move on and find another. But she knew it would only make matters worse. All she could manage was a wan smile, which she hoped conveyed her sorrow for him.

Returning her eyes to the table, she caught Daniel studying her.

"You care for him a great deal," he said.

Oh, no. "Excuse me, Your Grace?"

"The king, my lady. You care deeply for him."

"But of course, Your Grace." She sighed with relief and looked at William frolicking with her old countrymen.

"'Twas not a question, but an observation, Majesty." Daniel said, "You care for him not just as a sovereign but as a man."

The king was finishing a bawdy pub song at the top of his lungs. Anna laughed. "Your Grace, how could I not? Look at him—he's a delight to behold. And his fraternization will not lower him in their eyes but build his pedestal all the higher. Not many men could carry that off."

The king then rolled up his sleeve, about to grasp the hand of some brave lad who'd challenged him to arm wrestle. He met her eyes with a look that made her heart woozy and he broke into a grin. His forearm flexed with strain as the match began. He was using his left. Coins clinked on the table as bets were hastily changed.

Daniel's eyes fell on Bryan in the corner of the pub.

"Your Grace," she said, "the answer is unequivocally yes. His highness has the whole of my heart."

Daniel took her hand in both of his and squeezed it. "I am glad to hear you say it, Majesty. And to see that coming to your old home does not strain your attachment."

She locked his eyes. "I know things didn't start off in the most desirable of circumstances," she said, "but never doubt my devotion to His Majesty. For there is no one, not even my father, that I hold in higher esteem." But she knew he hadn't been commenting on her father.

"Then may you both be blessed, Majesty. And the duke as well."

Daniel turned to rise, his eyes falling upon Bryan again. Anna couldn't help a glance in his direction, not wanting him scrutinized. It must be terrible enough to see her here and so happy.

"Dance! Dance!" came the chants now, and the king, beads of sweat on his forehead, thrust his victorious left hand to her.

"They demand we perform for them, madam, and I tremble to refuse." Over his shoulder, he added, "The mangy lot!"

The crowd hooted with glee. She handed him a handkerchief to mop his brow while the players retuned to their instruments. The king donned his jacket and chain, the better to cut a handsome picture, and led her to a bare patch of floor by the bar. Throwing another wink at Mrs. Cleaves, he swung Anna away from him to bow and begin the dance.

"You never told me there were such delightful people in Beaubourg," he whispered as he twirled her in his arms.

"Why, you've met Mary, and me, and my father—are we not delightful?"

He pulled her into a parallel hold. "A touch more than that, my dear."

The beat gained momentum and they spun together in and out and around like spindles, their rich garments snapping and rolling in answer to the music. Reaching its end, he twisted her around, her arms arched over her head like a second crown, and stopped her in perfect time with the final note. The crowd roared.

Another brave soul yelled out, "A kiss, a kiss!"

"A kiss?" the king said in mock offense. "You say you want me to kiss the queen?"

"Aye!" shouted the patrons. "A kiss! A royal kiss!"

"Well," William said, shaking his head, "I suppose since you all missed the wedding . . ." Another hurrah of appreciation shook the flimsy walls.

He snaked his arm round her waist. "What can I do, lady? The people demand it."

He took her dimpled chin in his hand, drew her face to his, and kissed her, very proper, very quick. He held her face there, so close to his own. The corner of his mouth twitched . . . .

And he kissed her again as if they were alone in his chamber.

The crowd went wild. So rowdy were they, no one saw the door swing open. But all heard the guttural cry, like the sound of a dog being kicked.

Anna looked just in time to see the back of her oldest friend disappear into the night.

* * *

"Matron Mary," William said, trying to appear calm, "the room, if you please."

Mary shot a nervous glance at her mistress and bustled out the door, leaving he and the queen alone in Anna's girlhood chamber.

"I thought the whole thing came off spectacularly." Anna moved to the window. "You won them all over as I knew you would."

"All save one," he said, quiet.

Anna was silent. She would not face him.

"I felt your whole body go rigid in my arms when he left," he said.

"'Twas not how I would have wanted him to see me."

"You didn't want him to see you in the arms of your husband?" There was a dull ringing in his ears. "You want him to carry your torch even now?"

She faced him, eyes afire. "That's not what I meant and you know it."

"What makes you think I know your thoughts?" He prowled the stone, back and forth, back and forth.

She put her hands on her hips and looked at him the way his mother used to when he was being unreasonable. "Perhaps because I haven't been shy in giving my thoughts to you, whether you liked them or not."

William cursed under his breath.

"Am I not allowed to have compassion for my oldest friend?" He stopped his pacing.

"Only compassion?"

"For the last time, yes! Would you not have compassion on Margaux in a similar situation?"

He let out a mirthless laugh. "I never cared for Margaux. But you've made your feelings about Sir Bryan quite clear."

"Apparently not clear enough!"

"I beg to differ, my queen," he said, voice rising, "for I believe the entire countryside and half my lords saw you throw him your favor!"

Anna retreated to the window again. "I've told you, I didn't love him — not as he wanted."

"And yet all it takes is the sight of his backside for your feelings to return."

She whisked around, fists clenched. "How dare you — how dare you find fault when my heart is tender for a poor boy whose dreams have been shattered whilst mine have blossomed? And how dare you accuse me of lying about my feelings!"

"I — "

"I should laugh in his face? Shall I send for him now to watch you bed me?" She flung out an arm. "Shall I have him stand at the keyhole and hear us moan in pleasure while he writhes in torture? Is that what you'd like? Is that what you need to prove I love you?"

His brows popped up. "You love me?"

"That's entirely beside the point!" She threw up her hands. "How am I to trust anything between us if you constantly doubt what I say? Haven't I told you again and again I have nothing to hide, nothing to prove — "

He closed the distance between them in three strides. "You haven't said it before."

"Just today in the meadow, I showed you I have no secrets. Weren't you paying attention?"

He put his hands on her shoulders. "No, not that," he said, voice soft. "You haven't told me you love me."

She squinted at him. "How can you — in the middle of a fight you started — suddenly change topics?"

He just smiled. Waiting.

"Yes, Wills, I love you," she said. "Even when you're being a horse's ass."

He grabbed her dour face and covered it with kisses. "Ah, my darling wife, how glad you've made me."

"If calling you an ass gives you joy, I've a few other words I might share."

He laughed and hugged her, then let out a happy sigh. "I feared you would tell me that seeing him had rekindled old feelings."

She broke from him and sat on the edge of her bed. "I've never seen you so unsure of yourself."

"You're the only person who's ever caused me to quake in their presence," he said. "That includes when my brother wanted me dead." He went to his knees in front of her, taking hold of her hands. "You have the power to completely unhinge me. I hate that."

"How nicely you put things."

"Don't you understand?" he said. "I'm a king, and yet the changing whims of a mere wee woman brings me to my knees." She looked up to the timbered ceiling. "Oh, my 'just-Anna,' how I do love you."

Suddenly she grinned at him like a child just given their first pony. "You do?"

He laughed so loud the doves outside her window took to the sky. "Of course I do!"

"But you didn't say it."

"Yes I did."

"Yes, but not right away."

"Mother of Moses, Anna, give a man a minute to gain his wits." He slid next to her on the bed. They were both quiet. He started fiddling with the bed curtain's tassel.

"Nice drapes," he said at last.

She burst out laughing and fell back, holding her stomach. "Come here," she said, yanking on his hand so he landed next to her with a thump. They both lay there, gazing up at the newly formed cobwebs amidst strong beams, Anna still giggling.

"Do you still wish to keep your father's house from the scandal of royal intercourse?"

She sighed. "While I would be tempted, at the very least to prove a point, 'tis now one o'clock in the morning. Sunday morning."

"Hang the papal rules," he said.

"You realize your brother would have had you burned for such a sentiment?"

"I'm not my brother. Besides," he said between kisses and her pleasured whimpers, "you're still not with child."

One of his hands worked its way down her side as the other

clasped her head, pulling it to his hungry mouth. But she pushed him away.

"You're the king, sire," she said, "but even you can't flout the dictates of God. To gain princes or no."

He flopped next to her with a groan. "Are they the dictates of God?"

"Does not his Holiness speak for God?" She turned to look him over.

He raised an eyebrow. "Sometimes I think the Pope doth speak only for the Pope."

She shoved him off the bed. "Away with you, jester, else you send us both to the fiery pit."

He smirked, giving her an exaggerated bow, and backed toward the door. "And what a blessed way to go."

CHAPTER 11

My Life for a Queen

Palace Havenside bustled with preparations. The last jousting tournament of the year would be held on October twenty-fifth, St. Crispin's Day, with the traditional parade and feast. Everyone from the scullery maid to the Duke of Norwick hustled about, making last-minute arrangements.

For Robert, everything was according to plan. While he did not much like the queen—he found her daft, haughty, and annoyingly unmoved by his charms—the king found her otherwise, and that was the point. With Yvette firmly ensconced in her good graces, all he needed to do was turn the screw—delicately.

For now, the only problem left was his sister. Many assumed she had once been William's mistress and would soon be again, which made finding her a suitable husband something of a challenge. The man needed to be strong-willed enough to control her, yet weak enough for Robert to manipulate, an all but impossible balance. She had some years of fertility left at four-and-twenty, and any man would be proud to have her on his arm in public. Of course, in private was a different matter.

He thought of the Duke of Halforn, a wealthy widower with hopes to spend the rest of his days in the company of a doting wife, but he couldn't bring himself to inflict his sister on such an old and stalwart ally.

For the briefest of moments he thought of the upstart knave. Not only would Margaux be happy to throw him in the queen's face, he was handsome and young and pliable enough to mold to Robert's liking. Of course, William would never have it. The boy was too low of station and the king would not brook his rival flitting about court.

Cecile was a non-starter. Even if Robert begged him, he suspected mild-mannered Daniel would lose his wits when faced with Margaux.

Then it hit him like a charging war-horse: James's dead queen's bastard, Eustace. Enough stature to throw Margaux a bone, and young enough to respect Robert's own wisdom. Perfect.

* * *

"The whole palace is alight with revelry, and yet you wear a frown." Robert sat back against his large desk, feet and arms crossed. "Have you ever thought how many women would kill to live your life?"

"Oh, it's a fine life," Margaux said. "Another beds the man who should be my husband and saunters around with my crown on her smug little head."

"Jealousy ill becomes you, sis."

"What do I care if I'm becoming anymore? The king has rejected me." Her frown deepened. "Though mark my words: the queen's still not with child, and the king will soon throw her off for another."

"I thought you didn't want any 'little brats' as you called them," Robert said.

"So I'm to be a spinster? I'm ruined. And I have you, dearest brother, to thank for it."

He clapped a hand to his chest in mock offense. "Little me?"

"Yes, you—you and that conniving Yvette."

Robert walked past her to the window, tapped his forefinger on the leaded glass and turned to face her again. "Actually, 'tis I who have secured your future. I've arranged a marriage for you to which the king's agreed." Well. He was sure the king would agree.

219

"Truly?"

"Yes, my dear, and a fine one to boot. To Eustace, the Earl of Mohrlang."

"What?" She sprang from the couch. "The bastard son of James's whore queen? This is how you repay me?"

"Now, that's unfair. We all just *assume* poor Eustace wasn't King James's issue." He shrugged. "Who really knows but Queen Minerva? And as she's missing a head, we can't get the facts from her."

"She's missing a head because she cuckolded James and the resulting bastard—who was banished—is a child!" She shook with rage.

"He's a strapping thirteen-year-old. Give him a few years and he'll be man enough for you."

Margaux clenched her fists. "I won't have it, Robert. I don't care who says I must."

He chortled. "Now you sound just like your beloved mistress." She made a grunting noise like a charging bull. "Come, sister, you're looking at it all wrong. The wee earl is now allowed back at court. You won't be expected to lie with him quite yet, and who knows to what heights he will ascend?"

"I was to be a princess from the day I came into this world! I was to be William's wife, and you know it—"

Robert grabbed her, putting his hand over her mouth as though to stuff the words back in.

"*Was*, Margaux." He lowered his voice. "'Tis not your fate to be queen."

She shook free from his grasp and raised her hand to slap him. He caught her wrist and twisted it. "You'll do as I say." He let her wrist fall limp to her side. "And as the king has declared."

She dusted herself off, ready for another round.

"Sister," he said, gentler now, "even if William remained a prince, he wouldn't have taken you to wife."

"How would you know?"

"Because I know him." Looking at her there, frowning down at her shoes, he saw a glimpse of her younger self. He thought of all the times they'd played together, she and William. Did she only want him for his crown, or did she really have some affection for the man?

He sighed. "Despite what you believe, I'm trying to help you." She looked up, face mottled in fury.

"You're trying to help yourself and no other. Don't pretend otherwise. 'Tis not becoming, as you say."

"Think of me what you may," he said, walking back to his desk, "but you are to wed by Christmas."

"I'll make you pay for this."

"It will give me pleasure to see you try."

* * *

The king was out surveying the tournament lists while Anna prepared to receive a pair of shoes from Havenside's best cobbler, in honor of the Crispin brothers. She had just taken her gloves from Lady Jane and reached for a glass of wine, but Margaux snatched it away with a frown.

"Excuse me, Majesty," she said. Her eyes looked red. "But the wine smells spoiled to me."

"Let me taste it," Lady Jane said, reaching for the goblet. "My father was a cup bearer, and—"

But Margaux tossed the wine out the window before Jane could finish the sentence. "I'm sorry, Majesty—I'll have them send another pitcher."

A visitor was announced, whose name Anna didn't catch amidst the hubbub, but when she heard the sound of chain mail swishing behind her, she turned to embrace the king.

But this was not the king.

Bent on one knee before her was a golden-haired knight, the blue and silver colors of Beaubourg draped over his mail.

"Majesty," Bernard said, fidgeting, "the knight says he has permission for an audience."

As merciful as the king had been of late, he would never allow Bryan a private audience, and in her chamber no less. "Is that so, sir?" she asked Bryan's bent head. He looked up at her with pale blue, adoring eyes.

"Yes, Majesty," he said, "for I have urgent news from home, for your ears alone."

She at least had to find out what he was doing here. Perhaps her father was ill. It wasn't as if Bryan could do anything surrounded by her ladies and guards.

"Good sir knight," she said, "the king is the only man allowed my private audience." She caught Bernard relax at this statement, but Mary's eyes looked alarmed. "However, let us retire from the crowd so that you may feel free to speak."

Bryan swallowed, Adam's apple bobbing like a cork. She walked up the three steps to her bed dais. Her ladies shuffled to the east windows, pretending to watch the preparations at the stable yard.

"Annelore," Bryan whispered, "I've come to take you home."

"First of all, sir, I am your queen," she said. "And second, I am home. As you well know." He grabbed her hand. She snatched it away.

"Don't take liberties, Bryan," she whispered, "you'll have us both thrown in Stone Yard."

"I'm here to take you back to Beaubourg, to be with me and your father," he said, eyes ablaze.

"Bryan, you can't possibly —"

"I have a plan. At the tournament, meet me in my tent. I shall dress you as my squire and thence we shall flee —"

"What on earth makes you think I want to flee?" She put her hands on her hips.

Bryan glanced at her ladies and moved closer. "I know you must put on a show in front of others, so nod your head twice and I shall see you in my tent forthwith."

"I'm not putting on a show for anyone," she said, her voice loud enough for everyone in the room to hear.

Her ladies gave up their pretense and stared at the two. She waved them back to the window with a flick.

"Anna, this is what we've hoped for—the perfect opportunity. Why are you suddenly so contrary? Your letters —"

"Letters?"

"The letters you've sent," he said. "How you're counting the days till we can be together again." Her frown deepened. "Annelore, don't be daft." He reached for her hand again.

"I've sent no such letters. No letters at all."

He glanced at her ladies and sighed. "All right, I'll play along."

"I'm in earnest," she said. "I haven't written you a word since leaving Beaubourg—"

"You know that's not true. You said your heart was ripped asunder when you saw me at Mrs. Cleaver's pub. And the look you gave me—"

Her face was stone. "I wrote no such thing."

He pulled a folded sheet from his breast. "Here."

She snatched it from him. Scanning the neat curling words, she read her declared love for him, begging he come and wrest her from the grip of her horrid husband. No names were mentioned and the letter was unsigned.

It was not her hand. Very close, but not hers. "I didn't write this. Did you?"

"You've taken this far enough. I've gone through substantial risk to be here."

"Yes, it seems you've taken significant pains—falsifying letters and requests of the king—"

"Anna?" he whispered. "None can hear us. I beg you, drop this pretense."

She searched his face and knew he was telling the truth. He thought these letters were from her. Whatever cruelty their writer had intended was made manifest in Bryan's desperate face. To him, she was still in need of rescue, and here he was to extract her.

"Bryan," she said, tender now, "I'm so sorry. Please believe me when I tell you I didn't write to you." She tossed the letter on her bed. "Go and examine my old letters to you. You'll see the difference in tone and in hand."

His face fell as he watched the letter fall to the duvet. "If you regret them that's one thing, but to claim you didn't write them . . . it's hard to believe you."

She grabbed his hand and pressed it. "Then believe this. I love the king. And it would grieve my very soul to leave him."

He chortled his disbelief.

"Remember when you came back from the knighting?" she said. "You talked about how you were drawn to the king and I teased you about it?" He gave a wary nod. "Well that's how I feel now, but multiplied by four months of days—and nights."

"No—"

"Forsooth, Bryan, I love him! Not merely as we are all to love our sovereign, but as a wife should love a husband. Like my parents—"

"Stop!" He threw up his hands. "All this pomp, these riches, have blinded you."

"Do you think so little of me?"

"Apparently so."

"Bryan, please—"

"You'll come with me and fulfill our dreams together." He took her hand as if to whisk her away right then and there. "For once in your life, just do as you're told—"

Her patience evaporated. She raised her hand to slap him. He caught her wrist and pulled her to him in a hard embrace.

"Perhaps I need to jog your memory." He kissed her with force.

Anna untangled herself and shoved him off, sending him tumbling backward into the bedpost, knocking him to his knees.

"My lady?" Bernard said, now at the foot of the dais.

All were frozen, even Bryan. She strode to him, a towering mass of velvet and rage. She slapped him with all her might, across his lovely face. The face she used to go to sleep imagining, the face she once believed would be her companion through this life. She slapped that perfect face so hard his lips bled.

His hand leapt to his cheek. He stared up at her, mouth and eyes wide. "Sir," she said, "you will leave my presence at once and never seek it again."

Her door guards had since entered the room and stood flanking Bernard. She gave them the slightest nod.

"You are fortunate indeed the king is not at home, for he would not show you such mercy. These men will escort you out and you will not enter these walls again."

The guards climbed up the stairs and pulled Bryan to his feet. He struggled against them, writhing in front of her. "It grieves me to have things end this way. But end they must. I was your friend and now I am your queen. If you will not honor the request of the former, then I command your obedience as the latter. Goodbye."

She turned away. She heard his feet dragged against the stone, heard the murmurs of her ladies—and the giggles from Margaux and Brigitte. She'd been a fool. A fool to carry on with him so, leading him down a flirtatious trail she'd never have consummated, king or no. Thank God William was out, for he'd have had poor Bryan's head on a spike. And how could she explain this?

Mary touched her shoulder. Anna hugged her hard.

"Tush, tush. He should never have come. He knows his place, he knows the king's wishes. He should not've come."

"But he thought he was acting on my wishes," she said.

"He's always been a dreamer, that one," Mary said.

"He could be killed for treason, the things he said." She massaged her head with her fingers, then picked up the discarded letter and handed it to Mary.

"What treachery is this?" Mary said. "No wonder he's half-mad."

"I shall have to tell the king of it."

"Are you sure you should tell him everything?" Mary said. "I do worry about young Bryan's life ending too soon."

Anna folded the letter, stashed it in her bodice, and laced her fingers through her supple gloves. "I'll tell him. And I pray for his mercy. Besides, we must find out about these letters, for they intend harm to us both. And I could not conduct an inquiry without His Majesty's knowledge—or his help."

She smoothed her skirts and clapped her hands for the attention of the room. Her stomach lurched. "I wish to ask you a service. I do not ask you anything untoward, though you may think it at first." She cleared her throat. "You have all witnessed the zealous outburst of Sir Bryan, a knight from Beaubourg. He and I were friends since childhood. I made my views quite plain to him, as I have before. I have not imprisoned him, which he rightly deserves, out of compassion and the friendship I once bore him."

She paused, looking at each eager, upturned face.

"What I ask of you is this: please keep the incident to yourselves until I have an audience with the king. I feel 'tis my right and my duty to tell His Majesty, not have it reach his ears from another source, twisted and falsely construed. Due to the constraints of the day, I shall not have a moment with the king until we retire. Do I have your word?"

"Yes, Your Majesty," came the solemn chorus.

"If I have not kept my word in telling the king, you have all liberty to share your observations to anyone you wish tomorrow."

"Yes, Majesty."

She caught Margaux's wide blue eyes. Could the lady stoop so low? She thought of how fastidious Margaux was with the mail. Surely not. Seducing William was one thing, but this? Margaux might be jealous and spurned, but what would such a horrid act gain her but disgrace and banishment?

She took a deep breath and a much-needed gulp of fresh wine. "Now, let us see about these shoes."

* * *

William lay stretched out, head resting on the back of his stuffed leather chair, legs extended across the low chest, feet in Anna's lap, she in her robe and shift, he just shirt tails and shorts. He wished the whole of him was in her lap, but there were other matters to attend to. Matters that twisted his insides. So instead of merry-making, they sat before the dwindling fire in his bedchamber, grazing on fruits and cheese.

"Then I said to him," William said, "'I shall brook no drunken jousters. Feed them, but no wine until the tournament is finished.'"

"That seems reasonable, especially after last spring." Anna kneaded her knuckles into his heel pad. Lord, it felt good. A companionable silence hung between them while the logs crackled along, their violent pops sending embers to the stones.

226

"Sir Bryan was here today," she said, switching her ministrations to his other foot.

"I know." He looked at her intently, judging her reaction, his gut seizing.

She stopped her hands. "I told my ladies not to say anything."

"I know that too." He sat up, giving her his full attention. Robert had seen the guards throw the knight out and had questioned them. He'd then cornered Margaux, who spilled over with enthusiasm telling the story. Angry at first, and even though it had be a torture to think on, William now wished to hear Anna's side of things before he drew conclusions.

She sighed and gazed into the fire, biting the side of her lip as she did when choosing her words carefully. "I asked that no one speak of it because I wanted to tell you first." Her eyes flitted to his and held them, unguarded and earnest. "I didn't feel it fair to either of us to have you hear it secondhand."

William leaned his forearms on his knees. "I trust you'll tell me exactly what happened."

"We were getting ready to see the shoes. Heaven knows how he got past all those guards, but there he was, kneeling at my feet and asking for an audience. He claimed he had your permission."

William chuckled in what he hoped was a casual way. "A likely story."

"That's what I thought. Ridiculous to think you'd have allowed him in the palace." She went on, sharing each painful detail. He startled when she got to the letter. No one had mentioned a letter.

"Anna, did you keep it?"

She reached inside her robe pocket and pulled out a well-worn parchment.

Dearest and Gallant B —

It tears my very heart every moment of every day that we are parted. When the king forces me to be with him I only imagine you. I cannot stand one more minute in this despised palace! I am disliked by all my maids and constantly hounded by the insatiable king. And yet he leers at my maids and I know it is only a matter of time before he takes one to his bed. Oh that he would! Then I would be free. Make haste to me in whatever way you can. But only in secret!

Continue to send your letters, for they are my only solace. I love you I love you I love you!

Forever yours, A

His rage rose. He knew she had not written it—the tone told him that much—yet he could not help but react to seeing written there his very own fears. He took a long breath and spoke as calmly as he could manage.

"I'll send Daniel to seek and confiscate the rest." He frowned. "'Tis most worrying—we must find out who has been sending these. 'Tis treason to forge the hand of the queen."

"I can't imagine anyone close to me would do such a thing, but it must be so . . ."

He shook his head. He remembered how Robert thought her not ready for court—and truly, she wasn't. But that was something he loved about her. She would never do anything so wicked, so it never occurred to her someone else might.

"He also grabbed me—and kissed me." She blushed.

William sprang to his feet at that, needing to punch something, but calmed when she told him how she'd slapped the knave and sent him on his way.

"The whole thing made me feel so horrid, yet what was I to do?"

He turned to her, mentally and emotionally appeased, but his body still pulsing. "He not only spoke treason to you but attacked your person, both of which are punishable by death."

"I know," she said. "But how do you send your foolish friend to the Yard, let alone to a traitor's death, when he honestly believed he was doing your bidding?"

"You don't have to," he said, sitting on the chest in front of her. He took a long, steadying breath. "That's my job."

"Think on it this way. What if Daniel had done something he thought was what you wanted, something not only against your wishes, but also a capital offense? You wouldn't have him killed."

"Daniel would never do such a thing, for he's smarter than all of us put together."

"Robert, then." She rubbed his hands as she had his feet, working her thumb into his palm.

"I see your point." He paused to give a grunt of pleasure, finally, blissfully at peace. "So you're asking me to show him mercy?"

She covered his hands with hers, giving him a curious look. "Wills, I don't ask you for anything. I told you because you're my husband and no person should come between us."

He frowned at this speech. "Truly? You don't want me to give him pardon?"

"That's, as you say, beside the point." She shook her head. "I told you I would never use my influence for my own gain or anyone else's. For me to beg your mercy would go back on that promise. You must do what you think best."

He kissed her forehead and rose again to stare at the fire. "And what if I asked your opinion?"

He heard her rise, felt her dainty arms slip around his waist, pressing her cheek to his back. He clasped her hands against his chest. They stood there silent for a while, breathing in time with each other.

"If you asked my opinion," she said, "I would tell you the man is no danger to anyone anymore. He finally knows his errand was in error and in vain. He's wounded in heart, embarrassed and angry, but there's nothing he can or will do."

"Humph."

"Furthermore," she slid around to his front, resting her chin on his sternum, "to make a spectacle out of him gives more weight to the incident than it deserves. If you feel you must lock him up so he can cool his heels, then by all means."

"Ah, my lady, you are very wise, indeed." He tapped the tip of her nose with a finger. "In fact, I shall let him keep his entry at the tournament." Anna blanched, but kept her peace. He held her waist. "He shall joust and fight and then go home, perhaps a victor in at least one attempt if not in what he came for. Though I will have to think of some punishment."

"That's more benevolent than I could've imagined." She stood on tiptoes to kiss each cheek.

"'Tis not for his sake but yours," he said, "I won't allow your heart to be pained, and I'll be damned if I'm the cause."

He searched her charming face. She looked at him as if he were the Lord Jesus and she in the need of healing. He would do everything in his power to keep it that way. With a stab, he knew he would fail her one day. It was inevitable. But right now, in this moment, she adored him completely and without question. For now, he would savor it.

"William, King of Troixden, you're the most wonderful of men," she said. "I couldn't have dreamt you up if I tried."

He kissed those soft, trusting lips, moving his hands up her arms to her shoulders. He had only meant to give her a peck of returned gratitude, but, well, why not take away any trace of her old love's imprint?

Sliding his hands up to cup her face, he drew her deeper, his tongue churning with hers, swallowing her murmured mewls. Did that knave ever kiss her like this? Taking his time and his pleasure, making her pout for more. Did she press herself against him, eager, craving, wanton? He need not imagine what reaction she evoked in the young knight, for how could any man not burn for her? But she . . . did his Anna pull the nape of Bryan's neck, urging him into her, did her eyes spill over with longing and delight when they met his? Had he supped at her breasts . . . .

William pulled away, breath heavy, cock angrily hard, possessive, beneath his shorts. "I must have you, Anna," he said, snaking off his shirt, letting his clothes fall in a lump at his feet. "Right now."

She was not repulsed by the carnal heat he revealed, did not recoil at the hunger in his eyes, though perhaps she should have. He didn't know how gentle he could be this night. If at all. Somewhere, in his sensible mind, he knew this was no way to behave — there was nothing for her — or him — to prove, but he was beyond rationality, led only by a driving need to lay to waste this damn knave and his own damned jealously.

He backed her against the bedpost, clawing off her scant coverings. He stood, panting before her like any beast. She locked her eyes on him and gave a small, swift nod. As if it were the starting horn to a joust, he launched at her, swallowing her whole with his body, his mouth, his hands. A whisper in his brain wondered if he were too rough, too quick for her, but he could not hold back. She'd possessed him and he must possess her.

He lifted her, using the bedpost as a counter point, and she wrapped her arms around his neck, one hand gripping his hair, yanking his face to hers. He stiffened even more thinking she felt this urgency too. Lancing him self inside her, he nearly came as she cried out.

"Yes, Wills," she growled.

She latched her lips to his neck as he rolled his hips into her, crushing her sumptuous ass against the wood. He could feel her womb as he dug, racing, straining for release, for peace of body and soul.

Flinging her head back she wailed incoherently, shaking and clenching all up his shaft and with one final thrust, as her screams died out, he shattered into ecstasy. Both body and soul.

* * *

The air was cool though the sun glowed with all its might, as if in hopes of outshining the spectacle below. Horses whinnied and kicked the dirt, metal clashed against metal, men yelled orders. Crowds dressed in a rainbow of jewel tones moved to their seats while ladies waved favors at passing gallants.

In the midst of it all sat the queen, glowing in velvet the color of moss, cuffs trimmed with beaver fur, a spiked crown of gold and drooping pearls atop her head. The throne next to hers was empty, as the king would be the first to ride in the joust.

Amongst the tangle of flagged tents Anna knew was a heartsick knight hoping against hope that his love would poke her head through the flap of his tent. William hadn't imprisoned Bryan, only taken his lands to the crown, leaving him his house and small garden patch. When the trumpets sounded she saw him trotting his steed into line with all the others.

Robert was behind the king. Third was the tall Timothy of

Ridgeland. Behind him, Bryan. The line lurched forward to present itself to the crowd.

Something didn't feel right. William was saying something about joyous unions, brave saints, but she couldn't focus. And now it was her turn to wave to the crowd. She stood and smiled. The king pointed his lance at her, extended steady and straight as an arrow.

"Majesty, the honor of your favor," he said.

She kissed her handkerchief and tossed it to him, acutely aware that the last time she had made such a gesture was to the knight three horses down.

"I shall keep it to my heart as your very own," William said, giving her a wink. He was so jolly, so blithe. Why could she not be?

Bryan's turn was suddenly upon her. He reined his horse, face still covered in gray steel. "Sir, I bless thee in your quest," she said.

"'Tis not your blessing I seek, Majesty," he said, "for another carries your favor."

"Indeed, sir knight, and the one who carries it will defend it with all valor."

Bryan lifted his visor, to gasps from those around her. Taking his lance from his squire, he held it aloft. His eyes still on her face, he lowered it to Margaux, directly to Anna's right.

"My lady," Bryan said, "you are more beautiful to behold than the sun itself."

Margaux gave the queen a wary look, then batted her eyelashes at Bryan. "Why, sir, you do flatter."

"Nay, I speak only truth, goddess of light," he said. "Please, kind lady, put me out of my misery by honoring me with your favor."

She reached into her bosom, pulled out a handkerchief, and kissed the silken square. Tying it to the tip of his lance, she bent low, allowing him to see the creamy crevice she'd pulled her favor from.

Bryan took it, kissed it, and shoved it in the armor at his chest. He flicked his eyes to Anna to see how she was taking this performance, but she turned her head quickly to acknowledge the next man in line.

Margaux issued a little puff of annoyance.

"My lady," he said, trying to recover their repartee, "it appears I am taking too much time admiring your charms."

"I will be watching you, sir," Margaux said.

"I shall do you proud, lady."

Anna watched him shut his visor with a clang and trot off to await his turn at arms.

* * *

Robert knew his place. This first joust with the king was ceremonial. He and William would merely skim lances, Robert taking a slight hit for show. And yet if he were to best the king in this tilt, or worse, if something dire were to happen, no one would fault him . . . .

His horse twitched while they waited for the call of charge. He gave the king a nod signaling his readiness, then closed his helmet. The joust was announced. Digging into his horse's belly, balancing his unwieldy weapon, he galloped toward his liege.

William's blow to the shoulder caught him off guard. He'd been expecting the king's trademark move of threading his opponent's lance and flicking it out of his hands. Robert tumbled off his horse, dangling from the saddle, his foot caught in the stirrup. The horse reared, wild feet rising above him.

In all his armor he couldn't roll. He instinctively held up his arm to protect his face as he saw the hooves come down. But there was no impact. He had been pulled just shy of the raging beast.

"Your Grace," came an anxious voice, "Your Grace, can you hear me?" Robert groaned and made to remove his helmet. The man stayed his hand. "Your Grace, let me help you."

The mysterious savior had just removed Robert's helmet when he saw the king approach.

"Sweet Jesus, Norwick," William said, falling to his knees, "are you all right, man?"

Robert squinted at the king, then looked to his shoulder where his rescuer hovered. The man had flipped up his visor to reveal pale blue eyes wide with concern.

"You," Robert said.

Bryan whipped out his lady's favor, mopping Robert's brow.

"Give me that!" Robert snatched the handkerchief. A looping M was embroidered in blue on one lacy corner. Good Lord, how many piles of manure was this heel going to step in?

As the king reached to shake the knight's hand, Bryan snapped his visor shut and tore off, leaving his sovereign frowning after him. William turned back to Robert, bent over him. "Are you all right, my friend? Can you stand?"

"Aye, sire. It appears you need no warming up." He checked his mouth for cuts and his face for blood. The king helped him to his feet with much applause from the crowd. Robert felt shaky but waved and grinned, the consummate showman, as William escorted him to the royal tent. While entering, they both caught sight of Margaux running across the lists, false concern stamped on her face.

"I would take the horse over her ministrations," Robert said, arms outstretched while his armor was unstrapped. Waves of relief swept over him with each buckle released.

"Did you not say you wanted her married to Lord Mohrlang?" William raised his brows.

"Yes, Majesty—all that need be done is your signature on the betrothal."

The king nodded his sweaty head. "I didn't know you disliked the lad so," he said. "In the meantime, wish me victory, dear cuz. And God speed your recovery." He turned to go, then stopped, regarding Robert.

"Your Grace," he said, "I don't know what I would've done if I'd lost you." A pang stabbed Robert's heart. "We have our differences, you and I, but you must know you're ever dear to me."

With that His Majesty was through the tent and into the adulation of the arena.

* * *

Anna watched the field. Distracted by Robert's fall, Ridgeland, who was next to joust, had dismounted and was chatting away with other nobles. At the other end of the list was the king, mounted to take Robert's place against Ridgeland.

The crowd, still deep in the breathlessness of a near death, ignored the field. The king spoke to his squire, visor up, leaning one hand on his downturned lance as he waited for the first trumpet to arms.

Fully mounted and still cloaked in some mystery, Bryan guided his horse to the start, sneaking into Ridgeland's position.

The caller, similarly sidetracked, but noticing a horse snorting at the ready, yelled out, "The Earl of Ridgeland!"

Bryan rammed his heels into his horse's belly. It neighed and lurched forward in a mad rush of spittle and rolling eyes.

"Halt!" the crier called as Bryan whizzed by.

Bryan unsheathed his sword and held it aloft. Anna was out of her seat. The king still had not looked up.

"WILLIAM!" Her guttural scream soared above Bryan's war cry.

Everything happened at once: the king looked up in alarm at his fast-approaching assassin, he reined in his horse so hard it reared, pawing the air. His sword was out in a flash, but for naught.

Bryan let his own sword fall clanking to the ground, slowing his horse, arms slack, head and body slumped. All his fight gone. He held up his hands in surrender. Anna fought for air.

Bryan offered no resistance as men surrounded him in short order and dragged him from his horse. The king himself wrenched the helmet from Bryan's head.

"You," he said. Bryan looked at William as if drunk. "Take him to the dungeon. Tomorrow I shall deal with him as I should have months ago."

No less than ten men heeded the order, jostling the woebegone knight toward the palace for the last time.

* * *

Despite some popping joints and a sore arm, Anna found William was in lively spirits that evening. The dancing had begun and he led

Anna in a volte. While not so bold as he'd been at Mrs. Cleaves' tavern, it was obviously hard for him to keep his hands to himself.

And how on earth could a man eat a goose so sensually? But William had done it, with all that finger sucking and flesh tearing and eye locking. In another frame of mind she might have crinkled her nose at him in disgust, but tonight it made her blood quicken.

While they spent nearly every night in each other's company, these evenings did not always end in a sweaty pile of exhausted appendages and twisted sheets. Even kings grew tired or had headaches. Even after their furious coupling the previous evening, her parts still sore, something about this day had roused in her a raging passion. And even though this was a feast day, she was not so sure the threat of godly recompense could keep her from him.

It was as if she were bewitched. The music was the most beautiful she had ever heard, every conversation the wittiest, the food the most sumptuous. She was madly in love with the world—a world that had almost come crashing down about her but hours before.

"Majesty," Robert said, appearing as if from nowhere, "will you do me the honor of a dance?"

She left her throne and let him lead her to the floor. William raised his eyebrows as they passed and she gave him a shrug.

"A night for celebration." Robert said, making a small circle around her.

"Indeed, Your Grace."

"I feel, Majesty, we did not quite start out on proper footing."

"Oh? I hadn't noticed."

"We both care for the king. We should not be at war with each other. Indeed, we may be able to help each other."

"And what would I need your help with, Your Grace?" It was her turn to circle around him. Upon facing him again, she saw his eyes alight, seductive, holding her gaze. She felt her heart stop.

"I suppose you don't need my help," he said. "Yet."

"And could I trust it if offered?"

He broke into a broad smile, the most sincere he had ever shown her. And Lord, he was handsome.

"The king trusts me. And you trust him, do you not?" His eyes were back on her. She swallowed.

"He is the only one I trust in this whole court."

The dance ended. He gave her a sweeping bow and a kiss on her hand. "Just remember, Highness: he's the only one I trust as well."

* * *

"My queen," William said, strolling to her throne. She had returned there after her odd dance with Robert to gulp a glass of wine. Ladies Jane and Stefania stood by her side, giving each other the knowing glances of seasoned gossips. "You look to be enjoying yourself this evening."

"Why yes, Majesty," she said, "the revelries have made me glad of spirit and heart."

Giggles from the ladies. He took her right palm and brought it to his mouth as if he meant to consume it as he had the goose. He leaned to her ear, his whiskers tickling her cheek as he whispered, "Would that all these gathered were gone."

He turned his head slightly and caressed her cheekbone covertly with the tip of his tongue. She closed her eyes and shivered.

"You concur?" he said, lips just brushing her face. She could not think straight.

"What is the time?" she managed, still unable to open her eyes lest she seize him then and there. What was wrong with her?

William inhaled deeply, taking in her scent. Her eyes fluttered open. "Does the time matter, Highness? For even if it be not past nine, I can send the whole court away."

"Majesty, as much as I desire your most private of audiences, we cannot disappoint our people by retiring so early."

He gave her a pout, which always made him look like a little boy. "Will you really deny me tonight?"

"'Tis not I who deny you, 'tis God."

"Well, if He and I have words, will it ease your mind?"

To deny one's husband was sin. To desecrate the saint's day was sin. To burn in lust was sin. She was damned any way she turned.

"My love, give us another hour," she said. "The dancing has just begun and I hear there's to be another mask." She let her eyes linger as she took in his frame. "And there's much to be said for anticipation."

"Indeed." He swept low before her, his brows bobbing, and took his leave.

* * *

"Oh, he was made a complete fool by the king," she heard a male voice say, echoing down from the balcony above her. "His Highness frightened the sword from his very hands."

"I wouldn't say complete fool, for he did save Norwick's neck," said another.

Anna looked sidelong at Jane and Stefania, then tipped her head slightly, hoping they'd take a hint and go learn the identities of the speakers.

"Touché, touché," said the first, "but you didn't see him receive the Lady Margaux's favor. 'Twas a pathetic show." He lowered his voice. "All for the queen's eyes, of course."

Anna's heart sank. What in the world had happened to her carefree friend? How could he have gone so mad? Thank God he'd dropped his sword. Perhaps William would spare him a traitor's drawn-and-quartered death and give him the quick axe instead—oh, but she could not bear to think on it. She was so saddened by him and so angry with him all at once.

The anonymous companion laughed. "The Lady Margaux? Now there's a perfect way to get under the skin of both their majesties . . ."

The men had moved their conversation out of earshot. She frowned. Her eyes searched the room to find her father in a dance with Mary, she puffing along to keep up with the duke.

"Is it true, Your Majesty?" Lady Jane said, coming to Anna's side. "Did Sir Bryan truly charge the king?" Jane had been given leave to attend to her infant son for the day and had missed the drama of the lists.

"I'm afraid so," Anna said. She went cold remembering—the

flash of steel and horse, William unawares, her horror— why wasn't he looking?—her scream of terror. Dear God, no.

A court jester galloped suggestively atop a broken lance past the king, bringing her back to the present. As the fool bounced by, the king slapped his rear and made some sort of witty remark that brought chortles from those near enough to hear it. As she considered William from afar, her lust, momentarily dispelled by her ghastly recollections, came roaring back. Her eyes lingered on his wide mouth, his broad chest. The tips of her fingers ached. She could stand it no longer.

She rose and strode across the Great Hall, falling at his feet, wine velvet skirts unfurling on the stone. "Majesty," she said.

He was standing with the young Eustace, Earl of Mohrlang, Robert at his soon-to-be brother-in-law's side. The engagement was announced that night. The little earl was puffing out his chest as if to compete with the strapping men around him.

"Queen Annelore," William said, taking her hand to rise, kissing her knuckles modestly, "what is your pleasure?"

She flicked her eyes to the throne room doors, empty and dark, inviting, leading to the royal chambers. She leaned toward him, shielding her lips with hands like parentheses.

"You are," she mouthed.

William raised one thick brow then took her hand. "Excuse me gentlemen." And left said gentlemen behind, their own brows quirking.

They both nearly sprinted to the king's chambers, half of William's clothes already shed by the time they cleared the closing doors.

He gave her that goose-smacking grin. looked her up and down, and shook his head. "Again, way too many damned garments."

She strode to his desk and brandished a letter knife. "Then relieve me of them, my liege."

"If you insist." He chortled, taking the knife from her with no hesitation. She didn't think she could bear wearing this gown again anyway. It would always remind her of his near death, and the sealing of Bryan's.

Putting the blade in his mouth, he gently removed her crown, placing it squarely in the center of his desk. He did the same with her necklaces, his delicate fumblings with clasps sending flames hissing through her veins, his restraint excruciating.

When the last of her jewels were winking near the candles, he brushed his lips to the nape of her neck and whispered. "Don't move. Don't even breathe."

She felt him sheath the knife down her back, the flat of it against her spine, then all at once lacings ripped, her lungs expanded, and her bodice hung off her by the sleeves. She gulped air.

"I'm not finished," he taunted, right by her ear. "Hold. Still." He sliced off her sleeves with the ease of cutting through butter, one side then the other, barely before she could blink.

He sauntered in front of her, blade behind his back. He flicked his eyes to her skirts then back up. "You're sure?"

She bit back a grin. "I've never been more sure."

His eyes grew. "Of anything?"

She laughed, loving him so, wanting him so. "I think I am more sure of you than anything."

He grinned right back. "Correct answer." He prowled behind her and did not merely cut the ties, but tore through the skirt entire, the wrenching rip of silks violent and somehow deeply comforting.

She heard him disrobe behind her, the clank of his buckle hitting stone reverberating to her waiting, wanting crotch. He nestled up against her, his heat swallowing her back, his member pressed against her buttocks. Wrapping his arms around her, he cupped her aching breasts through the silk of her shift and hummed.

"Dear God, Anna, how you undo me." He sucked her shoulder, slowly, devotional, devouring, and brought his hands to the scoop of her shift. Without his lips leaving her, he tore it in two like it was no more than a spiderweb, its remnants falling to the floor like mist, any inhibitions she might have had going with it.

Snaking a hand to her belly he pressed her against him, his erection quite insistent now. He trailed his other hand down, threading fingers through her hairs, alighting to her wet lips. She gasped and jerked in response, thrilling to the fact that even after all their couplings he still brought this heart-stopping sensation to her with just a flick of his finger. But she would not be idle this night, could not let him lead her blissfully blind down this pleasure path. This night, she needed him to know she wanted him, and him alone. This night, she needed to look in his eyes as she took him inside her, needed to feel, see, smell all of him, alive. Virile and vibrantly alive.

She bucked him off her and ran to the bed, jumping onto its pillowed smoothness. She sat on her haunches, knees spread, breasts perky, smiling at his startled look. She crooked a finger and he wasted no time, launching himself, lion-like, on to the bed next to her. She bade him lie down and bent to hover over him, taking his mouth, kissing him deeply, his hands finding her rear.

She had to taste him. Everywhere. Tripping her hands along his torso, her lips followed suit, grazing on his neck, a slow lick to his collarbone.

"To what do I owe this devoted treatment," he said between grunts of gratitude. "I hope I don't have to almost die every day to deserve it."

She stopped, lifting her lips from his sternum. She studied his face, his soft wide lips, his dark stubble now in need of a trim, his proud nose and deep brow. And those eyes, rich dark pools of blue like the sea in winter. She recalled their wedding, the fear they'd struck in her, how they'd scorched and startled her, how they scorched and startled her still, but now in a way she craved like food itself.

"Nay, my liege lord, my husband divine. For you deserve this every moment every day." Though even now, she could not help her cheek. "But dodging death does help."

He laughed, deep in his chest, that same laugh from the tennis court all those months ago. "Oh Anna, you do keep one humble."

Her response was to continue her progression. Yvette had schooled her on what was next. Initially she had balked at the idea, it seemed somehow wrong, just not done, but being here with him now, knowing how her heart stopped when his was nearly stabbed, knowing how much she wanted to show him what he meant to her, to honor him, all her squeamish prim ideals melted at the joy that he lived.

Besides, as Yvette bluntly pointed out, he did the same to her. Multiples of times and to quite pleasing results.

So she worked her lips down his chest, finding the trail of hairs, following, slow, tasting the salt of his sweat, smelling his scent of cedar and oak, smoke and wine, and his unmistakable musk.

Her chin hit the tip of his cock and he hissed. She glanced up at him and caught his eyes as they widened in surprise. She licked her lips and smiled, feline-like.

Grasping him at his base, she marveled at his size. Certainly she'd seen him before, but not this close. Not where she could see the slight rise of straining veins, the glistening pearl of seed at the tip. She took a deep breath, then took him in, slicking her mouth down, stopping just before she gagged. William let out a roar she'd never heard before.

She twirled her tongue along his shaft like Yvette had taught her, on a squash no less, and moved her mouth up and down, sliding his tip across the roof of her mouth. He tasted only of salt. She was glad she had practiced. Apparently William was too, for he clenched and thrust in uncontrolled need. Seeing how she'd sent him beyond reason sent her own veins hot again, her breasts aching, her folds yearning.

"Stop, please, not yet," he yelped, eyes crushed together, face rumpled.

She removed her mouth, but kept her hand at his base as she mounted him. Plunging on to his cock, she braced herself on his taut stomach, swirling her hips, their rhythm soon working together. He opened his eyes, almost amazed it seemed, to find her there.

"I can't hold much longer," he said through panting breaths.

She ground into his pelvic bone and just nodded, unable to speak. She was too close, too flooded with fire like a match scratching across stone. She would explode in moments.

"Anna!" He yelled her name as she came, shattering to pieces over and over again, both their bodies coiling and flinching until she collapsed, limp, against him.

She let herself rise and fall to his breathing for long, quiet minutes.

Eventually, he kissed the top of her head. "Remind me to dodge a broadsword tomorrow."

"No more dying," she said. "Not tomorrow. Not ever."

* * *

Anna was surprised by the humidity of the dungeon. She had expected cold and damp, not hot and stifling. She adjusted her bodice, feeling overdressed and sticky.

A palace guard led her into the depths. The cells here were mostly empty, but the smell of human suffering lingered. The guard stopped and she peered into a large, shadowed cell where Bryan sat on a stool.

"Her Majesty the Queen," the guard called, her title echoing down about her. The guard moved a respectful distance away. Bryan remained motionless, staring through her.

"Oh, Bryan, why? What on earth possessed you?"

Finally, he looked at her. "You're the one who dashed our dreams at the feet of a throne."

She heard a noise behind her and a *shhh*, but looking back, she saw only the guard.

"You can't still think I wrote you those letters," she said. "I would never lie to you—certainly not at the hour of your death." He gave a slight nod. She moved closer to the cell. "Some of the happiest moments of my life have been at your side. Never doubt that. You were always such a joy to me, such a pleasure. It grieves my soul that it has all come to this."

He jumped up and seized the bars. "Why can you not leave me to die in peace?"

She moved toward him, grabbing the bars herself. "How can you say that? What of Beaubourg? What of your family? How could you cast them aside—"

"Like you've cast me?"

"Bryan—"

243

"Better to have me out of the way, I suppose." His lips twisted. "The better to frolic with your king."

"You've no right to diminish us. He means more to me than—"

Bryan let out a groan and jerked his hands away. "Dammit, Anna, must you gut me as well as the executioner?"

"I thought you were still convinced—"

"How could I be?" He returned to her, clutching the bars so hard his knuckles went white. "It was his name you called, not mine. It was your scream—for him—that stopped me." He turned his pale eyes to hers and she saw the sorrow in their depths.

"'Tis all laid bare now," she said as he moved back to his stool and sat, cradling his head in his hands.

"At least be contrite in your confession. Perhaps the king—"

"Will slice off my head instead of disemboweling me?"

"He's been better to you than you deserve. James would have torn you open on the spot."

"Don't you see I know that?" A wail escaped him. "Don't you think it kills me to shame the man I swore my life to? And that my love should be in thrall to him, and me knowing he's a better man?"

She took a breath. Must this be the last memory she had of him? "Why must we fight? Now of all times?" She knelt down to see straight into his face, not caring if her skirts were ruined. "Can we not be at peace, you and I? For we were always so."

His shoulders shook. "Oh God, Anna, I wish—" He lowered his hands, revealing red eyes. "I wish I could hate you both."

"I'm so, so sorry, Bryan."

He rose slowly and she followed suit. She again took hold of the bars, hard and cold in her hands. He rested his forehead against the iron and stroked her hand with one finger, finally coming to rest on her wedding ring. He gave a rattle of a sigh, then looked her full in the face, a single tear dropping down his cheek.

"I'm sorry too." He turned his back on her and walked into the depths of his cell, a dark, hunched figure in the gloom. He spoke barely above a whisper. "I'm sorry I can't give you the peace you seek. You'll have to find absolution from your God and your king."

* * *

Ragged gray clouds obscured the shining sun of the previous day, the damp creeping in, making it feel as if the palace itself had a hangover. Still musing over the evening's public and private festivities, William chewed on his thumbnail, reviewing documents Daniel presented to him. Other than his friend and two guards, his chamber was empty.

His doors burst open before his caller had a chance to announce. The queen plunged in, face blotched and tear-stained, feathered cap still perky on her head. She stopped short when she saw Daniel, her face struggling to disguise her disappointment.

William rose hastily. "Your Grace, would you please excuse us?"

"I-I'm sorry," Anna said, "I see you are engaged, Highness. I should return later." She made to go.

"Not at all," he said, "Cecile just arrived himself, and we can continue this afternoon. Yes?"

Daniel bowed, gathered parchments to his chest, and took his leave. William went to Anna's side and held her as she shook silently.

"I know it's not right to bring this to you, Wills." She dabbed her eyes with a damp handkerchief. "But even Mary can't give me consolation."

"Tush, dearest, what's the matter?"

She smiled weakly as he guided her to the fire, which sputtered, sluggish like the rest of the palace. She took off her hat and sank onto the bearskin rug, her face still and pale.

She did not look at him as he took his place by her side, crossing his ankles, arms about his knees. While he knew she was overly prone to tears both of joy and trauma, there was something in her face he'd not seen before. Sad, joyless, yet fierce.

"Please, Wills—"

"Anything."

"I just need you to listen. Not be the king nor the rival lover." He nodded. "I've just been to see Bryan." Her voice broke at his name. "And I grieve for him so." Finally she looked from the fire and into his face, breaking into fresh tears. "Stupid, stupid boy! I'm so angry with him and yet so, so wretched. I don't know whether to blame myself, for I am certainly not guiltless—"

"Nay, Anna," he said, "whatever he thought, there's no excuse to try to kill a king."

"I know." She sighed. "I relive that moment over and over, wondering if I could have done something different—"

"Your scream saved my life."

She sniffed and sat tall, eyes bright from tears. "He said when he heard me scream for you and not him, he dropped his sword."

"Tell me all of it." He listened as she recounted everything he'd just heard from Daniel—for Daniel had been on his way to the prisoner when the queen appeared. Daniel said he decided not to make his presence known, so as to overhear any further confession from the knight. But now Anna was adding bits to the story his friend had been too cautious or too kind to include—like her weeping at his feet and telling the knave how sorry she was.

"And he just stood there, hands on the bars, staring at me like a phantom. He said he knew my heart was yours and he would be happy to go to the grave. I pled for his mother and sister and brothers but he paid no heed."

"He didn't beg for his life?"

"Nay," she said, looking into the fire as if she could divine answers there.

"Anna, he's a fool."

"But he's my fool. And I will grieve his passing." She winced. "'Twas his friendship that helped me through my mother's death, and here I can do nothing to save him."

William took her hand and turned it over, smiling faintly at her upturned palm. "All you need do is ask." She looked up at him. He continued. "I daresay you didn't think of such circumstances when we made our little pact."

"William," she said, her tone hard, "I shall never forgive him for trying to take you from me." He'd never seen such fierceness on her face. "When I replay it in my mind, I can't help but go further. I see your bleeding, dying body . . . I'd have killed him with my own hands."

She darted her eyes away and swallowed hard, steadying herself. "'Tis true that I love him as much as anyone would love a brother. And that is why I weep for him."

William nodded, face somber.

"He was there when I skinned my first knee." She gave a little laugh, lost in memory now. "I treated his first bee sting. He wrote me sonnets. He taught me to fight and I taught him to plant. He's a part of almost every childhood memory I have, happy or sad."

She looked at William again, her eyes so full of sorrow.

"But Wills, I was wrong when I thought he was incapable of harm. Something in him changed. And yet—" She made to rise but turned instead into the side of the leather chair, hiding her face.

"Anna . . ." He felt a mixture of anger at the sway this knight still held over her, and joy at the honesty she had shown.

He turned her to him and wiped the tears from her cheeks with his thumbs. "His death will give me no pleasure." She reached a hand to stroke his chain of office, fingers rubbing the bumps of jewels and twists of gold.

"You're the king," she said. "You'll do as best befits the rule of law. Just . . . be quick about it."

* * *

The only sounds were chains dragging over marble and the clang of the guards' boots as they ushered the prisoner into the throne room. After Anna's visit to Bryan that morning and her talk with William, she had no heart to sit staring while his punishment was doled out. But neither could she bear to miss what was said.

She stood unseen behind the throne's tapestries. She grasped Mary's hand as if to break it as the matron bit her lips and trembled for the both of them. Robert, Daniel, and the king sat enthroned. The jailer and grand master general stood at the foot of the dais. The manacles stopped clanking. It took so long for William to speak that his booming voice made the women jump.

"Sir Bryan, Knight of Beaubourg, you are accused of treason, attempted regicide, and attempted molestation of Her Royal Highness the Queen." Another pause. "These offenses carry the sentence of death twice over. What say you to the charges?"

Mary and Anna looked at each other, startled. It was highly unusual for the accused to be allowed to speak in such a case as this.

Bryan cleared his throat. They heard a shuffling of chain. "Your Majesty, I wish you no ill for you deserve it not. You know my purpose. And your queen is lost to me by your hand and her choice. Do with me what you will, for I look with eagerness toward my heavenly home."

"Some would argue that be not the direction you shall fly, sir." That was Robert.

"Aye, Your Grace," Bryan said. "But the conditions of the devil's house could only improve upon my situation."

"You are ready to die, then," William said. Anna pulled Mary's hand up to her chest.

"Majesty," Bryan said, "I was ready to die the moment I entered your service. I am, as always, at your command."

Anna glared at the tapestry, wishing she could see through it. What was happening? Why all this silence? *Oh William, be done with it —put us all out of this misery.*

"Nay," the king said, quiet but firm. "We shall not have you killed." She heard urgent whispering. Robert? "In saving the life of our dear cousin, you have saved your own."

Robert snorted. "Majesty, do not spare him on my account."

"If it were not for your haste," the king continued, "His Grace would have been crushed. A life for a life."

"But—" Bryan started.

"And as you aborted your attempt on our own life, we shall stay your execution." Anna heard the king pace behind the throne. He tapped the tapestry three times. So, he knew she was there.

"Majesty . . ." She heard a loud thunk and chains clanking. Bryan must be on his knees. "Majesty, I beg of you—"

"Do not think you shall in any way remain free." She heard the king stop his pacing. "You are forthwith stripped of your knighthood and all other honors thereto, though your family shall be provided for out of the queen's good graces. You shall spend the remainder of your days in Stone Yard. In time, we are sure we will need someone to make an example of."

She could hear heavy breathing. Bryan's? Was it relief? Bitterness?

"Do not misunderstand," the king said, voice low yet echoing through the chamber. "The next time we lay eyes upon you shall be the day of your death."

She heard Robert scoff, then heard the rustle of parchment. Daniel. A scratch of a quill made Bryan's fate official. She smelled the soothing odor of melting wax, heard the parchment crinkle with the imprint of the royal seal. She saw it in her mind's eye, the thick gold ring with crowned griffin, thistle, and rose entwined in its paws. She spent many a night fiddling with it on William's right middle finger. Someone blew on the seal and flapped the parchment about, cooling the blood-red wax. Finally, the sound of William's footsteps as he returned to his throne broke the tense silence.

"Guards," he said, as if asking for a drink, "take him to Stone Yard. Be sure there is nothing about his person or in his cell that may aid him in hastening his own death. And feed him well, for we want him in perfect health as he contemplates his crimes against our person and Her Majesty's."

Again the chains swung and chimed as Bryan was thrust to his feet. The same dragging that had started the sentencing now receded into the Great Hall, the men remaining silent in their places.

Anna bit her lips, tears running down her cheeks. William had spared Bryan's life, for her. An act of mercy from his perspective. But not, she feared, from Bryan's.

CHAPTER 12

Good Christian Men, Rejoice

A nna watched the cotton clouds of snow dip and dive, blanketing her beloved garden in unyielding chill. She was waiting, eager, for her father.

The Duke of Beaubourg had been invited to court for the Christmastide celebrations. The king had made him Master of the Horse, a position whose influence was seventh on council—a high honor indeed. He was due in her chambers after his first Council Table.

Bernard finally escorted him in, bedecked in a thick new chain of office, his face alight.

"Papa!" Anna was beside herself with pride. She followed their embrace with a little curtsy. "The chain suits you, Your Grace, and the position even better."

"Aye, my lady," he said, kissing her hand, "and the king claims you had nothing to do with it."

"'Tis true." She led him to her roaring fireplace. "I had no idea until he told me two weeks ago."

"Surely you had some part to play?" He accepted mulled wine from Lady Yvette and settled into a chair.

"The king knows I make no demands upon him. Now tell me, how went Council Table?"

"Oh, 'twas an honor, to be sure." His eyes danced. "That husband of yours certainly knows how to put up a fuss for an old man."

"I'm glad for it—you deserve the post. Why, who else in Troixden knows more of horses?" She took a sip of her wine. "I've been to council myself, you know."

"I do know." His smile faded.

She frowned. "You were the one who told me to expand my mind."

"'Tis not that, my sweet, for I'm sure you give them a well-needed workaround."

"What, then?"

"There are whispers—some tension at table." He sighed, not meeting her look.

"Father, whatever is the matter?"

"Dear heart, you know I cannot bear to hear anyone even imply ill of ye."

"'Tis no secret I have few friends at court, and council resents my outspokenness and influence on the king, but I've never known you to let idle gossip worry you."

She caught him steal a glance at her belly, then quickly look out at the iced-over fountain, a mountain of snow.

"Father, do you mean to imply . . . are people really talking about my private performance with the king? At council?" Her stomach lurched. She was sick to death of sorrowful looks—Margaux's, self-satisfied—the constant whispering, the disappointment in William's eyes when she had to tell him she bled. And now her own father.

"My darling daughter, as a queen, nothing about you is private."

She crossed her arms over her chest. "Don't you think the same worry is my constant companion?"

"My dear." He shook his head and smiled. "It's only been five months—pay those hounds no mind. I, of all people, know these things take time."

"Indeed." She paced to the east windows, watching the progression of low, smoky clouds over Stone Yard. "It took mother more than ten years to bear me, and she much younger than I."

"Aye." He paused. "And yet she carried seven children before you, though only three born and those not lasting."

"Forgive me. This is just so . . ." She returned to his chair and took his hand. "I only mean, why would people have the gall to make comment so soon?"

"And I only mean that your strongest supporter, save the king, is me. And I will do everything I can to protect you."

"Protect me?" She turned from him and walked back to the fire.

"Laureland grows more restless by the day. When spring approaches, they may take to arms."

She felt lightheaded and sat down in Matilda's old chair. "But if we had an heir, they perchance would settle knowing the crown continues."

"It would be an unwise man," he said, "who pinned his hopes of peace on a pregnancy." He took his warm wine from the fireplace and handed it to her. "And the king is not an unwise man."

* * *

The gloom of mid-December deepened as incessant rain turned to snow a week later. His Majesty's chin rested on his upturned hand, elbow on the council table. With the other he spun a small dagger.

Cecile, Norwick, Ridgeland, and the grand master general sat before him, their debate noisy as they interrupted one another, the rest of council sitting taciturn, waiting to see which way the tide turned.

"And I say," Timothy rose from his seat to his foreboding full height, "Norwick is right. Let us not be cowardly. Let us stand strong and courageous against these usurpers!"

"How is it cowardly to send an envoy?" Daniel said.

Robert rolled his eyes for the hundredth time. "Why send an envoy to confirm what we already know?"

"Aye," the general said, "they only delay the inevitable. The throne must be secured and peace restored."

William, head throbbing, closed his eyes.

"For all we know," Daniel said, "Her Majesty is with child even as we speak—"

William flung his dagger, its point landing squarely in the middle of the table, cutting through all other speech. "If the queen were with child we would be the first to know it. Get your meddling spies out of her bedchamber." He pushed back his chair and turned upon Robert. "And you, Norwick, act as though we have somehow lost all military understanding."

"Sire, I merely advise against redundant caution," Robert said. "We begin to look a fool to the world when our own people can be stirred up by foreigners."

William was hot with rage. "You dare sit there and call us a coward?"

"I only say we shouldn't be caught with our pants down."

"Ah, so now we're not just a coward but a bare-assed coward?"

Robert dropped his gaze and held his hands up, palms out.

William took in the hangdog faces of his most trusted advisors and walked to the windows, back to them all.

"Desiring the blood of our people not be spilled is not cowardice," Daniel said.

"Aye," the general said, "but when some of the people want your blood, some must be spilt to save the rest."

William had had enough. He strode back to the table and wrenched his knife from its place. "Not if I can help it."

With that he left them, silent, to seek haven in his wife's arms.

He found her in the privy dining room at supper with the Archbishop of Bartmore, both bedecked in purple.

"Your Eminence," she was saying, "I do not hold to the heresy of Luther, yet I believe the Scriptures may be instructive and bring good cheer to those who read them, as they have to me."

"Well, well." Bartmore sniffed. "The Duke of Beaubourg must have some interesting ideas about raising daughters."

"Come now, Your Eminence," the king said, "must you also set fire to her father?"

"I only mean to say, Majesties, that the Scriptures are not fit for the people, and less so for women. They are the purview of learned men, not for idle curiosity."

The queen took a sip of wine, looking as if she'd like to choke the man.

"Your Eminence," the king said, "do you really have the impudence to degrade the queen in her presence, and over a meal she's most lavishly provided for you?" If one more person insulted his wife today, there'd be hell to pay.

Bartmore tut-tutted. "I never presumed to insult. 'Tis an academic matter—nothing personal is implied."

"Your Eminence," Anna said, her tone even, "what may be academic to you, a man, makes sport of my very soul. For I am subject to the whims of so-called 'learned' men. And yet I have a mind, given to me by God, and, feeble as it may be, I will use it to better my person, my circumstance, and my soul."

"That may be," Bartmore said, gazing at her as if she were a particularly charming performing monkey who had just pulled a coin out its ear. "But the Scriptures are not for the eyes of just anyone."

William opened his mouth to speak, but the queen was too quick for him.

"And if God's Holy Word be the most wise, the most instrumental in working for our improvement, and I be schooled in Latin and Greek, why ever would I not read and know my Lord the better?"

Bartmore looked to the king for support, but William simply raised his goblet. "My queen," he said, beaming with pride for this woman who feared no man, king or clergy alike, "may God strike any man down who wouldst dare deny you."

The queen returned his toast, sipping just a taste of her wine. She looked pale. He knew all of this inclement weather was wearing on her. He could kick himself for letting her parlay alone with this insufferable churchman.

"Tell me, Archbishop," he said, "what of this young vicar of

Havenside, Multman? I hear he aligns with the Franciscans, preaching good news to the poor."

The archbishop scowled into his wine and took a finishing gulp. "He is young and has many radical ideas. I worry he may unsettle the shaky peace we hold in the city."

"How lucky then," William said, "that you live far enough away to not be disturbed by the reprobates about Havenside."

William summarily ignored the mighty archbishop for the rest of the meal, which, thanks to his own late arrival, did not last long. When Bartmore took his leave, William kicked his feet up on the table, crossed them, and grinned at the queen.

"Look at you, my little theologian."

"You know I take my faith seriously," she said.

"As well you should. And never let anyone shame you for it, even I."

She narrowed her eyes at him. "Even when it hampers your own advances?"

He rose and took her into his arms, taking her spicy, flowery scent into his lungs, filling his heart with the power to cast out his demons. "God save me, even then."

* * *

"Your Grace, I have given thee this warning before," the archbishop said as he left chapel with Robert the next day, steering him from the rest of the departing worshipers.

Robert stroked his chin. He did not like the man any more than the king did, but unlike the king, he saw the churchman's potential usefulness. The man wanted to be cardinal, ambition that could be easily exploited.

"The queen's dabbling in theology will only incite our already troubled realm," Bartmore said. "You have heard the reports as well as I. Any hint of heresy from that woman or from court and we are at war. Our people will be to arms, not to mention our neighbors."

"Our rebellious, heretic friends in the northeast would hardly contest the king if they believed him married to one who shared their ideals."

"Then you admit the queen is no friend of the One True Faith?" The archbishop looked ready to foam at the mouth.

Robert forced him against a pillar. "I say no such thing, Eminence. And even if the queen be a heretic, that is no reflection upon the king."

"Her influence over him grows by the day," Bartmore said, regaining his dignity as Robert allowed him to straighten. "Did you not see how they sat and tittered together, completely disregarding mass? 'Twas disgraceful. And the people are thirsty for blood. This is just the thing to rile them."

Yes, just the thing. "Archbishop," he said, guiding the priest into the Great Hall, "the king be still a man with a mind of his own whom none will influence against his will. I should know."

"His will is pliable, Your Grace."

"Perhaps." Robert said. *Perhaps for me.*

* * *

"How dare you enter my rooms unannounced!" Margaux's blonde curls quivered at her temples.

Robert had left a cowering Bartmore to speak with her about her upcoming nuptials. He advanced to where she sat hunched at her writing desk, forearms over a parchment.

"What occasion has brought you to chicken-scratching, my dear?" He stood over her now, craning his neck to see.

"How is it any business of yours?"

"Because, dear sister, you have a nasty tendency to insert yourself where you are most troublesome."

Her eyes became slits. "I could say the same for you, dear brother."

"Hand it over." She flattened herself over her writing. "Don't make me take it by force, sis."

"'Tis not your right!"

"You wouldn't be writing to your new pen pal in the queen's hand again, now would you?" He leaned on the desk.

"'Tis not true! You say yourself my hand is chicken scratches. How could I copy the queen's?"

Robert bent to her ear, feeling her tremble at his closeness. "You may have convinced Daniel, but you don't convince me. Hand the letter over. Now."

"Nay!"

Robert grabbed a large handful of her hair, yanking her back. She let out a cry as he thrust his free hand to the desk, ripping the parchment from her now loosed grip.

His eyes roved over it. Whatever he had imagined, it had not been this. "'Tis a list of plants."

"If you must know," she said, "I'm helping the queen order more herbs for her garden."

"Then why hide it?"

"Why were you so eager to see it?"

Robert leaned in to her again. "Margaux, I don't know what you're up to, but I'll discover it. And if it in any way impinges on my own goals, I'll find a way to banish you from court. No matter whom you're married to."

"All you care about is your own ass on the throne," she said, folding her arms in a huff over her chest, "or your precious little boys' asses."

Robert turned to leave, then checked himself. He strode back to her desk, too quick for her to react, and grabbed a wooden box there.

"Stop it, Robert, that's none of your business!"

He attempted to pry the lid off, but it was locked. "Where's the key, Margaux?"

She lunged for him, missing both him and the box as he took a swift step to the side.

"Give it back—those are my papers!"

He grimaced, giving the box one more pull, to no avail. He went back to her desk and picked up a small blade.

Shoving it into the keyhole, he pried the box open and pages of parchment floated to the ground. Margaux jumped to recover them at the same time he did, but she was too late.

In his hand he held the evidence Daniel had been searching for the court over. Line upon line of carefully copied script to match the queen's hand. Lines crossed out and started again, the name Bryan repeated over and over until it was just right. His heart sank. As much as his sister annoyed him, he did not want to see her in Stone Yard. Or worse, headless. He grabbed her by the arms and shook her so hard it jarred her blonde curls into disarray.

"Every time I think you have gone far enough, you go further." She looked frightened, cornered. "Do you know what this means? This is treason! This means Stone Yard!"

Tears streamed down her cheeks. "Please, Robert, please. You can't tell—you must protect me! If I ever meant anything to you—"

His heart felt like it was in a blacksmith's heated vise. His mind spun. Could he really keep this from Daniel? From William? Looking through the damning sheets once more, he came to the last. Another list of herbs, identical to the one he had found her scribbling. But this came with directions and in an unrecognized hand.

Wild carrot seeds, anise, pennyroyal, smartweed, pinch of clove to cover taste in spiced wine. One dose daily, or after relations. His blood ran cold. She was rocking back and forth, holding herself, shaking her head. He seized her again but she craned her neck from side to side and would not look at him.

"What have you done?"

"'Twas not for her but for me!"

"You defend what I haven't accused and seal your guilt!" He shook her again, unable to help his fury. "My God, you've kept the queen barren. And now running low on supply, you're ordering more!"

By all rights she should be killed. The king would not be merciful here. A knave attempting his own life was one thing, as were some forged letters, but interfering with the life of an heir, and with his beloved queen? William would swing the axe himself. And how could this not reflect upon Robert?

"Does anyone else know of this?" He was frantic now, combing through the papers, throwing them all on the fire. "What of that simpering wench Brigitte?"

"N-nay. No one. I'd stopped anyway! I couldn't stand it —"

"And what of the apothecary?"

"I-I had more than one. The rest I get from the gardens."

At least she'd been smart there. No one would trace a request for anise as anything sinister. "Margaux, you must never speak of this to anyone. Ever. Not even to me."

After he tossed the last page on the fire, he came back to her, dragging her to her feet.

"You'll leave court and the queen's service immediately—you'll make some excuse of preparations for your wedding. You'll stay with my wife and have no contact with anyone save myself. Do you understand?" She stood there, limp. "Do you understand?"

She nodded and wiped the wet from her cheeks.

"You and Eustace will take a three-month wedding tour. You will proclaim wedded bliss and your wish to retire to Mohrlang until I, and I alone, recall you to court. If ever!" She let out a little cry, which he ignored. "I've got to save both our necks now, for no one would believe me ignorant of your damned plots."

He dusted off his jacket, making sure even the smallest piece of telling ash was gone. He grabbed her chin and forced her face to his. He looked into her frightened eyes and swallowed the lump in his throat.

"If you speak of this to anyone," he said, "if you disobey in even the smallest detail? Mine will be the last face you see."

It was a sparkling Twelfth Night. Even the snow shone like diamonds in the light of the high moon while streams of glittering partygoers fluttered from the Great Hall to the roaring bonfire in the palace's manicured square. Performers blew fire, minstrels roved, jesters plied their witty craft, and all faces were red with spirits.

The revelries had gone on all day, and it was only now that the king and queen could steal a private moment together before the official start of the evening feast.

King and queen lay sated, naked, and intwined in bed, covers pulled up, William's fire crackling merrily, their matching royal purple garments hanging in wait. Their crowns of office sat on the king's desk. Anna stared at them, nestled on a single pillow, their golden points almost touching, the fire giving them a life of their own.

"Look how they glow, Wills." She nodded at them. "'Tis as if they have a flame inside and yearn to be one."

He smiled, following her gaze. The last time they'd worn them, she had trembled at the sight of him and he'd feared the worst. And here he was now, knowing he'd been given the very best.

"They reflect their wearers." He rose, pulling on a shirt and his shorts as he went to fetch an ebony box from behind the crowns. "My dearest Anna, I have a gift for you."

Striding back to the bed, he held the box in outstretched hands, worrying the corner of his lip. She still had the power to make him tremble like a lovesick boy. He rather thought she always would.

Anna opened the box and gasped. Resting on a pillow of green velvet lay a ruby near the size of a robin's egg. Wrapped around it was a band of engraved gold. She drew the precious stone out of its case, turning it reverently with her fingers. Their crowns had nothing on its glow, for this stone blazed like an ember, pulsating. A long, thick gold chain hung from its top, uncurling as she lifted the necklace. She looked at William's face, for once at a loss for words.

"I take it you like it, then?" He said, admittedly relieved.

"Wills," she whispered, staring at the stone. She lifted the small parchment below and read the verse, written in his hand:

I am thine, thou art mine, This shall be a sure sign: Locked fast thou art, within my heart, And lost forever is the key—So thou inside must ever be.

"Oh, William!" Tears sprang to her eyes. "I shall treasure it always." She turned the jewel in her hand and read the engraving: *Locked fast thou art, within my heart.*

"I'm happy to hear that," he said. "For 'tis my heart I give you."

She drew the necklace over her head and let the ruby fall against her chest. "And I shall wear it always against mine own, so our hearts shan't be parted." She grasped his hands in hers, pressing them to her smooth, damp cheeks and showering them with kisses.

"You never speak in halves, my dearest." He said with a chuckle.

"And you, dear husband, are my sun and my moon, and now, you're to be one thing more."

She pointed to a four-inch-square, plain wooden box on the chest by the fire, a small leather strap and his own wax seal upon it.

"Open it," she said, her eyes restless, eager. Slipping on her discarded shift, she slid out of bed, tiptoeing after him as if they were about to play a childhood game.

He obeyed her command, and opening the gift, found a tennis ball of pure gold inside.

"Why, whatever—" He reached in to pull out the ball. As he loosed it, he knew it was hollow, and something inside made it chime like tiny bells.

"'Tis lovely, my dear, but . . ." Seeing a small parchment inside, he unfolded it carefully.

The king's set and match. —A

Realization slowly sunk in. His set, his match—he'd won the game. He held in his hand a golden rattle. Fit only for . . . .

"You're to be a father to a true heir of Troixden." And the smile on his wife's face could have lit the palace. Too overcome to say a word, he opened his arms and she rushed to his chest.

No wonder she'd been tired and pale of late. No wonder her breasts had felt fuller in his hands. "Are you sure?" he said when they finally pulled apart, smiling like idiots through their happy tears.

"I've missed my bleeding for the last two months."

"Two months?" He looked into her eyes. "Why ever did you wait to tell me? So many things could've been dampened with this news."

"I wasn't sure. I—I didn't want to start bleeding and have nothing to tell. I couldn't bear to raise your hopes, only to dash them."

William hastily reviewed the past months. How had he not kept track himself? He'd been preoccupied, of course. Good Lord, they must have come together more than threescore, and not always in a gentle fashion. But she still held on to the child. It truly was a miracle.

"Weren't you afraid to come to my bed? What if our joining had harmed the child?"

She cupped his face in her hands, running her elegant fingers over his whiskers as if she could smooth them away and with it all his fears.

"I couldn't let myself believe it was true. And, if you recall, I've been a bit hesitant these past few weeks, at times to the detriment of thy royal mood, O king."

He swept her up in his embrace, her feet leaving the ground as he swung her wide, both of them laughing so hard their waiting attendants burst through the doors.

He did not put her down. "We shall join thee in a moment, dear friends."

The king hooted with glee, spinning his laughing queen as she kissed his neck. And all was merry and bright.

The End

The Realm Series Continues
with . . .

God & King, Book II

Queen Annelore's condition hasn't quieted the religious and civil discontent of the sword-rattling northern regions of Troixden, forcing William to face the hardest decision of his reign: whether to shed the blood of his countrymen, or break with Rome. While he struggles, one of his most trusted advisers still plots, waiting to seize power. But what power does he hope to gain—is it the throne, or something more sinister? And how are his plans woven into the strain and suspicion building amongst Anna's courtiers?

With the world crashing down around them, can William and Annelore's marriage survive?

Crown & Thorns, Book III

King William has more to worry about than the religious tension in his own lands. His country has unwittingly been made a pawn in the vast European fight for land, power, and religious freedom, and many think his cousin, the Duke of Norwick, would make a more decisive king. Especially since Queen Annelore has still not conceived a son and heir. And as the threat of invasion and civil war grow, she will have to make a decision that could very well break her heart. When friends become enemies and enemies wield incredible power, will the kingdom of Troixden—and William and Anna's marriage— survive?

Betwixt the Sheets Editions of all books available 2025!

www.jennielspohr.com

Major Characters

King William II (or William, Rex) ~ King of Troixden, brother of King James

Lady Annelore ~ People's Queen, Duke Stephen of Beaubourg's daughter

Robert, Duke of Norwick ~ William's cousin and friend, current heir to the throne

Daniel, Duke of Cecile ~ devoted childhood friend of William and Robert

Sir Bryan ~ Annelore's childhood friend and suitor

Mistress/Matron Mary ~ Annelore's nursemaid and surrogate mother, renowned healer, and midwife

Lady Margaux ~ Robert's sister, also William's cousin

Lady Yvette of Havenside ~ Robert's mistress, lady-in-waiting

Stephen, Duke of Beaubourg ~ Anna's widowed father

Minor Characters

Julia, Duchess of Beaubourg ~ Anna's deceased mother

Duke of Halforn ~ elder statesman, councilor

Archbishop Bartmore ~ highest church official in Troixden

King James ~ William's eldest brother, deceased

Lady Jane ~ pregnant lady-in-waiting

Bernard ~ Queen Annelore's master chamberman

Grand Master General ~ head of Troixden's army

Timothy, Earl of Ridgeland ~ casual friend of the king, councilor

Gregory, Duke of Duven ~ casual friend of the king, councilor

Queen Matilda ~ William's mother, Queen Consort; ruled as regent until eldest son, James, came of age

Queen Minerva ~ King James's unfaithful, beheaded consort

Eustace, Earl of Mohrlang ~ bastard son of King James's Queen Consort, Minerva

Kindly Note: Troixden, sadly, is completely made up, based on the politics of the time. It is about the size of Luxembourg and is located in the author's mind where modern day Belgium sits now.

Acknowledgments

What fun it has been to revisit Troixden and add more spice to the mix! I want to thank my readers and friends for the encouragement —especially Yvonne Roberts for bringing "smexy" back (smutty + sexy). Your wit and wisdom has meant the world. The whole team at Greenleaf and Rivergrove have been a joy to work with as well.

About the Author

Called "much funnier than Phillippa Gregory" by the illustrious Nancy Pearl, Jennie Spohr's award-winning four-book series based in early Renaissance Europe, *The Realm: Heirs & Spares, God & King, Crown & Thorns,* and *Sword & Shield* has garnered high praise. She has a Master of Divinity, of all things, and lives with her brood and animal menagerie in Seattle.

You can find her at www.jennielspohr.com and the following social media accounts:

 facebook.com/jlspohr
 instagram.com/jlspohrwriter

Made in United States
Troutdale, OR
09/22/2025

34767601R00166